ALONG THE FORGOTTEN COAST

THE CORAL SERIES
BOOK 2

ALONG THE FORGOTTEN COAST

A NOVEL

JENNIFER ODOM

WordCrafts Press

To my great-aunt,
Allie Bentley,
who ran a store like the one in
Along the Forgotten Coast.

Well. Peter Cordero's law office had located my father.

I only hoped he wasn't some creep or pedophile like all Mama's other boyfriends. If she hadn't mentioned him in that blood-stained note, we'd never have known he existed at all.

"Hey! Earth to Coral!" Peter tossed me a grin from the driver's seat of his brand-new car. "Were you even listening?" His courtroom stories had grown long and detailed, and my thoughts had drifted away a good while back.

The cobwebs cleared as my double reflection mirrored off his sunglasses. He returned his attention to the road ahead.

I shrugged. "How can you be so giddy about meeting him?" I asked.

He snorted. "Giddy. I'm not giddy."

"What if it turns out bad?"

His smile broadened. "I bet you didn't hear a thing I just said."

"I don't understand you. You're taking two days off in the middle of a court case," I said.

"But I'm not giddy."

"Fine then. Why so upbeat?" He was the most focused person I'd ever met, and this was out of character. "You hate distractions. You hate broken momentum."

Peter, Grandma's long-time family friend with a family of his own, had arranged this ride up to the Big Bend of Florida on my behalf. Back in Ft. Myers, he was also my part-time boss and called me *Miss Smith* at the office whenever I came home on college breaks. Later this evening after he dropped me off with Matt and Grandma who were following in the car behind us, he'd head straight back to Ft. Myers. We'd needed two cars, since there was little leg room in the back of Grandma's Mustang. He'd asked me to ride along with him, probably so he could ply me with fatherly advice the whole time. And then there was Grandma. Peter, always the protector, wanted to make sure she got settled in safely at Carrabelle. There was no leaving him out of this trip.

He chuckled from the driver's side.

"Oh, I get it," I said, dragging out my words. "You get to break in your new car."

He waved me off. "Just another car."

I crossed my arms. "Or maybe for some reason you think my fath... this dude... is going to be some bright, shining improvement over Mom's other guys?"

According to what Peter had learned, the guy's name was Ralph— which sounded like some old man, though he was only about forty. I bet he was fat, hairy, and ugly, too.

If he turned out to be a loser, I'd cross him off as a relative and forget about it.

If...

And now that Mama was gone, I'd truly be alone, the last in the line of my family.

"Watch him be a dud," I said. "Just watch."

"Have faith. And jot that down in your little book of wise sayings."

I turned away. "Too cliché. Besides, I already have that one."

"Then how's this? Never judge a case before it's tried."

Peter, in his forties, was a good man. He had always been there for me, even before Mom died. I fluttered my hand. "Truth is, you're simply overjoyed to help me out. Right?"

"You know it."

Jokes aside, Peter's nonstop storytelling—well, not all of it, he always had a tale—and his uber-positive attitude all morning— seemed a bit exaggerated.

I knew what he was up to, though. Peter was standing on his head in order to distract me from the utter terror that lay ahead of me.

Because on the inside, I was chewing my nails off.

"Thank you, Peter."

He snapped a nod. "You bet, kiddo."

I certainly wouldn't be making this trip without him—or Matt Flores and Grandma Rosella Flores back there. I gazed into the side mirror at their car behind us.

It was Grandma who'd insisted on this trip. "Wild horses couldn't drag me away," she said. "Back in that hospital, I nearly lost my chance to see you through this. And you can bet I wouldn't miss it now for the world."

In her weakened condition, she shouldn't be going, and it horrified me that she would try.

"Sick or not, Coral, we can't tie her down," Peter said. "If we left her behind, she'd drive up here on her own, and you know it."

Grandma Rosella. The stubbornest mule in the barn.

For the first time in many miles, I smiled.

Back in Las Vegas, Sol Flores burst out of his office and sauntered down the hall to his small display area. He set his hand on the countertop. "My mother's dying, Eddie, let me borrow your car."

"But…"

Sol raised his voice, a tactic he practiced on his ex. To overpower and shut her down. It worked with employees, too, especially the young. And Eddie was just twenty-one.

"You don't expect me to drive my new Mercedes all the way to Florida, do you? I haven't even worn the new off."

Eddie stared at the register.

Sol crossed his arms. "My mother's dying, Eddie."

"But…"

"Look." Sol dangled his keys. "See these? You get to drive my car. Home to work. Work to home. What's the difference, that's all you do with your car, anyway, right?"

Eddie lived with his mother only a few blocks away. A disabled widow, she needed him home, and it saved money on his college expenses. Lucky for Sol, school was out, and Eddie wanted to work every hour he could to sock away the tuition money. Even luckier for Sol, the kid kept his car in tiptop shape.

Eddie stared through the plate glass windows at Sol's silver Mercedes. He turned slo-mo to gaze at Sol. "Me? Drive that?"

"Heck, yeah."

Eddie raised a shoulder and tilted his head as if to say, *I guess so.*

"The keys will be in my office. All you have to do is open and close the shop every day like I've shown you. You know the routine."

Eddie was dependable. And Sol always leaned on him when

he didn't feel like opening or closing. "It's your dream-come-true, Eddie. You've been asking for more hours, right?"

"I'm… I'm not sure about my car, though. How good it runs."

"Oh, it'll do."

Anything that shiny ought to run just fine.

Back in his office Sol removed the Mercedes key from the business key ring and dropped it in his pocket.

Eddie could fend for himself and walk those few blocks to work. The boy's house wasn't that far, really. And Sol shouldn't be gone all that long.

Sol would simply ring him up from down the road and say, *Whoops, sorry, Eddie. I forgot and ran off with the keys.*

And Eddie would be fine. Just fine.

Around noon, Sol stopped off at his house with Eddie's little red car.

He walked into his kitchen and turned in a circle. *Snacks.* He settled on a brown bag full of chips, raisins, and prunes along with some bottled water and tossed it over by the front door.

In the bedroom, he grabbed a travel bag and laid out things. He folded a few short-sleeve button-ups and shorts. He glanced down at his flip flops and wiggled his toes. "*Meh.* It's Florida. One pair's good enough." This trip couldn't take too long.

"Nearly forgot." He reached into the closet again. "A suit for the funeral."

As he laid it on the bed with the rest of the clothes, a sudden heat—similar to what rolls off asphalt at noon—scorched his heart. He pushed the feeling aside, clamped his lips, and re-focused on the task at hand.

He stepped into the bathroom and grabbed the shampoo, did a double-take as he bumped the pink bottle of conditioner, and then turned away, leaving it sitting on the corner of the tub. His ex, Paulette, left that.

Five years ago. Or was it six?

He growled at himself for dwelling on those things, then dug around under the sink to find his shaving kit and stuffed it full. Odd. Most everything he packed started with an *S*. But that led his thoughts to the word she liked to call him—*selfish*. Sol slammed the cupboard door. He could think of nothing more, so he grabbed the paper bag of snacks and stepped outside to toss it into the front passenger seat.

Unspent energy drove him back into the bedroom, where he grabbed his other things and verified the well-being of his car key on top of his dresser. The only person with access to his home was Matt—and his ex, Paulette. But she'd never come by. The image of her pretty face and long red hair passed through his mind, and a second ripple fluttered through his chest.

He shoved the feeling aside as he always did, walked out the front door with his final load, and locked up.

Out in the driveway, he hung the suit in the back of the car, and tossed the bag in the trunk. *Florida here I come.* He backed out of the driveway and then burnt a long streak of rubber down to the stop sign.

"Been wanting to do that for a while," he muttered. Of course, he wouldn't do it in his own car.

He paused at the stop sign to adjust the mirrors and seat, then stepped on the gas again. It was time to get moving and straighten things out down south.

He sped along, admiring the various reflections over the well-waxed hood. Eddie certainly cared for his paint job. Good kid, that Eddie.

By the second stop sign, Little Red stuttered and vibrated. *Putt, putt, voom. Putt, putt, voom.*

Sol lifted a thumb and looked down at the gas gauge. Less than a quarter of a tank. He searched for a logo but couldn't figure out what kind of car it was. Didn't matter. A small car like this ought to get pretty good mileage.

He revved the engine until the sputter evened out and then once again, burned rubber.

A few blocks later, he pulled into a gas station and put in five dollars' worth. There'd be something cheaper along the way.

He put away the dripping nozzle and circled the car. At the sight of Eddie's back tire, he leaned down to take a closer look. Then he examined the other three.

A scowl accompanied his sigh. Looked like he'd have to watch things in the rain—because every one of those tires looked a little bit smooth.

I glanced Peter's way as the sun climbed higher over our vehicle. The courtroom lawyer caught my eye and returned to his stories. I squirmed and recrossed my legs in the other direction. As much as I loved his tales, my eyelids were battling sleep.

He'd sacrificed a great deal to bring me up here. I didn't want to insult his kindness by dozing off.

Meanwhile, I sneaked another peek in my passenger-door mirror at the black Mustang behind us.

Though Rosella wasn't true flesh and blood, when I was twelve, she moved me in with her—a long story—and after Mama died, she told me to call her my grandma. She might as well *be* my grandma. I've lived with her since that time, and loved her like my own.

I'd only met Matt, her real grandson, a week and a half ago. And despite my initial hesitation about him being the son of Grandma's horrible offspring, Sol—he neither looked nor acted like the man—I couldn't help but fall for him.

His good genes came from Grandpa Eduardo, Rosella's husband and the hero of my childhood.

And right now, I wanted so much to trade vehicles so Matt and I could chat.

Matt wanted the same thing. I could tell by the looks he gave me. But here I sat in the front car, all because Peter said he needed to discuss a few things with me. That was earlier in the day but not a peep so far about anything like that.

We reached Ocala, and Peter exited I-75. "Looks like we'll get off here."

"Highway 27?"

"We'll pick up 19 in Chiefland, take that to Perry, turn west on 98, and be in Carrabelle before dark."

"Hmm." The directions were simple. But not so much the decision I would soon have to make.

I peeked at the Mustang again. No matter which way this turned out, Grandma had come along as backup. Matt too.

Because at Carrabelle, along the Forgotten Coast, I'd figure out whether I wanted to introduce myself to my father or walk away and forget him.

An hour from Ocala, we hit Chiefland. Peter swung us into a fast-food joint where speckled sun scattered over a parking lot beneath the oaks. Grandma and I climbed out to find a restroom and order coffee. My legs rejoiced in the stretch. But Grandma balked when Matt pulled her walker out of the trunk.

"I don't need that," she said, shutting the door.

"Yeah," he reminded her, "but safety first."

She grasped the walker anyway. "I hate this thing."

I closed my own door. Good for her. With that independent spirit she'd regain her strength in no time.

She and I stayed together and then returned to the car, leaving the guys at the register.

She sat inside the car, and I returned the walker to the trunk and leaned against the open passenger door. Why get in when it was so beautiful outside?

Matt shouldered open the glass doors and came out first with a cardboard tray of coffee in his hands. "Just like his Grandpa Eduardo," I said as he approached but kept any comments about the tall, dark, and handsome part to myself.

"Yes. His character, too," Grandma added. She'd always emphasized its importance over looks when it came to advising me on boys. "Looks are fleeting," she'd say. "But character lasts."

Of course, good looks didn't hurt a bit.

Matt approached and flashed those gorgeous dimples as he set the carrier on top of the car. "Hi, there." He leaned in toward Grandma. "As you requested, m'lady." He handed her a cup. "Cream and sugar and *un poquito helado* all stirred in."

I pointed at him. "A little ice, right?"

He winked at me across his shoulder, and I grinned as he straightened and motioned for me to follow him a few steps away. "Good job," he said as I turned. "I mean, with the translation."

I smiled.

"But hey," he said with a slight shrug. "I'd been hoping we could chat before this, but…"

"Me too…" I tipped my chin toward the restaurant where Peter now emerged, carrier in hand.

When he set the carrier on the curb in front of his car and approached, Matt said, "Looks like it'll still have to wait."

Rats. Not one minute to ourselves.

Joining our group, Peter bowed and waved his arm in that uber-polite way of his—which allows him to get away with doing the stinkiest things. "Pardon me, *Coralcita,* could you allow Matt and me just one short minute? *Por favor?*"

Coralcita means *little Coral,* his way of heaping on the charm.

Might as well.

He wrapped an arm across Matt's shoulder and led him away even farther. But not before Matt tossed me a grin over his shoulder.

"Say, Matt, I was just thinking…" Peter began. His audibility faded quickly, but I could tell it was some detail regarding that co-executorship meeting back in Ft. Myers.

Over the years, Grandma had told me several times, "My son, Sol, will get plenty of money, but I don't want him involved in handling my will or funeral affairs. Especially those. I won't be cremated, and I won't be turned over to science. No, ma'am."

And only recently had she confided, "You and Matt will be handling my affairs—with Peter's help, of course—when the time comes. Sol is too greedy."

Hence the big meeting with Peter a few days ago. And that's what shook me up.

I'm not her real grandchild.

While Peter and Matt discussed business in the parking lot, I knelt down beside Grandma. "Mmmm. How's your coffee? Mine's just right."

"Delightful," she said. Not one to dwell on frivolous conversation, she had a way of switching subjects. "Matt's a good driver, you know."

I welcomed the topic of Matt. She never used to mention him or show me his picture. In fact, I thought she was hiding something nefarious from me. With Sol for his father, anyone might suspect that. But that joke was on me—another story for another time.

"Not reckless at all," she went on. "Matt was hoping to talk to you."

"I know."

Her eyes sparkled as she took another sip and dabbed her lipstick with a napkin. "Patience, dear."

"Sol's going to be livid, you know. About this inheritance thing."

"*Pfft!* Don't you worry about him. He's not dangerous. He's chronically irritated."

I laughed. More like chronically angry—not to mention selfish and greedy. So many times, I'd heard his loud, negative attitude through the phone. It never fazed her, though.

"He'll come around. Are you still praying for him?"

"Trying not to miss a day," I said.

She patted my arm. "Good girl. Then between you and Matt, he doesn't stand a chance, does he?"

"You're praying too, aren't you?"

She held up a finger. "God's listening. He's there. Don't think for a minute He's not."

Meanwhile, I cast a glance toward Peter, still monopolizing Matt's attention.

The nerve!

Grandma gave my arm a pinch, and I returned my gaze to her.

"Patience, my sweet. And guard your heart. Above all things, guard your heart."

I smiled. Maybe I should write that down in my book of sayings. How did one guard her heart?

About that time, Peter and Matt headed around to the driver's side of the Mustang where Peter punched the air with Latino enthusiasm. "Come on, everyone. Let's get as far as we can before Grandma gets worn out." He leaned into the Mustang. "Still comfy in there?"

Grandma grinned back.

And wait, was that a wink in Peter's eye?

"Oh, Matt's a fine driver. Wonderful ride," she said.

The rascal.

I circled around to Peter's car and grabbed our drink carrier from off the curb.

Peter had always filled that special father-figure slot for me—and had always been there when I needed him, full of wisdom and whatever.

But this!

P eter tapped my shoulder, and I squinted into a lowering sun.

"Wake up sleeping beauty, ten more miles."

I roused, sat up straight. "Ten?" Somewhere along the way our vehicles had curved around the Bend of Florida. The Forgotten Coast, they call it.

My heart leaped into overdrive. "Oh, no," I whispered. "This is it, isn't it?" Reality had arrived. I was about to see my flesh and blood father for the first time.

If it hadn't been for my mother's dying note, or Peter's research, this wouldn't be happening. Despite the seatbelt, I wrapped my arms around my knees.

"Listen, now, Coral," Peter said, interrupting my thoughts. "I want you to stay calm."

His voice took on a serious tone. "I mentioned it before, and here's what I've wanted to discuss."

"Discuss?"

"Say. Here's what I wanted to say. Much better word."

I nodded.

He gripped the wheel with both hands, the sun low and straight against our faces, flickering between the tall pines. "Your welfare is more important than some stranger. If you even get a hint of wanting out of this place, just call me. I'll be there. We'll toss your stuff in the car and head right back down to Fort Myers. No questions asked."

My heart skipped a beat. The reality of Peter actually leaving us here and heading back to Fort Myers now sank in.

"Peter, I can only imagine what you've had to give up for this trip…"

"Don't mention it."

No father could be more thoughtful, caring, or protective.

"Are you hearing what I'm saying?"

I nodded. Swallowed around the lump in my throat.

He used one hand now to emphasize his words. "You're under no obligation to stay, meet, speak to, or accept this person as family. This man's never been in your life, and he doesn't have to be a part of it now if that's what you want. He doesn't even need to know you're in town. Remember, I will come if you need me."

"I appreciate that, Peter. I really do."

Yes, there was always Peter.

Sol headed out of Las Vegas on Highway 15. It seemed to lead
in the right direction. South. After a bit, he'd find his way to I-10
and then head straight east.

Easy peasy.

He reached for the radio, turned the knobs, banged the dash,
but not a sound came out. Dead silence.

Puh!

He gave up, settled his hands on the wheel at ten and two, and
stared around at the boring landscape. Sol had nothing else to
do but think about that situation in Florida—and his upcoming
inheritance.

But dwelling on his inheritance—wait, no—his mother's death—
the whole thing felt like a wad of garbage in his chest.

It hurt that she chose Sol's son, Matt, to settle her inheritance—it
stung like bees to get leap-frogged over like that. His mother couldn't
be in her right mind, and Sol didn't deserve that kind of treatment.

He slapped the wheel. He'd show 'em.

For the time being, though, he didn't feel like thinking about it.

He spent a while counting the approaching cars and made a
game of guessing their make. It passed the time. Before long, he
grew bored with it. Besides, it made his eyes ache.

Sol started a new game, alphabetizing the things he'd packed.
He recalled an item for most of the letters—until he reached U.

And then it hit him… he'd forgotten his undershirts.

And undershorts.

"Noooo…."

That fact barely struck home before a troubling green sign

appeared just ahead. Its white printed words announced his arrival in Barstow.

He frowned. "Barstow? *Barstow?* That's in California."

He slowed enough to read more signs. Barstow Insurance. Barstow Bank.

He slammed his hand against the steering wheel. "Stupid road signs. Why didn't I have some kind of warning?"

From Barstow, Sol needed to find his way south to I-10. All he needed was a map.

Yes, he had a phone. But he liked maps. Hold-in-the-hand, hard-copy maps.

His stomach rumbled.

What he needed first was food. Nobody could think on an empty stomach.

Then he'd find a map.

He pulled off Highway 15 at the first place he found. Peggy Sue's '50s Diner. Good. Looked like a prime place to eat judging by the crowded parking lot.

Even before he reached the door, the fifties music from inside reached out to greet him. He sang along to Elvis wailin' about a hound dog. "Love those old tunes," he said aloud.

Inside, he was greeted with even louder music. Painted mannequins of Marilyn Monroe, Elvis, and other stars decorated the room. "My kinda place."

He climbed up on a counter stool, took a menu and studied all the famous names attached to the dishes.

The waitress approached.

"Yeah," he said, glancing up at her cute little fifties outfit and then back at the menu. "Uh, gimme one of these Marlon Brando burgers here."

She chewed her gum and scribbled on her pad as the jukebox switched over to *Put Your Head on my Shoulder*. "And to drink?"

"A Coke."

As she sashayed away, a shadow blocked the light behind Sol, and a gentleman, maybe close to seven feet tall and fair-haired like Sol, brushed by and perched on the stool beside him. He took a menu and smiled down at Sol. "Evening."

Sol nodded and then glanced sideways at the man's shirt. Palm trees and surfboards on a yellow background. Just like Sol's shirt. Hard to miss. This guy looked like an over-sized surfer dude. Maybe he was. Had the big white teeth, the tan.

The waitress returned with Sol's order. "What will you have, sir?" she asked the newcomer.

"Same as him, he said, sliding his menu back to its vertical position beside the sugar.

Eventually their food was served, and for a while, Sol and the stranger ate in silence.

As Sol polished off his onion rings, he sneaked another glimpse of the man's shirt—and then of his own—just to compare the designs again.

"You noticed my shirt," the man said, finishing his burger and washing it down with the Coke. "You shop at Wally-world too?"

Sol shrugged. "Guess so." Sol's ex had brought his home. If he could call Paulette that. They'd never married.

Then one day when their son Matt was a teen, she'd walked out. Disappeared. But not before an argument and her loud declarations of his selfishness.

"She'll come back one day," the stranger said.

Sol glanced around for the waitress. One day? She'd already served them. Why would the dude say that?

The man grinned and shook his head.

Sol frowned and turned his eyes away as he re-digested the comment. Then he swiveled around to face the man. "Say, do I know you?"

The man's eyes twinkled. "Call me Mike."

"You following me or something?"

"Not really. But I am heading east."

"Whaddya mean?" Sol asked.

"Florida."

Sol shook his head. This made no sense. *Crazy idiot.* He reached for the ticket and counted out the exact amount, minus a tip, and rose to leave. He couldn't get out of there fast enough.

But Mike stood and blocked his way.

"Hey!" Sol's head tipped back as he looked up at the Goliath.

The giant's voice was calm. "Leave a tip. You know better."

The pressure in Sol's veins rose. Nobody'd ever called him out on his lack of tips before.

Nobody but his mother. Oh, and maybe Paulette.

The man held his place like a brick chimney. Sol couldn't squeeze out if he tried. "Oh, all right." He pulled out his wallet again. Laid down a dollar.

The chimney held fast.

"For Pete's sake." Sol fished out a five and laid it down. He didn't dare take back the one.

"That's better."

Sol clamped his lips tight as he stowed away his wallet.

Busybody.

R alph Stone stepped into Carrabelle's darkness and fog. He snapped the cottage door shut behind him. Not quite a slam but a clear rebuff to Millie and her obvious hints inside.

She knew he didn't need no dang wife. He slung his work apron over his shoulder, the one she'd laid out all clean and pressed by the door just now, and swiped his knuckles across his mouth, scraping away the bacon grease.

Nah, he didn't give a clamshell how wifely she wanted to carry on. It made no never mind to him that she got up every morning at four to cook him bacon, eggs, and toast. Ralph wasn't falling for any of her tricks. Sure, that was all nice. She was nice too. He even loved her. But he didn't need no wife. Didn't need to be tied down.

Didn't need no kids.

That's the way things were, and that's the way they'd stay.

He stalked along the broken sidewalk for several blocks, but thoughts nibbled around his brain. A picture of Millie's long lashes and big brown eyes filled his imagination. His pace diminished. Millie did mean well. And he ought to have kissed her good-bye. No need to hurt her feelings. Maybe he should turn around... *Enh.* He was already late. He'd make it up to her at ten when she came in to work. Ralph turned into the next street. Within a block, he reached the side porch of Aunt Allie's ancient corner store and its mammoth mulberry tree. Its overhanging limbs nearly hid the corroded stop sign.

Aunt Allie, though very dear to him, was not his real aunt.

She rose with the chickens, so he stepped lightly, as usual, like he had for the past twenty years, avoiding any chance encounter with her.

Ralph paused beneath the sign like he did every morning and inclined his ear to the sounds across the highway. Sounds of the Gulf. Well… the Carrabelle River. Same thing, nearly. It was all connected.

He tipped his head to concentrate on the sounds and smells around him. And this morning not a frond rustled. Not a wave slapped. No hint of a storm today. He breathed in the usual heavy odor of low tide—decaying oysters and marsh mud—and inclined his ear toward the faint racket of fishermen up the river at the icehouse. Sounds filtered easily across the water. The voices, one of them surely his old friend Zeke's, mixed together with the clatter and bang of ice loading into their refrigerator-sized chests for today's catch.

Ralph picked up a stone and rolled it between his fingers. He zeroed in on the carved Captain's Table sign on this east end of the bridge. The other sign, planted at the west end, was next to the restaurant. Ralph carved them as gifts when Dad bought the building.

Before Ralph's rotten decisions.

If only he could back up time and undo it all—carry out his and Zeke's childhood plans—to endure the rigor of boat life, ride the waves of an angry black sea, or squint into blinding ripples ahead of the sunrise. But Zeke—like Aunt Allie—could pry the truth out of anyone. Even Ralph.

So Ralph stayed away. From both of them.

He inhaled and hurled the stone. And just like other mornings, his rock missed the sign and disappeared into the darkness. He shook his head and moved toward the incline of the bridge.

Ralph stepped between the fog-slippery lines of Highway 98. He'd barely set out when headlights behind him thrust his shadow post-haste in the opposite direction. He scrambled toward the limestone surface in front of Aunt Allie's store—just as a massive produce truck thundered by, its tailwind whipping the apron against Ralph's face. *Dang!* He snatched it away and thrust up his arm in a universal salute—along with a curse-word. "Boy, if I were a cop right now…!" he yelled.

Seconds later the truck's lights blazed across the palms behind the Captain's Table where they swung in hard behind his restaurant.

Oh, wait. Today was produce day.

Arms pumping, Ralph took off sprinting.

Ralph had spent four years in the Army, and now, after sixteen years, he still kept in shape. He walked to and from work. He watched his weight—most of the time—and even jogged a little. Still, he craved activity. Manly things. Not stuff like standing around in a restaurant, but real activity.

Barely out of breath, and proud of it, he reached his three-story building. No sir, he'd never let himself go.

But as he rounded the corner behind his building, he pulled up short. There stood his pimple-faced cook Larry in scraggly silhouette—outlined by the truck's colorful brake lights. Their red glow dimmed as the knucklehead driver climbed out of his truck and headed around to lift its back door.

Ralph glanced back at Larry. Well, well, well. For once, his cook was on time. But there he stood, smoking a dang cigarette, messing up the air, and completely oblivious to Ralph. Ralph hated cigarettes at his back door and didn't want the smoke drifting into his kitchen.

Mew! One of the restaurant's kittens—Ralph's orphaned kittens—no bigger than a sandpiper—stared up at Larry. Larry lowered his cigarette, "Get away from me you rodent!" He scooped a foot beneath its belly.

Ralph opened his mouth as Larry's foot swung up—and the cat sailed in a perfect arc into a leafy clump of young sabal palms beyond the truck.

It landed against the foliage and slid down to safety, but still…

Knucklehead, with his back turned, missed it all. But now he turned, made eye contact with Ralph and paused, most likely recognizing him as the person he'd almost plowed down on the road just now.

Larry, observing the knucklehead's gaze, twisted around to see what he was looking at. At the sight of Ralph, he froze in his tracks, his mouth open.

Yeah.

Ralph's fists curled.

Everybody knew how Ralph felt about those cats.

What Ralph did next might have been a little different had the produce driver not been there.

Ralph signaled for Larry to come close and then stepped around with his back to the driver. This was none of his business.

Ralph gritted his teeth. "You got two choices, you kitten-kickin' punk. You big bully."

The kid glanced at Ralph's tattooed biceps all back-lit in red from the tail lights. He swallowed hard. A second kitten moved into the space between them.

Mew!

Ralph took a step toward Larry. Jabbed his thumb toward the bushes. "I can send you sailin' into the palms like the kitty…"

Larry blinked, stepped back, but kept his eyes on Ralph's unflinching glare.

"Or you take off runnin'—back home to your mama." Ralph

spat the last word. He leaned into the kid's face, and the next two words came out nice and slow. "Now choose!"

The boy nearly fell into the gravel as he spun around and took off down the road from which Ralph had just arrived. He didn't live far, of course.

"And don't come back," Ralph yelled. "Oh. And just for your information," he added, "cats ain't rodents."

He whirled around to face the driver, mouth agape, and the back of his truck still closed.

"Stupid kid," Ralph told him. "Nobody kicks my kitties around."

J essica Parker's old gray Toyota crawled west along Florida's Highway 98. Today, her first appointment as a home health nurse would land her west in Apalachicola. On the return trip, she would meet her new patient at the B&B in Carrabelle—an elderly woman recovering from sepsis.

Jessica never minded such distances, and the slow scenic drive along Florida's Forgotten Coast allowed her time to think. And she certainly needed it after her boyfriend's bad attitude back at the apartment this morning.

An hour before her alarm was set to blare, he'd snatched off her covers and yelled about the cereal she'd brought home. The wrong kind.

But she'd gotten even with him by slinging open the front door and emptying the box all over the parking lot. Now he had nothing. Well, at least the crows and seagulls loved her. Next time, he'd be smart enough to put his preference on the grocery list. Or keep quiet.

But all's well that ends well, and the spat was soon over. He apologized and made it up to her by fixing her a large Styrofoam coffee-to-go.

It wasn't exactly a lovers' quarrel, but more like a roommates-with-benefits tiff. At least they ended in a truce. But his days were numbered. If there were any other rentals along this coast—something she could afford by herself—he'd be out on his ear. She'd send him right back to Tallahassee.

Lately he was even slacking off his half of the bills. Freeloader.

Near the curve in Carrabelle, she grasped the top of the cup and lifted it midway. *Eeow!* A splat of hot liquid scalded her leg.

The lid was loose. "My scrubs!" With the cover still in her palm and the squished cup sliding between her fingers, she steadied it against the gear-shift. She'd have to pull over.

She steered to the right across the limestone parking lot of an old store with her non-dominant hand and gasped when it smacked the barely balanced cup. Coffee slopped across the steering wheel and drained onto her scrubs.

She winced. This couldn't be happening.

Her boyfriend's grin—no, his smirk—came to mind then—and that wink he gave her as he leaned across her driver's seat to place his peace offering in her cupholder. "Have a nice day," he'd said, and backed away with both hands on the window.

Only now did the actual truth sink in. He'd loosened the lid on purpose.

Vengeful thing.

Jessica glanced up at the grayed boards of the old store in front of her vehicle.

Coffee trickled down her leg as she maneuvered the car into park. She fished under the seat for a box of tissues. "Look at this mess," she moaned as she pulled out a handful, mopped up, and returned the cup to its rightful place.

Her lips clamped together. She'd never let on to her boyfriend how he'd pulled off his dirty little trick. What a child. Starting today she'd keep her eyes open—for an apartment of her own.

She glanced down at her near-empty coffee cup. There were so few places along this Forgotten Coast where she could find a cup, or even a bathroom.

And this didn't look like one of them.

She studied the store's salt-filmed windows and cracked open the car door. Rusty signs lined the building's weathered clapboards and boasted lots of sodas—but no coffee.

The place was open, though, and worth a try. Wet fabric clung to her knee as she pushed the door wide and dabbed at it using up the rest of the tissues. One good thing—the busy print would hide most of the stain. But she'd have to smell the coffee-perfume all day.

She exited the car and climbed the sagging wooden steps.

The store's screen door squeaked as she pulled it open and stepped in. A bell tinkled somewhere in the back.

Jessica took in her surroundings. Wow. She was used to weathered buildings along the coast, but this building wasn't just weathered. It was ancient.

Wooden counters lined the sides of the long narrow room.

Store-length shelves, sparingly stocked with dusty items, covered the walls behind the counters. Gee, this was a museum. Straight out of the 1800s.

"Anybody home?" she hollered.

"I hear you," a woman called out. The voice was elderly but strong. "Coming."

Jessica studied the curved glass cases with their gum and candy—mostly small individually wrapped pieces—the antique register, and the assortment of cans, borax, bug spray, chicken feed, and school supplies on the shelves.

At the far end of the central area sat an old wood stove and behind that a third wooden counter. A sign on top read, "Pull string to ring bell if you don't see me." A sturdy string reached from there to the back of the building.

Through a door in the back of the room shuffled an old lady with white hair like Einstein's.

"Mornin', I was just turnin' off the gas stove," she said, her voice warbling but sturdy as she caned her way into the room.

Jessica detected a faint hint of coffee and hoped it wasn't just the smell of her own clothes.

The little lady's cane tapped forward and then paused ten feet away. The lady shielded her eyes from the glare of the single bulb and probably the front door too. She squinted at Jessica.

"Are you my granddaughter?" A strong sense of expectation, more like a demand, accompanied her question.

Jessica had heard this very same thing from former patients at the Apex Retirement Village. They always hoped for the grands who never seemed to come.

"I'm sorry, but no. I just came to see if you had any coffee."

"*Hmph*. Must be my bad eyesight. Or these old glasses," the lady said, lowering her hand. "Anyway, coffee's almost done." She motioned to a sitting area of ancient orange crates and broken chairs fitted out with a variety of flattened homemade cushions around the cold Franklin stove. "Here. Have a seat. Sit a spell."

A whiff of stale ashes and pine kindling met Jessica's nostrils as she hooked her purse over the arm of the only straight-back chair and sat down. "I don't have too long," Jessica said. "I spilled my coffee in the car."

"I'm sorry to hear that. You must be on your way to work."

She nodded and brushed at the stain on her leg. The spot hardly showed against the seascape design of her scrubs. But its dampness remained. "It'll be dry soon."

"I thought you were my granddaughter just now. There was a dream I had."

"Oh?"

The lady squinted, "You do believe in dreams?"

Jessica nodded. She'd had a few herself.

"And with the light behind your head just now you looked exactly like the girl in my dream. So much like my granddaughter."

"I'm sorry," Jessica said.

The woman leaned both hands on the cane and then took a seat in what was probably her favorite spot, a shabby armchair rocker. "She'll come back."

"I hope so. What about your children? Do you still have them around?"

"One daughter. Gone. Except for the granddaughter. I've had that dream twice now. I know she'll return. She'd be thirty-four by now. Just about your age."

"I bet she's beautiful."

"Nadine. That's her name. It means hopeful."

"I hope she does come back."

"Left us some twenty years ago. Fourteen years old. And I've asked the Lord to put His big angels around her. To protect her. Draw her to Himself."

Jessica hoped so. For this lady's sake.

"I'm Alice Bentley, by the way. Call me Aunt Allie. What do you call yourself?"

"Jessica," she said, shifting.

"Might be a minute more on the coffee. I don't usually have requests. So, it's no charge."

How could Allie afford to run a store like that?

Allie laid her cane across the chair's arms and rested her pale hands on top. The skin was papery and full of age spots. She still wore a wedding band. Her cane's tip had long since worn away and left behind a hollow metal tube.

Allie mentioned the weather and asked about Jessica's daily drive.

Jessica explained how beautiful and relaxing the drive was and then added, "I could get you a new tip for that cane, Miss Allie. We've got plenty where I used to work."

Allie lifted the cane and pointed its hollow end in Jessica's direction. "See this hole?"

Jessica nodded.

"That little hole once saved my life."

Jessica observed as Aunt Allie planted the cane on the store's worn floor and stood. She seemed as spry as any old lady Jessica had ever seen.

"I'd love to hear that story," Jessica said. "About the cane saving your life."

Aunt Allie headed for the kitchen. "That coffee's probably done. You run back to the car and get your cup. Mine are all glass."

Jessica stepped outside, grabbed the mostly empty Styrofoam cup and a few dollars from the glovebox and stepped back inside. She wasn't about to let this little old lady give her the coffee for free. The store's screen door slammed behind her. *Whoops.* "Sorry! Didn't mean to slam the door," she hollered.

"Come on to the back, Jessica," Aunt Allie called.

The store, with its high beadboard ceiling, was dark and cool, and for the second time, Jessica blinked to adjust her eyes. She stepped past the Franklin stove, the counter behind it, and crossed the area between it and the kitchen. A dizzy joy stirred inside her like that of a young child allowed into a wonderland.

The next thing she knew, her feet were standing upon the smooth floral-patterned surface of Allie's ancient kitchen. Curtains hung below the sink and around the room in place of cupboard doors.

How simple and quaint. "I've never been in a kitchen like this."

"Once you fill your cup, come back out to the stove, and I'll tell you that story."

Jessica poured her cup, topped it off with cool water from the faucet, and snapped on the lid—a better job than Nick had done—but not before taking another glance around. She left the money on the heavy oak breakfast table and caught up with Allie as she reached the Franklin stove. "I'll have to leave for work in a few minutes," Jessica said. "But I've got just enough time to hear your story."

"That's all right. I know you have to go. And I'll keep it short." Allie sat and leaned forward with both hands on the cane.

Her sharp blue eyes struck Jessica as fierce behind the glasses.

"One evening I was closing up shop—counting out the register. Wasn't much in there. My cane was up there on the counter to my left. I'd laid my newspaper on top. And in came these two big strappin' boys."

"No, not a stick up…"

"Yes, ma'am," she said. "And, oh, Nellie, I read the meanness in their eyes. 'Whadyou boys want?' I said, 'I'm closed now.'"

Jessica shifted in her chair.

Aunt Allie pointed to the register along the east counter. "Right over there it happened."

Jessica nodded.

"They had no gun, but they stepped forward—those two big old boys. Well, I jiggled that cane layin' there under my newspaper, had it pointed straight at 'em. Placed two hands on it under there. 'Course, they couldn't tell it was just a cane. All they saw was that hole in the end."

Allie banged her cane on the floor and Jessica jumped.

"'Shoo,' I told 'em, 'before I blow your brains out with this shot-gun.'" She chuckled. "You should've seen them back away and then turn and run out that door. Like two scared rabbits. Got in a car and took off down that road. And I haven't seen 'em since."

Jessica laughed and shook her head at this woman's spunk. "I'm glad that turned out good for you."

Allie nodded.

Jessica stood and collected her purse. "I'd like to stop by and visit again if I could."

The old woman leaned on her cane and rose. "Anytime, Jessie. Glad to have you. Oh. And here," she shuffled past Jessica and toward the front window where she came around behind the candy counter. She took a Snickers bar from its box under the glass counter and held it out to Jessica. "You take this now. Enjoy it for a snack."

Jessica, unsure of what else to do, took the candy. "Thank you. I appreciate it."

Aunt Allie shuffled away from Jessica, one hand on the counter, and one on her cane. "You have a nice day now."

Jessica wondered if Allie's granddaughter would ever show up. She hoped so. In the meantime, Jessica would return. A hundred horses couldn't keep her away.

I sat upright as Peter slowed the car to a crawl. He pointed out the little green sign up ahead. "Carrabelle, Florida. We've arrived."

Highway 98 curved dramatically through the tiny little town. We passed quaint shops along a boardwalk to our left. Between that and the sparkling waters rose a captivating jungle of sunlit masts, waving flags, and furled sails from a long row of docked fishing and pleasure boats.

But we weren't here for that. We were looking for a restaurant called the Captain's Table.

We rolled forward, and there at the base of the bridge we found the sign. A small routed one just like Peter had shown me on the Google Earth maps. We crossed over the river, curving left to the west end of the village. And there on the left at the bottom of the bridge rose a concrete and glass structure along the water much taller than all its neighbors. According to Peter, my dad had inherited it from his father.

Who would have been my grandfather.

"There it is," Peter said, "in all its glory. Your dad's restaurant."

The weather was hot, but I crossed my arms to suppress a shiver. "Well, it's clean, right? I'm not sure what I expected to see."

"Clean's important," Peter said.

"And… it's got decorative potential."

"Spoken like a true dress designer. Always fixing things up."

"Yeah." It did need fixing up. "You've got to admit it's drab and unfinished."

"Maybe he's not so good at decorating."

I squeezed my arms and wondered what his talents were.

Peter pulled over and put the car in park so we could take a better look. After a minute, he turned his face to me. I'd seen that look before.

"I'm sorry, Peter. I haven't even met the man, and here I am criticizing." But then maybe I was just getting ahead of things in case this turned out to be a big letdown.

"I've heard restaurant work is hard," he said. "Maybe he spends all his time running the place. Needs someone with creative ideas to come along."

"Don't say it like that. You've already got me talking to him."

"Running a restaurant and keeping it profitable could be a good sign. Maybe he's the responsible type," Peter said.

I took a deep breath, reached for my cup to see if I had a little sip of coffee left so I could take a Tylenol.

As I reached for the cup, Peter took my fingers and gave them a squeeze. "Look at that. You're shaking like a leaf. Remember what I said. Even one hint you want out of this…"

I nodded. Blinked hard. "Okay," I whispered. "Got it."

After taking my Tylenol, we made a U-turn with Matt and Grandma's Mustang following tight behind us. For several minutes there I'd forgotten about the two of them.

Peter pointed across the bridge back toward town. "That was your bed and breakfast back there," he said. "We'll check it out in just a sec."

In the meantime, Peter allowed his car to crawl as we studied the building again. We coasted by the Captain's Table, its near-side shaded from the lowering sun.

He cleared his throat as we crested the bridge. "I checked and triple checked our sources, Coral, and to the best of my knowledge, I haven't brought you up here to meet someone with a criminal record. There's no wife that we know of."

I turned away from the scene, gripped my knees, and blew out a long slow breath.

"There is one good thing—your dad was honorably discharged from the army."

Well, there was that. I could only hope this man was different from all Mom's others. He might even be an American hero— seeing how he was once in the Army.

Might be.

Though few seemed to exist, there were some good men around— Eduardo, Peter—Matt.

But I'd also seen more than my fair share of the rotten ones.

I wasn't going to get my hopes up.

After Sol left the diner, he was still rattled by his encounter with the giant and gave scant thought to topping off the car's gas tank. He made his way through San Bernardino, stopped for a map at a Quick-Stop, but found nothing. Nobody had maps anymore. But he lucked out when he asked for verbal directions, and found himself just before the last little stretch south to I-10.

And there was the sign. Finally. He turned left and swung onto the road. A few more miles and he'd be home free.

All he had to do at that point was follow I-10 to Florida.

Scenery flew by as he pressed the accelerator, and by the time he remembered he should have located a gas station back at the last stop, the vehicle jerked and *sput-sput-sputted*. His gaze shifted to the gas gauge where the needle pointed straight at the bottom end of the red E, and he filled the air with his choicest curse words.

A quick look around at the barren, stick-dry surroundings and he muttered a few more.

"Just what I don't *neeeeeed!* Come on, car. Not here. Not here," he coaxed. Up ahead—maybe a mile away—stood a familiar-style gas station sign. "See? C'mon, Betsy. There's gas right up there." But it was no use. Betsy's engine fizzled to a stop. "Dadgummit!" He whacked the steering wheel with his hand, wrangled the tires onto the rocky shoulder, and thrust the vehicle into park.

With a turn of his shoulder and a lift of the door handle, Sol stepped out. Heat wafted up off the asphalt, bellowed out his shorts and shirt and threatened to melt off his chest hairs and other important parts. How did those pioneers do it?

He squinted and hoped that gas station wasn't some deserted relic like in the westerns.

A debate raged in his head—whether to hitch a ride or walk. He stood there, propped his back side against the broiling vehicle for one brief instant and then jerked away.

Decision made. He reached around to make sure he had his wallet and then clamped his lips tight. Here was the deal. If somebody drove past and offered him a lift, he'd accept. But only if the person looked safe.

In the meantime, he glanced down at his hairy toes. At least his flip flops were thick. He stepped forward over the gravel. Better get moving.

About fifty feet down the road, *beep beep!* He whirled around as a red Jeep pulled in behind his car.

A Jeep. Yes! That had to be good. In car language, that meant an outdoorsman, not a bandit or a murderer.

He trotted back the short distance, spent his energy, and by the time he reached the side of his car, had to lean forward to gasp for breath. Not like back in the day, for sure. Sweat dripped off his brow and onto his wire-rimmed glasses.

Well, he had good reason to be out of shape, being indoors all the time. Other folks got to swim in pools and have vacations. Sol? He had responsibilities. Had to work all the time.

He slid a hand across his sweaty bald spot and then straightened. He wiped his glasses on the tail of his tropical shirt. Shoulda brought a hat.

Good thing somebody stopped. Out here in this sun, he'd either be dead or burnt by the time he reached that gas station.

He waved at the driver still inside the Jeep but couldn't make out a thing through the windows. "Hi, buddy."

The door opened and a set of long legs clad in khaki pants and flip flops touched earth.

The man's torso leaned out, and Sol's hand froze in mid-wave. It was Mike. The giant. Sol dropped his arm.

The brute grinned at him, went around to the back of his Jeep, and opened it up.

Sol gaped as the man came back around with a big red gas can. Come to think of it this man looked more like the Terminator. Sol swallowed and took a shallow breath of oven-hot air.

The man extended the can on his three middle fingers. "Looks like you've run out of gas. Think you could use this?"

"How'd you know?"

"Happens to the best of 'em. Good to be prepared. How 'bout you pop open your gas cap?"

By the time he pulled the lever and came back around Term was already pouring in the gas. Fumes rose around him.

But as Sol glanced at the ground by the man's feet his mouth fell open. All he could do was point like an idiot to the fat rattlesnake that lay coiled on the rocks. "S-snake!" was all he could get out.

The giant turned and nodded, wedged the side of his foot beneath the reptile and flipped it up and over the embankment as if it were no big deal. He continued pouring in the gasoline.

Sol felt the blood rush from his face. "Are you nuts? What did you just do? That…that thing could have bit you."

The man shrugged. "I'm fine. Just fine." He tipped the rest of the gasoline into the car. "I do appreciate your concern, though."

Sol stared as the giant re-screwed the black cap onto the empty jug and handed it over to Sol. "Fill the jug and keep it full for the long roads. You never know what could happen."

Sol reached around for his wallet. "Well, thank you. How much do I owe you for this?"

"Never you mind. Just pass on the good deed," the man said as he hopped into his Jeep and turned his key.

Sol gripped the handle of the jug as the guy slammed his door.

Hey, that was convenient. Sol hadn't made out too bad. Free gas. Free gas can.

But on the way to climb in he noted his tires once again. And now they all seemed pretty low. Better get those tended to right away. Maybe that would be free too.

Sol watched as the red Jeep pulled onto the asphalt, passed on by, and moved down the highway. He didn't give a care if he never saw the dude again. Helpful or not. Big people like that gave Sol the willies. Even if he had saved Sol's skin.

He thought back to the incident at that fifties diner and the way the dude stood in Sol's way until he left a tip. And then waited there till he gave an even bigger tip.

Who was this guy?

Enforcer was a pretty good label. But no…Sol thought about it a little more before he turned the key. No. Terminator was a better name. Like that guy in the movie. Yeah. Just like him.

And call him Term for short. Term. That was it. Sol laughed out loud at the new nickname as he started his engine and let down the window. Then just like the giant, he turned his wheels onto the asphalt.

A glance at the dead radio reminded him he couldn't turn on some rippin' loud music to go with his close call of nearly having to walk a mile to the gas station up ahead.

He gathered up some speed to close the gap between him and the gas station. He returned his eyes to the road and squinted. Looked like a dark blur in the distance. Something up there on the left shoulder. As he drew closer, he coasted past another broken down traveler going in the opposite direction.

Sol slipped on by avoiding the guy's hopeful gaze. He couldn't help him. His gas can was empty.

Let somebody else stop, some do-gooder going in the same direction.

Besides, this running out of gas thing had already slowed Sol down, and he wasn't interested in more delays. And his tires… He needed to fill them up too.

As he reached the gas station, his tires crunched as he circled around to the air pump. *Free,* it said. His kind of place.

But there, blocking his access, sat that same dadgum Jeep. With nobody in it. He'd have to park behind it and wait his turn.

Sol rolled down his window and turned off the motor. He craned his neck across the passenger seat and toward the front of the station where he might spot the giant. Where was the guy anyway? Not a sign. Probably in the men's room.

A tap on Sol's left shoulder nearly made him jump out of his skin. He whirled around. "Wha…?"

There, ten inches from his face, leaned Mike's big face. The Terminator.

Sol backed away. "What are *you* doin' here?"

"Did you pass it on?"

The vision of the broken-down but hopeful traveler flashed across Sol's mind.

"What are you talking about?"

Term crossed his arms and stood tall.

Sol gripped the window's edge. He leaned out and stared up. "I couldn't stop. I needed air." Besides, it was more than a hundred degrees out there.

"They're still out there. You can get air when you get back."

"But the can. It's empty."

Term grinned and motioned toward Sol's trunk. "Fill it up, then."

There went that free gas. Looked like Sol wasn't getting ahead on this deal. But there was no arguing with this brute. Sol popped his trunk and climbed out. Term circled around to the passenger door and opened it up. He tossed Sol's snack bag into the back seat and plopped himself inside.

Just like some dadgum teenager.

"Make yourself at home," Sol muttered. He grabbed the handle of the gas can and yanked. But the gas can didn't fly right out as Sol expected. "Hey!" He tried again. "This…this thing is full!"

"Let's go," came Term's voice from inside. "Let's get on down there. The lady's about to have a baby. Quit wasting time. It's broiling out there on the road. More than a hundred degrees."

"Like I said…." Wait. No, Sol hadn't said that about the temperature. Not out loud.

Sol stared at the gas can. Slapped it a few times to make sure he wasn't imagining things, and came back around to climb in. As he turned the key, he frowned at Term and pointed at his own eyes. "I saw you with my own eyes. You emptied that gas can back there."

Term grinned, rolled down the window, and leaned his elbow out. "Okay, Sol, just step on it, please."

And furthermore, what did Term know about the car back there? Sol hadn't seen a woman, just a man standing out there.

As they approached the broken-down car, and Sol pulled onto the shoulder, Term spoke up. "You go ahead. I'll watch… or step in if you need help."

Sol shifted the car into park and stepped out. He hollered the obvious. "You out of gas?"

The man approached, his body language clearly that of the grateful. He motioned toward his car. "Yes, and my wife's about to have a baby. We were headed to San Bernardino."

Sol eased the door shut. "I think I can help you, then." He stepped around back to the trunk. He was no good with mechanics, but he could pour gas into a tank.

The man lifted his ball cap and ran five shaky fingers through his hair. "You don't know how much we appreciate this."

As Sol brought the gas can around, he could see the woman in the passenger seat. Maybe Term wasn't so daft after all.

"Glad to help," he said.

Shaky reached for the gas can. "What's your name, sir?" he said as he took it from Sol's hands.

By now, Term had stepped out and stood near the back of the couples' car. "Tell the man to empty the can, and then hang onto it. The same way I told you before."

Sol frowned and wondered why Term didn't tell the man himself.

But he did as Term said. "Just keep the can. It's yours. And pass on the favor."

"Oh, thank you, sir," the man said as if Term wasn't even there. "But what's your name?"

"Here," Sol fished out his wallet, found a business card. He held it up and then laid it on the fender of the car. "Sol Flores. At your service in the CBD business. Las Vegas."

The man nodded as he poured. "Thank you. Thank you, a million times, over."

From inside the car, the lady let out a yelp. "It's getting close, honey. Hurry."

The gas can was nearly drained out. Sol backed toward his own vehicle. "San Bernardino's not that far. It's straight up that way. You'll see the signs. I just came from there."

The man nodded, capped the can, grabbed the card, threw the can in his trunk, waved, thanked Sol again, and leaped back in his car. He spun rocks as he sped away, arm out the window, waving.

Sol watched as the vehicle grew small in the distance. Then he and Term climbed back in. As he made an illegal U-turn and picked up speed, Term spoke up. "How'd that feel?"

A mile of dry landscape flickered by before he answered. "About a hundred twenty degrees is all."

"You know what I'm talking about."

The gas station grew larger as Sol considered his answer. But he had nothing. Besides, he still needed to air up his tires.

But as he circled around to the air pump, Sol stared at the empty space where the red Jeep had been. "Where's your vehicle?"

Term grinned and offered no answer. They stepped out, and Sol aired up the tires as Term stood by. Sol stared up at the man, waiting for some kind of response.

"Ah, don't you worry about the Jeep. I can get another."

"But where'd it go?" Filling the tires gave Sol time to mull things over. He put away the hose and came back to the car. Term had once again planted himself in the front passenger seat.

"Coupla things, Ter—, I mean, Mike." Sol cleared his throat. "Listen," he said, crossing his arms. "I'm not callin' you Mike. It doesn't suit you. You don't even look like a Mike. Your name's Term. And that's that." He slid behind the wheel.

Term scratched his chin.

"First, how'd you know my name back there?" Sol continued. "And how'd you know about the woman and the baby?"

Term shrugged, but Sol waited. He'd about had it with all these weird things happening.

And then there was the filled-up gas can.

"Call me whatever you like," Term said. "And now that I've lost my ride, I suppose you don't mind if I hitch a ride out to Florida with you, do you?"

Sol gazed past Term and through the passenger window. This guy was a pirate. A dadgum pirate.

On the other hand, he wasn't particularly dangerous.

He turned the key in the ignition. "Fine, whatever." What else could Sol say? He shrugged his shoulder. Free gas. Help. Whatever.

At least the dude didn't stink.

I fell in love with The Cozy Inn, an old two-story bed and breakfast with plenty of porches and lots of gingerbread, flowers, and foliage.

We got settled in and unpacked. Grandma needed a nap.

But not Matt. He brought everything in and headed out to explore to village.

"If you need me," Peter said, "I'll be taking a long nap up in Matt's room before my drive back."

Before I could ask any questions, Peter was halfway up the stairs.

But he turned and bent low to peek between the balusters. "Coral, I apologize that you and Matt didn't get to visit on the way up. But," he winked in that mischievous way, "I think you'll find plenty of time." He started to turn again but stopped. "Oh, yes. And delighted to see y'all worked out your differences back there in Ft. Myers."

Peter was talking about our mutual suspicion before we first met. But that's another story…

I grinned, closed our door, and turned to Grandma. "I've never stayed in a bed and breakfast before," I said. "But I love this one."

"It's certainly cozy," she said.

I could tell by her voice she was exhausted.

"I agree with Peter. But take things slow, Coral. There's no rush."

I didn't realize she could hear what Peter said from the stairs.

"I declare, you sound just like him," I said.

She laughed and kicked off her shoes.

Grandma still had her old spark.

Once I settled in at the B&B, my stomach began to complain. Lunch was wearing off, and my insides were whining for supper. So, as Grandma napped, I sat in the armchair and sipped on bottled water. I studied the coupons and list of restaurants on the bedside table. The Cozy Inn, instead of meals, offered breakfast or discounts at a variety of restaurants in town. The Captain's Table was on top of their list—alphabetically at least.

My father's business was only a short walk over the bridge, and I knew we'd be down there, but I couldn't bear to go just yet. I wondered what Matt would want to do. One thing for sure, we'd be bringing Grandma's meals to her for a while.

Within minutes, I fell asleep in the chair. But I didn't sleep long. The front doorbell woke me up. I stepped down the hall and cracked open the front door, and a girl about my age with long chestnut hair and freckles stood there. I glanced at her name badge, hardly believing the nurse had made it here already.

"Hey there…" She had a southern lilt to her voice.

I liked her immediately.

"I'm Jessica, the home-health nurse and I'm looking for Ms. Rosella Flores."

"Great," I said, opening the door wide and showing her down the hall to our room. "We've been expecting you, but this is amazing. I'm Coral."

"Amazing?"

"I mean fast. And a relief to see you. I thought it would take days."

"I was just on my way back from Apalachicola," she said, stepping in and setting down her bag. "So, I decided to go ahead and stop by. Thought we might as well get acquainted, especially since Mr. Cordero called the agency yesterday and urged me to stop by so he could meet Mrs. Flores's caregiver."

At that point, she glanced over and realized Grandma was asleep. "Oh," she whispered. "So sorry."

"It's okay," I said. "Grandma's tired but never very concerned about losing sleep. She'll be fine with your visit."

We woke Grandma and guided her into the chair while Jessica gave her a once-over. Of course, Grandma never met a stranger, and freckle-faced Jessica would likely end up being her friend. Turned out Jessica lived at Lanark, a little town to the east, and served patients all the way to Apalachicola.

After the exam, Jessica nodded and tucked away her stethoscope and blood-pressure cuff. "Miss Rosella, you certainly are in good shape, and I'm impressed, especially considering your long trip today. But again, I am really sorry I ruined your nap. Maybe you can finish it now."

"Never you mind, Jessica," Grandma said, shifting in her arm chair. "I'll be taking all the naps I can stand and then some." She waved an arm toward the bedroom's bookshelf. "And in between, I'll have plenty of entertainment."

"That's good, ma'am." The nurse tipped her chin in my direction. "And I can tell you're in good hands."

"Oh, indeed," Grandma said.

"Just be a good patient for me now. Don't you go exerting yourself. I'll be back in a few short days to check on you. Here's my number if y'all need me." She handed us each her cream-colored card with a pink stethoscope on front. Cute.

In the meantime, someone came clomping down the stairs, then knocked on our door. I answered, and there stood Peter buttoning his cuffs. As tired as he looked, he seemed determined to head back out. The judge had only delayed the trial a few days. As I mentioned, this trip was a real sacrifice for Peter and all his associates.

"Would this happen to be Mr. Cordero?" Jessica asked.

Peter stuck out his hand, and I introduced them, thankful they'd met, and left them to chat while I ducked into the hall to set up the coffeemaker. It was well stocked with cups, lids, and a variety of flavored coffees, so I made Peter three strong cups of hazelnut for his trip.

Recognizing Peter needed to leave, Jessica kept the conversation brief and then said good-bye.

After she left, I leaned my head into Grandma's room where Peter sat perched on the other chair.

"Coffee's all set. But what are you going to do for supper?" I asked him, wondering if he'd stick around that long. No doubt I'd be on pins and needles till he lodged somewhere for the night. He planned to do so down the road. Otherwise, there was no way he could safely reach Ft. Myers. I hoped he wouldn't fall asleep or forget to let us know when he stopped. He wasn't forgetful, though. His mental lists were long and dependable.

"Don't worry. I'll stop and eat somewhere." Peter hated fast food. "I've got a room in Ocala, and in the morning, on to Ft. Myers. I'll be there by lunchtime. You know how it is. I've got plenty to think about. There's nothing like pondering a case to keep a lawyer awake."

That and all the phone calls. "I feel bad you spent your time entertaining me on the way up here," I said, "you lost all your prep time."

He shook his head.

"You're one in a million, Peter. Thank you."

The front door squeaked open, and I peeked around the corner. Matt stepped down the hallway and brushed against my arm as he paused in the doorway. Our eyes met, and he grinned down at me.

"Well, hi there, Matt," Peter said. He uncrossed his knee and leaned forward. "Glad to see you back from scoping out the town. I wanted to thank you for a very satisfying nap on your comfy bed. It's all broken in for you."

Matt saluted. "Absolutely."

"How was the town?" Peter asked.

"It's a tiny place, but there's a lot to see," Matt said. "Aside from the major mission, that is." He caught my eye again. "We'll have a lot of fun."

I liked the sound of that and rubbed my fingers across the warm spot where he'd brushed against my arm.

"But," he added, "business shuts down early around here, so we'd better figure out where we're going to eat."

"Seafood?" I asked.

Peter stood, yawned, and pulled out his keys. "Looks like things are all in order here. The little nurse seems fine, the bed and breakfast is comfy. So…" He turned to Matt. "You all take good care of your Grandma, okay?"

Matt nodded. "Yes sir."

Then Peter turned to me. "Coral. Remember what I said. Call me if you need me."

I nodded. "I hope it won't come to that."

We bowed our heads and prayed for Peter's safety, Grandma's health, and discernment and wisdom for our new situation. After the amen, we hugged Peter and told him good-bye. Then he left for Fort Myers.

Out on the porch, Matt and I waved until he turned left and his taillights disappeared. Why those disappearing taillights brought a tear to my eyes, I don't know.

Of course he'd be back when everything was resolved, because all our stuff wouldn't fit into the Mustang, but it was sad that he had to leave.

I hoped he'd remember to play loud music if he got sleepy and to call us when he got to his room in Ocala.

Sol blinked hard as he gripped the steering wheel. Enough of this endless battered ribbon of asphalt. He turned his gaze to the endless miles of long-armed saguaro cacti and scrubby brush flying by the windows—and their vivid color. The sunset glowed off them like some old Technicolor movie and made his eyes want to cross.

Before long, the spectacle faded under the sinking sun, and Sol's eyelids grew heavy. His back and neck began to cramp. A nap would be great right now.

It wasn't long before rectangular green signs with luminescent white letters began to flick by. Tucson exits coming up.

He blinked hard, shifted in his seat, yawned, and squinted into his rearview mirror. Behind him, the same saguaros stood in black silhouette against a blood red sky. Sol wanted to turn around, enjoy a good long stare, but he couldn't. So, he forgot about it and returned his gaze to the highway in front of him.

Paulette would have raved over this. All of it. At one time, they would have reveled over it together.

He yawned a second time, twisted his neck left and right, and adjusted the mirror. He blinked slow and hard, one eye at a time, to wet the inside of his grainy lids.

"You miss your woman?" It was Term.

Sol snapped a glance toward the man. He'd almost forgotten about him. "What? Now you're reading my mind?"

Term grinned and leaned to gaze into the sideview mirror. Its rosy reflection brightened his large head.

Dude ought to quit grinning about everything.

His woman. Huh. They weren't even married. And furthermore, it wasn't any of Term's business.

Sol clicked on his headlights. Up ahead, the final dusky tips of pink light disappeared off the distant mountains, and the dark took over. How many hours had they been on this road anyway? Seemed like forever. If Sol didn't stretch his arms and legs soon, he'd be a cripple.

Term lifted a hand and pointed toward the approaching exit. "Get off here," he said.

The man seemed pretty sure of himself.

Sol knew nothing of this highway, or this city, so he followed Term's directions. All he knew was that parts of this highway more or less paralleled the border of Mexico. One exit was as good as another. He turned onto the ramp.

"Always wanted to spend the night in Tucson," Sol said. Truthfully, he'd never even thought of it. But it sounded good conversation-wise.

He hadn't brought up the subject yet, but he wasn't about to shell out two hundred bucks for some hotel room.

Term straightened as they reached the stop sign at the end of the ramp. He pointed to the right.

Sol swerved to avoid a pothole. "How 'bout let's find a good parking place and camp in the car tonight? We could stretch out right here in these two front seats."

Term made no comment, and Sol proceeded down the indicated street. In his periphery, Sol took in Term's long frame and knees up near the dash. The guy had no right to complain about accommodations. He was gettin' a free ride, for goodness' sake, all the way to Florida.

At the street light, Term lifted his hand to the left, which led them down another seedy street. It was lined with crumbling adobe houses, broken sidewalks, and a few small trees. The patched street with its weedy cracks wasn't any nicer. Term waved Sol forward. About a mile up the road, Sol approached a leaning corner streetlight.

"Turn in there," Term said. Bars covered the dusty windows of an all-night mart. A bulb glowed inside, and a lone car sat in the parking lot. Probably the cashier's vehicle.

Sol frowned as he turned in. "This safe?"

Term motioned him forward. "Park to the right, by the restrooms."

A scrappy tree and sagging wooden privacy fence enclosed two parking places and a dumpster. "It's pitch dark back in there," Sol said.

When Term didn't respond, Sol tapped his thumb on the steering wheel. "Well?"

"Well, what?"

"Is it safe?"

Term's teeth gleamed, reflecting the dash. "What more do we need?" He tipped his head toward the store. "In the morning, our breakfast is right inside."

Sol peered toward the parking space. "Well, you do seem to know your way around," he said, and pulled on in. He turned off the ignition.

They sat there in the quiet, he with his hands on the wheel and Term with his on his knees. The engine ticked and cooled. From across the fence a woman's impatient scoldings—in Spanish, it seemed—drifted through the air. Then a child's answer—the woman's voice again—a small dog's yapping. A distant baby cried.

"Plenty of drama goin' on," Sol complained.

The corners of Term's eyes crinkled.

A vehicle with a loud radio passed and rattled their car. Its sound diminished as it meandered down the street.

With the car parked, their breeze was now gone. A whiff of Sol's stale body odor floated up. "I can't sleep if I'm sweaty…" he said. "You wanna go first?"

"That's nice of you to offer," Term said. "But you go ahead."

Sol could have sworn Term mumbled something about progress, but he didn't care at this point. All he cared about was scrubbing up and closing his weary eyes. That is, if he could sleep under these circumstances. He climbed out, but not before checking his three-sixty. He shut the door and stepped away. "I hope they've got some decent soap in there," he muttered, then grabbed some things from the trunk.

The bathroom had plenty of soap. In the meantime, he put it to good use, scrubbed up with the paper towels, and dried off the best he could. But he needed to stretch his wardrobe, so he slipped back into the same old clothes. It didn't matter, he told himself, nobody knew him here in Tucson or anywhere else along this highway. Soon, though, he'd need to locate a handy dandy dollar store and get himself some underclothes and deodorant.

He gave himself a final swipe with a paper towel and swung open the door.

"Ahh." Nothing felt better than being clean.

Back in the car, Term had already stretched out and appeared to be asleep. Lucky for Term, he hadn't had to do any of the driving. Life of ease.

Sol locked the door, lowered his seat, and raised the window so nobody could get their hand inside.

He sniffed the air.

Thank goodness. Term still didn't stink.

Sol closed his eyes and relaxed. How come he had to work so hard at staying clean while Term always smelled like honey, or a vase of those—what were those little white…?

Sol drifted away before he could answer his own question.

Yet the disturbing script of his dreams was nothing at all like honey.

Sol stretched out in the front seat of his car. He tossed and turned as a marathon of dreams played out in his head.

The first one began with Term slipping out of Sol's car and perching on the car's front fender. Sol wondered that the giant didn't seem to need any sleep. "What are you doing?" he mumbled, half-waking. And Term, on the front fender, just smiled through the window.

Sol tried to curl up. He rested his knee against the console and stayed that way until he cracked his eyes open to find the passenger seat empty. Sol picked up his head and looked around, but Term wasn't there on the front fender. He closed his eyes and settled back down. He figured Term was in the bathroom.

He turned the other way and crossed his arms, drifting away for a second time as the dreams played on.

The giant appeared again on the front fender and spoke through the window to Sol. "Don't you worry, now. Enjoy your sleep."

Sol stirred as the dream took a scary turn. A hand with a coat hanger wire reached through Sol's window. Paralysis sucked Sol's breath away. His mouth opened, but he couldn't move. Couldn't yell.

The wire loop in the coat hanger bumped against Sol's forehead. And Sol, with great effort, as if moving through quicksand, raised an arm. He groped at the window but found nothing at all. His hand dropped back, limp and open beside his leg. His slow shallow breaths returned.

On the screen behind his eyelids, Sol watched as Term snatched the coat hanger man backward and slung him in a long arc over the dumpster and across the wooden fence. Term brushed the dust off his hands and re-situated himself on the fender as if proud of a job well done.

Sol opened his eyes and sat up straight, his heart racing, and yet there was nothing to see. Nothing on the hood of the car. Yet Term wasn't in his seat. Sol sank back against the seat and closed his eyes again. Of course, time meant nothing during sleep and dreams. His buddy was probably still cleaning up in the bathroom. Sol relaxed again as sleep swept him away.

A new and surreal scene opened up.

This time he saw the store's front parking lot. A masked robber roared up in his jacked-up car and left it rumbling as he leaped out, a long-barreled weapon in his hands. Then Term stepped over, and with no effort at all, grabbed the criminal. He pressed the side of his head against the wall. Term held him there with one hand, and with the other, crushed his gun like a cheap plastic toy. He pulled off the robber's mask and tied his hands with twisted plastic bags out of the trash can. The gunman didn't stand a chance against the giant. Police pulled in and at the end of the scene, the cashier came out and identified the gunman as a high school bully. All ended well with the police cuffing and hauling the criminal away.

Once again, Sol cracked his eyes open and glanced toward Term's empty seat.

He glanced toward the parking lot. Empty.

Sol hoped he could remember all his wild dreams in the morning. Term would want to hear every one of them.

But then Sol gazed at the empty seat…

Had Term gone off and deserted him?

When Sol awoke the next morning, sunshine had transformed the corner where he and Term had camped for the night. Term, now in his passenger seat, sat with the door open and his knees outside. He appeared to be rubbing the sleep out of his eyes.

Sol hated to admit it, but he was glad the big dude hadn't deserted him.

He snapped his driver's seat back up to its original position and stretched his arms around behind the headrest—last night's dreams—and the aggravation of seeing Term's empty seat all night—how could a person get any sleep with having to worr—no, *wonder*—where his travel buddy had gone. The whole thing had worn him out.

"Hey." Sol eyed the giant's back. "Where'd you go all night?"

Silence. Maybe old Term hadn't heard his question.

"Every time I looked over at your seat, you were gone."

The giant gave a quarter turn of his head. "Nowhere at all, compadre. Maybe you caught me gone to the restroom."

Sol shrugged and opened his door. Just wait till they got down the road, and Sol told Term about all his nutso dreams. He turned his head. "You eat yet?"

The giant waved him away. "I'll get something. Thanks anyway."

"Suit yourself." Sol stuck a foot out and once again observed a single car in front of the store, only this one was different. Change of shift. Sol couldn't help but wonder if the little store ever sold much of anything and what kind of food it might stock for breakfast. From past experience, he hoped the food didn't give him gas.

He brought the other foot around. Glanced down at the pavement.

"What the heck?"

There, hung up on his shoe was a bent coat hanger.

Sol squinted into the sunlight as he wolfed down his sausage-in-a-bun breakfast. In the meantime, he changed his mind about telling Term anything about the dreams. He'd just keep his thoughts and questions to himself.

After finding that coat hanger beside the car, he had a whole lot to think about.

He swiped a knuckle across his lips and finished off his last bite.

Beside him, Term, who'd followed him into the store, cleaned his fingers and mouth on a napkin. Somewhere along the way, the guy had found time to shave. That, or Term didn't have much of a beard.

Sol ran his hand over his own facial stubble. He'd probably skip it for today. Anyway, wasn't a day's growth the *in* thing right now? His son, Matt, would know.

He turned the key in the ignition, and Term pulled in his legs and shut the door.

Sol put the car in reverse and began backing out. "Let's get out of this place and get back on the highway."

"Don't you want to walk around the block and stretch your legs?"

That would have been a good idea if he hadn't already started the car. "The sooner I get my carcass down to Fort Myers, the sooner I can set things straight."

Term raised an eyebrow and nodded.

And about setting things straight… For the life of him, Sol couldn't figure why his mother had designated Matt and some little neighbor friend of hers as co-executors of her estate instead of him. *Pfft! Kids!*

She acted like she didn't trust him—or thought him incompetent.

Baloney! Wasn't he a businessman? Those kids didn't know a thing. It made his blood boil.

Term turned toward Sol as if waiting for him to continue.

Right. The dude wouldn't know what Sol was talking about regarding setting things straight. "Mom's estate," he said. "She made a will and wasn't thinking clearly."

"I'm sorry for your loss."

"Oh, I haven't lost the money."

"I meant your mother."

Sol cast a quick glance at Term. "She, uh, she's not gone. Not yet. But she's pretty sick."

Nothing but silence came from the passenger seat.

Sol exhaled hard and followed the signs back to I-10. Why he'd mentioned this to Term, a total stranger, Sol didn't know. The inheritance—his mother's impending death. That was his own affair.

Silence filled the vehicle as they neared the east-bound ramp.

"Unforgiveness is an ugly slave-master," Term commented.

Sol started to respond but swerved right. He jerked the wheel back to the left to stay on the road. He'd better keep focused. So, where'd Term get that idea?

The next time he looked over, Term seemed to be studying the landscape out his passenger window. But Sol could tell by the shape of his cheek, the man had to be grinning again.

Still, Term's comment about unforgiveness clawed at him. Sol had every right to be upset with his mother. He fumed as he merged into traffic and then tossed another glance at the back of his travel partner's head. The old boy better keep his opinions to himself. After all, Term was the guest here.

A dozen miles passed but Term had nothing more to say. Sol re-focused on the road, thankful for the fairly light traffic and a working sun visor. Driving east in the morning was always murderous, and this southeasterly stretch kept the direct sun out of his face.

Now and then a clump of scrappy trees rose from the median and varied the scenery, and Sol couldn't help but stare beneath each one to check for illegal immigrants. He found none. For the most part Sol found nothing much to hold his attention, just the brown grasses, spiky weeds, and distant purple mountains that seemed forever out of range. And Term's busy-body comment that he couldn't clear out of his head.

"I hope she makes it, Sol. I'm sure she's a very special lady. Just look at you."

Sol nodded his thanks. But then wondered if the man was being sarcastic.

Term had given up on the side-scenery and now faced the front. He seemed genuinely interested in the countryside around him and made several comments regarding its beauty and something about *even in its fallen state.* Whatever that meant.

Well, it was beautiful in its own way—but pretty dadgum repetitive. Sol pressed on the gas, eager to get on down the road.

"Lots of shredded rubber on the pavement," Term commented.

Sol nodded, eyed a chunk as he passed it by. "Reckon these things can do some damage when they fly off."

"Big damage," Term said.

"I didn't realize it, but they're all over the place."

Term nodded.

As Sol focused on the black bits of rubber along the shoulders, his tires wove now and again onto the rumble strips *blam!blam!blam!blam!* Then he'd jerk back into his lane. "Sorry."

Term raised his eyebrows but kept his mouth shut.

Yeah, you do that.

Then as they approached the Willcox, Arizona, exit, *blam!blam!blam!blam!* Sol gripped the wheel and held it steady as he slowed. This was something else. Maybe a tire. Maybe his own tire.

He glanced toward Term, glad now for the comfort of having another adult in the car. Even if he was a busybody.

Term pointed toward the exit and info-sign. "Looks like a gas station up there. Maybe they can help."

Sol took the ramp and slowed even more as the car limped its way toward help.

Ralph stood in his usual spot behind the Captain's Table pick-up window. He frowned and did a double-take into the dining room. Today's lunch business had sailed right along with the front dining room nearly full. He stared at the young couple. It wasn't the first day they'd come in for breakfast and lunch. Most times they sat at the second table by the front door, which gave Ralph a straight-on view of them.

He took another look at the girl, same as he had each of the other times. A coupla times she'd glanced his way, but he pretended to be looking at the tickets hanging there between them.

She must have felt his stare, but maybe he'd fooled her by looking at the tickets.

This girl was the spittin' image of…*her.* Nadine.

What was the word? *Doppleganger?* One person who looks just like another. He turned and dropped a mound of fries onto the plate he was filling and laid it up in the window. Steam now rose above them and obscured his view.

Impossible. No way. This could *not* be Nadine.

She'd be close to thirty-five or so by now. The chances of her showing up here again were close to zero. But this girl—*this* girl— was barely out of her teens; twenty at most. She couldn't *possibly* be her.

He stepped left of the steam to catch another peek.

On the other hand, she could be some relative of Nadine's.

Nah. No chance of that, considering what Ralph knew about Nadine's family.

Millie, the waitress, and also his girl, approached from the other side of the window. She waved a hand in front of his face. "Earth to Ralph. What are you gaping at so hard?"

He turned away to flip a cheese sandwich and then glanced up again. "That couple at table two, Millie. Seen 'em here several days in a row."

Millie shrugged and laid her arm along the window ledge as he heaped up another steaming sandwich and fries. He slid the platter alongside Millie's hand. On her finger glittered the big ol' garnet ring he'd just bought her. Might not wanna get married, but he didn't want to lose his Millie, either.

She nudged the dish back in his direction and shook her head. "Pickle, Ralph. You forgot the pickle."

He forked one out of the jar and dropped it beside the fries.

Millie took the dishes. "What am I going to do with you?"

"I know everybody around here," Ralph whispered, "and they ain't from these parts. Learn what you can."

Millie rolled her eyes. "What am I, Ralph," she mouthed, "your private detective? Bed and breakfast. They've been paying with Cozy Inn coupons."

"Yeah, but…"

She turned the back of her up-swept hairdo in his direction and headed out to the dining room with the orders. He watched as she circled back for the tea pitcher. Millie wouldn't let him down. She always came through for him.

"Hi, y'all," she said as she approached the couple's table. With only one other waitress on duty, Millie had this room and the register to herself. "How's everything? Could I pour you some more tea?"

"Atta girl, Millie," Ralph muttered as he glanced down at the next ticket. He inclined his ear toward the window hoping to hear more.

"Sure, thank you," the girl said. The young man, busy with his food, just nodded.

"Enjoyin' your stay over at the bed and breakfast?" Millie asked. "Real nice place, I understand."

The kids agreed and thanked Millie as she topped off their glasses.

At that point the kitchen racket increased behind Ralph and overpowered what little bit of the conversation he could make out.

"Dang it!" Ralph barked at Larry, "Pipe down back there!" Larry, back to work again, after having been fired a few days ago for kicking around Ralph's kitten by the back door, returned the same day with an apology and asked for his old job back. Ralph made him raise his right hand and swear, "I'll never ever kick any more cats as long as I live, no siree, Bob," then hired him again on the spot.

To tell the truth, Larry could cook anything and everything, and Ralph needed Larry as much as Larry needed this job. In fact, maybe Larry was the reason this place was still paying the bills.

But right now, between Larry's loud cooking and Jack the dishwasher's banging and clattering, the noise was deafening.

Ralph shoved his way through the swinging doors and stepped behind the dining room lunch counter so he could finally hear. He busied himself by pretending to wipe down its long surface and straighten up the glasses.

Millie continued chatting up her young customers. "I see y'all had the grouper sandwiches again today," she said. "Captain makes 'em just right, don't he?"

Nods again from the couple and something that sounded like *excellent* indicated their satisfaction.

Meanwhile, the racket behind the pick-up window slammered on as loud as ever and leaked out into the dining room.

Ralph gripped the window and glared back inside but failed to catch either Larry's or Jack's eye. *Idiots.*

He lowered his gaze and got back to his eavesdropping and counter-wiping.

Millie kept up her patter. "So glad you guys enjoyed 'em. Y'all on your honeymoon?"

Ralph's eyes widened. He swiveled around to catch the look on the kids' faces. *Good grief, Millie.* She sure was sticking in the shovel.

The girl blushed as the couple shifted and grinned and shook their heads. The young man swallowed and spoke up. It was obvious they had some manners. "We're here on vacation with my grandmother."

"Ahh," Millie said. "Then I hope you're having a real nice time. She seemed completely unfazed by the unfiltered dose of discomfort she'd dished out and maintained her babble. "I've seen you two come in the last few days and noticed how you always order an extra meal to take out the door." She pointed to her name badge. "Name's Millie, by the way. I won't bother you no more. Holler if you need me."

The young lady nodded, and the fellow thanked Millie as she walked away with her tea pitcher.

Ralph slipped back into the kitchen through the swinging doors and let the whole deal rest while he busied himself with a few more quick orders. After a time, Millie returned to the serving window and had to ring the bell to catch his attention. He approached, took the slip she clipped, then leaned in close to whisper, "Just so you know, when that couple is ready to leave, I'll check 'em out at the register."

Millie shook her head. "Sorry, Ralphie." She nodded toward their now-empty table. "You're a penny short and a minute late. And tell me, why, oh why, are you acting so weird about those two?"

Drat. They'd slipped out without him realizing it. He leveled a finger at her nose. "Now you stop that. And don't you go callin' me Ralphie. Or I'll call you Mildred. Out loud. So everybody can hear. See how you like that."

She thumped her hands on her hips and shot him a tight-lipped glare. Behind her the front door opened, and daylight poured in. "Gotta go," she said. "New customers."

Ralph turned back to the kitchen. How could Millie understand all the things that happened before she came to town? She didn't need to learn about it, either.

And neither did his old buddy Zeke.

In fact, it'd probably end his and Millie's little two-some.

I stood beside Matt as he paid for our meal at the Captain's Table. Millie, our waitress, chattered on as friendly as usual. I always made it a point to glance around and try to catch a peek at Ralph, my father. He usually stayed back in the kitchen, but if he waited on customers behind the lunch counter, I'd catch a closer look at him—his muscular arms, tattoos, and white apron. He kept his hair cut like a soldier. From what I could tell, he seemed to be in pretty healthy shape.

Every time we hung out at the Captain's Table I filled in another piece of his puzzle—voice, mannerisms, and so on. And he seemed to be pretty good friends with Millie. If Peter hadn't told me he was single, I would have figured them for husband and wife. On the one hand, she was his waitress, and on the other, she seemed to have a lot of say-so. And today he hung out behind the counter more than usual, just polishing things up.

On the way out, Matt opened the door for me and treated me like a lady—protective, but not overdoing it.

We left the restaurant, crossed the busy road, and headed along the sidewalk for the bed and breakfast.

Matt winked and grabbed my free hand with a grin. "Honey-moon, huh?" His dimples creased.

Millie's comment was crazy enough, but now Matt had to bring it up again. I detected no ridicule in his voice, though, just the simplicity of the comment. Still, a hot wave rose in my face, and I gave him a little nudge. It made me grin.

"I couldn't figure what to make of her," Matt said.

I raised my eyebrows and nodded, happy to change the subject.

"I guess you're not used to that personality. But it's typical of the South, I'd say, and in some areas more so than others. This Forgotten Coast is very old-south."

"I can't help but like her."

My pace slowed as my thoughts turned to my dad's hazel eyes, receding hairline, and military haircut. We hadn't really spoken to him, but I'd heard his voice now.

Matt slowed as well.

"You know, I thought I'd feel something," I said. "But I'm coming up empty."

"You're talking about your dad?"

I nodded. "Like a warm feeling or something special when I first saw him. Or a connection of some kind. But I'm… there was nothing."

Matt waited for me to finish. "You're disappointed."

"The man seemed like any other stranger." I shook my head. "Not creepy, though, like Mama's…"

I glanced up at Matt. This would probably be a revelation for him.

But his expression didn't change.

"Like Mama's boyfriends," I said. "They ranged from really awful to downright frightening. And I mean *scary*."

"Don't beat yourself up. Maybe your lack of feelings is just self-preservation. Fear of the unknown."

"Yeah."

"Your feelings could develop…if he turns out to be okay," Matt said.

"My inner scaredy cat is telling me to run back to Ft. Myers and forget the whole deal," I said. "To live my life in peace the way it's always been." I paused on the corner. Matt too. "No, that's not exactly right—but in peace like the last eight years of my life. Ever since Grandma Rosella came along."

Matt gripped the Styrofoam carton, and we stood face to face.

"But you can't do it, can you?" he said. "Can't just walk away? You'd never know how it could have ended."

"Guaranteed forfeit. I'd lose out entirely."

Matt pressed his lips together and nodded. He totally got it.

Fact was, if I walked away from my one and only blood relative—who might actually be okay—all I had left was Grandma Rosella. Yes, we had our friends and neighbors in Fort Myers. And Peter. He would always be there. But they weren't the same.

Rosella, who wasn't even my flesh and blood—even if she recovered—would not live forever. A fact that had only recently hit home.

God sent her into my life when I needed her most. I'd been able to lean on her. But I could no longer depend on her as my fortress.

No, even without her I would still have God. He was always with me. Our fortress, according to Psalms.

Perhaps this *was* the time to expand my world. And start a relationship with my dad.

I hoped it wasn't a mistake.

Matt waggled the Styrofoam box. "Grandma's food is still hot. Want to do a one-eighty and re-walk the bridge?"

We'd be passing by the restaurant again.

All this time, he hadn't let go of my hand. He gave it a squeeze.

"Sure," I said, and we turned together.

"If it was me, Coral, I'd probably feel the same."

I reflected on my life before Matt, alone at my college apartment, contented with my lonely studies. That life seemed so morbid now. I shook off the thought of it and took a deep breath. I could never return to that solitary existence.

Matt studied me as my mental wheels turned.

I let him in on my thoughts. "Good or bad, Matt, my father exists. I haven't spoken with him face to face, but I've seen him in person. Like you said, if I walked out now, I'd always be wondering and could never be content. I've got to have closure of some type, even if it turns into a bucket of worms."

Matt nodded.

"The brave part of me wants to learn more. To give it a chance. And I'm trying to listen to that part."

Matt waited as I turned things over.

"But something did bother me back there," I said. "Did you notice how he watched us?"

"No, I noticed him watching you."

"You think he knows?"

"How could he, Coral?"

He couldn't. I'd never met him—and Mama never even bought school pictures. So, nothing got sent out—to anybody.

"This might be getting messed up," I said. "Maybe he's just a perv and ogles young girls."

Matt grinned. "But only the pretty ones."

I ignored the comment.

"For some reason, he's trying to figure out who you are," Matt said. "I know this is probably very obvious, and I never met your mother—but do you by any chance look like her?"

I shrugged. Mama had short hair, sometimes orange, or purple—sometimes black. I had no idea what her natural color was. I couldn't even picture her face alongside mine right now.

We walked along in silence for several paces when Matt spoke again. "Seriously, though, if you're getting a bad vibe or feeling weird about him, we can leave today."

"No, no, no." I'd already chosen the brave part. But I needed more time. "This is not as easy as I'd hoped."

We neared the restaurant on the opposite side, and I paused. "I am sure of one thing, Matt. I probably do want to meet him. But I'm not quite there yet."

At this point I couldn't imagine anything that could change my mind.

Millie immersed herself in the new customers, an elderly couple. She offered them menus and friendly talk, as well as the usual questions about where they were from. Out-of-state retirees. And the missus complimented Millie's beautiful ring.

Millie beamed and twisted the garnet around with her thumb, a new habit developed because of its weight. It wanted to swing around backward. The restaurant was the perfect place to show it off.

"Why, thank you." She extended her fingers. "My birthday present." Her Ralph knew just what she liked.

Repeated compliments came from the customers. Millie retracted her hand and left them to study the menu.

But it didn't stop Millie from sneaking one more glance at her jewel. Her heart ached that Ralph had never included a single diamond among his gifts. Maybe one day. Over the years, she'd done everything possible to make their relationship permanent, but he couldn't seem to take the hint.

Couldn't, or wouldn't.

Truth was, she could buy her own birthday presents. But getting him to propose was another matter. The way things were going, he might never budge.

Millie returned for the couple's order, but with some distraction. Like the midnight frets, this problem of Ralph staring at that young girl wouldn't leave her head. She needed space to sort things out.

Of course, the girl and her young man were a couple. But Ralph wouldn't be staring at a guy that way. No, it was the girl. A child barely out of her teens. Half Millie's age. *Half Ralph's age.*

Hmmph!

Millie set the menus in the rack. She touched her hair. Glanced at her worn nails. Truth was, she might need to up her game.

Could her Ralph, a man who'd never been unfaithful at all, be on the prowl… for a younger woman?

72

As the little red car limped along the exit ramp, Sol complained. "One hour into the day," he said, "one hour, and we're already stuck on the highway with a bad tire." The vehicle turtled along at fifteen miles an hour. "And what is this place, anyway? This exit?"

"Do you want to pull over so we can see what's going on?" Term asked.

Sol leaned into his left sideview mirror. "I can already tell you what's wrong. Tire's flapping like a broken shoe. And no, we don't need to stop. There's a station up ahead there."

"You wouldn't want to bend the wheel, though."

Sol hadn't considered that. "Yeah, but that's not my problem. It's borrowed."

"It could cost you money."

Sol paused a brief second and then pulled onto the gravel. "Well, if you put it that way…"

"Allow me," Term said, opening his door. "Just pop the trunk, and I'll check for a spare."

Sol stood outside just off the broiling asphalt and worked up a sweat watching Term jack the car and change the left-rear tire. Within a few minutes, the giant had bolted on the miniature spare and stowed the tattered one in the trunk.

"You coulda left the stupid thing laying by the side of the road, you know," Sol said as they climbed back. He mopped the sweat off his forehead and wondered why Term hadn't worked up a sweat. "You must be supernatural, man. It's hot out there, and you're not even beaded up."

Term winked. "And, yes, to your comment."

Sol tucked his chin and frowned as he turned the key. "Whaddya mean, yes?" He didn't dare meet Term's gaze.

When Term didn't explain right away, Sol sucked in a breath, checked his mirror, and pulled back onto the pavement.

Term finally spoke. "The wheel's attached to it, but yes, I know I could have left the tire lying beside the road."

Sol exhaled. Nodded. "That's what I thought you meant."

At the gas station Sol cussed and argued with the attendant. No, he didn't want new tires, and yes, he'd wait until the truck delivered a retread. Sol refused to put a brand-new tire on somebody else's car, and he didn't care what the man said about the extreme heat and the safety risk. The guy just wanted to sell him a new tire.

No, thank you. Sol would wait. Even if it did take a couple of hours. He pulled the vehicle up to a little mesquite tree near a large propane tank.

It seemed these far desert regions took some time for deliveries. When lunch hour rolled around, he and Term were still seated in the plastic chairs of the lobby watching *Gunsmoke* on TV.

Term seemed unfazed by it all.

"I'm sick of TV. How long does it take to get a dadgum tire delivered?" Sol whined.

"We could take a walk and get a bite to eat."

Sol slapped his knees and stood. "Fine. Let's go."

Sol winced as they left the air-conditioned lobby. The blast of hot air felt like an oven. Maybe the idea of walking down the road wasn't such a good one.

"There's a restaurant past that RV park," Term said.

Sol gave him a side-eye.

Half an hour later, they approached the plate glass windows of Aunt Susie's—a small but clean restaurant with potted cacti out front—and swung open the door. "Food at last," Sol said. "I'm starved."

"And air conditioning," Term added.

A young waitress greeted them and led them to the lunch counter where she laid out their menus. Her nametag said ANGIE. Term nodded a friendly greeting but Sol didn't bother.

The giant laughed as they took their places. "Makes me think of old times," he said, "like back in Barstow."

It did seem like a long time ago. "Yeah," Sol said. "Old times." Same shirts too. Only his was getting a little stinky, and—he leaned toward Term and sniffed the air—nothing. How'd the guy do it?

After they ordered and the waitress disappeared, Sol commented, "Scrawny little chick, huh?"

Term shrugged. "She's under a lot of stress."

"You know her?"

"Her husband's in the hospital."

"Oh." Sol paused. "What makes you know so much?"

Term waved the question away as Sol's cell phone rang. It was the gas station manager. Sol listened and then punched the red button.

"Dadgummit! Talk about waste of time. Our retread won't be in until tomorrow."

After lunch Sol and Term killed some more time watching TV in the 24/7 gas station, charged up Sol's cell phone, and took turns getting cleaned up. Come to think of it, Sol hadn't noticed a cell phone on Term at all.

Sol checked his own phone and found a place in the nearby town to buy underwear.

They set out in the heat, but Sol had to put up with Term's off-road nature walk past a variety of cacti, prickly bushes of all types, bugs, and hidden sleeping creatures. He just couldn't understand the big draw of it all. "Most of these plants look the same to me," he complained. "And now all my body parts are sweating again."

Term laughed and kept up his stride.

"What are you, some kind of naturalist or something?"

"You might as well learn something while we're here," the man said. "Every square foot holds wonder—the rocks, the sand, the insects, and," he winked, "even snakes."

"You fanatics. Let's get on down to that dollar store. Two-day-old underwear's not my kinda thing, you know. It's annoying."

After the shopping spree, they backtracked to Aunt Susie's restaurant. Sol's feet were developing blisters between his toes. "Eat again now or walk back in the dark," Term had said.

Sol gave in to the early meal. "Shoulda bought bandages," he said. "Too late now."

"You can always drive barefoot," Term told him.

Sol swung open the door and took a deep breath of the air-conditioning. It welcomed him with open arms. The waitress, Angie, was still inside working.

Sol and Term gravitated to the same seats they'd had last time. To their right, a skinny seven or eight-year-old child sat at the far end of the counter. He appeared to be doing some kind of math homework.

"Math's a lot of fun, huh?" Sol said.

The child gave him a weary look and returned to his figuring.

Sol remembered back when his own boy Matt would come into his cannabis shop after school to do his homework. On the sly, of course, since it was against the law, Matt being underage in that kind of shop and all. Good kid, his Matt. Always hardworking.

Sol eyed the child. Sort of like his own little guy.

Angie stepped over. She remembered them from lunch, and Term returned her greeting. When Sol didn't respond the right way, Term side-tapped him with his foot. "Use your manners," he whispered through a grin.

"Oh, yes," he said, detaching his thoughts from the child. "Evening Angie, how are you tonight?"

She sighed and nodded. "Doing okay, thank you." But this time she seemed very tired as she handed over the menus and stepped away.

"That's Angie's boy, a second grader," Term said, dipping his head toward the little fellow.

Sol nodded. When Angie returned, he ordered first—steak, crinkle-fries, and lemon pie. As before, Term ordered exactly what Sol ordered. Minus the pie.

After Angie brought their order, the boy asked his mother for a piece of lemon pie too.

"Shh," she whispered and stroked his cheek. "I have to pay for what you eat, honey. We'll be home in just a little while. And the lemon pie's all gone."

Sol couldn't help but overhear.

The boy worked a few more problems, shut his book, and then laid his head on top of his notebook with his face to the wall.

Term looked at Sol. Shrugged. "Do it. Go ahead."

How could the dude know what he was thinking? Sol picked up his dish of pie and gestured for Angie to take it over to the boy.

Emotion washed over the woman's face. "Thank you," she mouthed and pressed the back of her hand to her lips.

She set the pie down and tapped the boy's shoulder. His eyes lit up as he picked up the fork and dug in. His mother whispered something and pointed toward Sol. The boy smiled, his mouth full.

"What do you say?" Angie whispered.

"Thank you, sir," he managed, despite the dessert in his mouth.

Sol nodded in return. "You're welcome."

Term nudged Sol. "Go ahead, say it."

"Get him a glass of milk to go with it." The question of how Term would know what Sol was thinking flickered once again through his brain, but he didn't pursue it.

Angie blinked hard and walked past them to get the milk. "Thank you," she whispered.

"Good job, Sol," Term said and mumbled something about progress. Again. He soon finished up his steak and fries and laid down his money. "I'll be right outside."

Dude needed to quit mumbling and interfering with his thinking.

Sol took the check, figured a customary fifteen percent, counted out the exact change, and stepped out beside the potted cactus with Term.

"Did you do things right?" Term asked.

"Always," Sol said. Yeah, he could have left a little bigger tip. But he wasn't going to bring that up. Back in the day, tips were only ten percent. Even that amount seemed high. Why didn't they just pay the waitress for her work? Why rely on the customer?

"Oh, no. Tell me what you were thinking. Right there when it first hit you. And you know what I mean. Show me with your wallet."

Sol stood there. Huffed in and out. Why should he have to tell Term anything? He opened his wallet so Term couldn't see inside. Fingered a twenty.

Term crossed his arms. "*Pfft!* I'm snorting, Sol."

"Snorting?"

"Snorting at you. Because you're so ridiculous. You knew in a flash what to do. Go fix it, Sol."

Sol stared up at the man in front of him with his big square jaw. Broad shoulders. Yeah. Term the Persecutor. Going after the contents of Sol's wallet like some kind of Robin Hood.

Well, he had news for old Term. Just because an amount flashed through Sol's mind, he wasn't going to just pluck out one of those hundreds. No. Not in his lifetime.

"Make it a game. Close your eyes and pull out a bill."

Aw, come on. A game? Sol didn't have to do whatever this giant said. Nobody was forcing him. Sol pinched the wallet. Hesitated. But he closed his eyes just the same, opened it up, and pulled out a bill. A hundred. He slapped the wallet shut. "Aw, gimme a break." Stupid game.

"You had that in your head, Sol. It was the right idea."

Sol gaped.

"Besides, you're rolling in money." He pointed at Sol's chest with every word, "You. Will. Never. Miss. It. Never." Then Term patted his back and nudged him back inside. "I knew you'd catch on."

Sol reached for the door handle.

Term stopped him. "And fold it small. Don't be obvious."

Sol couldn't imagine how Term could influence him with such foolishness. And yet here Sol was, following this nut's directions like some little chump in a schoolyard. What was wrong with Sol, anyway? Was he cracking up?

But he had that flash of an idea—before he figured that tip in there—yes, he'd thought of dropping the hundred. But only for a split second. A split second.

How the heck could Term know about that?

Must've been guessing.

He stepped back inside, caught Angie's attention, and reached out with the bill in his hand as if to shake. "It was a nice dinner. Thank you."

She reached back. Discerned the bill and looked down. "Oh!" Then she read the numbers on the bill and up went the back of her hand to her mouth again.

Then it struck him. That's just what Paulette would have done.

"Shh!" he whispered. He hoped nobody in this busy place was

watching. Sol didn't know what to say. "Just, just… Keep it quiet, now." He wasn't used to this kind of thing.

"Bless you, sir. So much," she whispered. "My husband—it's been hard lately with him in the hospital."

Sol stepped back. At least the woman wasn't loud. Paulette would have been. She was full of loud energy.

But that was neither here nor there. Paulette had nothing to do with this.

He lifted a hand, a half wave. "Enjoy it." Then he paused. "I'm sorry. Wrong word. Uh—just put it to good use. And—and you have a good evening. Good night, now." He backed out the door with her smiling after him, grateful and teary-eyed.

As he stepped down, a flutter rippled through his heart.

On the one hand, it felt pretty good.

But then he hoped this wasn't some prelude to a heart attack.

Sunset gilded the town of Carrabelle as Millie opened the front door of her cottage—she owned three—and swept the sand outside and down the steps. Sand was everywhere here, and though it was beautiful, it wasn't welcome in her house.

Ralph, would be closing up the restaurant soon and coming home. He hadn't dared to argue with Millie when she left work early this afternoon. But she had to get out of there. She needed space. Alone time to figure out how to deal with him and his antics and all those questions he was asking about that young girl. The kid was young enough to be his daughter for crying out loud. Shameful!

She'd show Ralph she could take a whole day off if she jolly well pleased. The thought of him and Larry and Jack trying to run things made her chuckle. Maybe tomorrow, she'd drive up to Tallahassee and get her hair and nails done. Find herself some pretty shoes.

"That oughta show you, Ralph," she mumbled. "Runnin' me, your only waitress, into the ground. Maybe you'll finally learn to get me some help in there."

A clicking noise across the street drew her eye toward Aunt Allie's backyard—the whole community called her that—where the old lady stood with her gnarled yard cane. Across the shoulder of her starched dress hung a muslin bag, which Millie knew contained her chicken feed.

Millie hadn't seen her neighbor for quite a while. She propped the broom beside the door and stepped across the weathered pavement—broken and crumbling through years of storms and hurricanes.

Millie usually worked past Aunt Allie's turning-in time, just past sunset. And besides, Aunt Allie's sitting-porch, on the opposite side of her store, faced the next street over.

"How're you doin' tonight, Aunt Allie?" she called out.

The old woman turned, her hair full and white, and waved. "Oh, just fine, Millie. And you? You're home mighty early."

For an elderly person, Aunt Allie's voice was surprisingly firm, and on most encounters, when it came to conservative politics and the importance of the Bible, strongly opinionated.

Millie adored her. She laid a forearm across a fence post and watched as Aunt Allie clicked an object in her hand for the chickens to gather in the pen.

"Hang on, Millie," she said. "Here, chickie, chickie." She tossed in a handful of chicken feed. Hens came running from all over the yard and skittered through the open door of their chicken coop. One little slowpoke wandered the wrong way, and she shooed her back. "Come on in. Come on in." As the last one entered, she pushed the door shut and turned the latch.

Aunt Allie stepped over to the fence and leaned both hands against her cane. "Would you like to come on around to the porch and sit a spell?"

It would be a delight to visit and rock with Aunt Allie on that porch that must be more than a hundred years old.

"Oh, I wish I could. But Ralph's comin' home, and I've got dinner about cooked." Anyway, everyone knew Aunt Allie went to bed with the chickens. Carrabelle was not a very late-night place.

They chatted for a few minutes, catching up on the local news.

"I'm sorry, Aunt Allie, I've got to get back inside and check my stove."

"Well, come on over anytime, honey, anytime you like. There's plenty of rockin' chairs."

"I'll do that."

"And bring Ralph. Haven't seen him for years and years. That young 'un used to come by and see me nearly every day before school. Oh, we had some good talks back then. That boy loved the… well, you just bring him on by."

Millie smiled. "I'd sure enjoy that." She paused. "Say, what was that clickin' noise you were makin' when you called in the chickens?" Millie had been curious since the first time she heard it.

Aunt Allie held up a little rectangular box attached to a worn string around her neck. Looked like metal. She closed her fingers around it. "It's an antique now, I guess. From my husband." She turned it in her hand and clicked it twice. "Used in World War II. Next time you stop by I'll let you in on it. I've got another one up on the porch. Looks like a little frog. Sounds just the same."

Millie nodded. "Tomorrow afternoon, then." She'd find a way to get her hair and nails done early. "Sounds just like someone cocking a rifle, doesn't it?"

"Well, come to think of it, it might. But that has nothing to do with the story. Stop on by. I'll fill you in."

Anyway, Millie was more interested in what Aunt Allie had to say about Ralph. Ralph loved the—what? What was she talking about?

At noon a few days later, the Captain's Table filled up quick. Millie was back today, serving as busboy, waitress, and cashier all at one time. As usual. She ran herself ragged trying to keep up.

Once again, she rang up the young couple from the bed and breakfast. After they left, another young couple occupied their favorite table by the door. These two had a new baby boy with a blue baby blanket over his carrier. Every now and then they'd pull away the blanket and peek in to admire him and talk baby talk.

When they finished, Millie rang them up at the register. "Treasure this time while you can, kids. Pretty soon you'll have very few peaceful interludes like today's lunch." They laughed and explained that today was a baby-doctor visit, and they already had two toddlers back home in the care of a sitter.

They left her a nice tip.

"Y'all have a nice day now," Millie told them as they headed out in the sunshine with mints in their hands and the carrier between them.

Back inside, Millie got even busier. Finally, she got around to cleaning their table when she found the baby blanket. "Oh, no, not again," she said, and snatched up the blue baby blanket. It must have slipped off their carrier. She raced outside and surveyed the lot. Nothing but rows of broiling parked cars. Her arm with the blanket dropped to her side. "Long gone," she muttered. "But who knows? They might come back."

She took the blanket, marched past the momentarily quiet register, and met Ralph in the back hallway. He was just coming in from the shed pantry with a hefty can of green beans in his hand.

She wadded up the blanket and tossed it against his chest. "There you go. Another one dropped beneath the booth."

"Another one?" he said, gathering it in his hand.

"And I couldn't catch them."

Ralph shook his head.

She thumped her hands on her hips, unappreciative of the way he didn't seem to care. "I wish you'd get me some help. If you'd paid attention and lent me a hand at the register today, I might not have missed this. But *noooo…*" she sing-songed, "Ralphie can't wait on the pregnant ladies or the ones with the babies."

"I was outside."

"Conveniently. It's been crazy all morning." She stared up at him. "Why do you have to act like that? Like squeamish or something about these babies and such. What are you afraid of? Whatever it is, you need to know it aggravates the fool out of me." She tipped her chin up. "*Ralphie.*"

But Ralph didn't rile.

Normally, he would. But this time he crammed the blanket under his arm along with the can of beans and pecked her on the lips.

She tucked in her chin. Her eyes followed him as he headed down the side hall to the kitchen.

"Please, Ralph, this is killing me," Millie called after him. "Just one more waitress."

He gave her a thumbs up. "I'll stick the blanket in lost and found."

Ralph dropped the can of beans off with Larry in the kitchen.

"Thanks, the teen said, eyeing the blue blanket over Ralph's shoulder. He nudged a pie pan full of fish and meat scraps toward his boss. "Saved you somethin' for your kittens."

Ralph took it. "Good. Back in a minute."

Little by little, Larry was redeeming himself from his earlier bad conduct. Saving scraps for the kitties was a step in the right direction.

On his way out the back door, Ralph stopped by the cardboard box full of lost and found items. He set the foil pan of scraps on the washing machine and then folded the blue blanket against his chest, pressing it flat. Inside the container were forgotten knick-knacks such as small games, toy cars, and dinosaurs.

Hardly anyone ever came back for them, but Ralph didn't want to risk breaking some kid's heart, so he kept them all. He laid the blanket on top but then recalled another baby blanket at the bottom of the box. A pink one they'd never come back for. He dug deep.

"Perfect," he said, as his fingers connected with the material. Toys clattered together as he tugged it out of the box and tossed it over his shoulder. Once again, he picked up the pan of scraps and headed out the back door into the sunshine.

"Here, kitty, kitty, kitty!" he called in his best high-pitched voice. Within seconds, seven mewing fur-balls came running and bumbling over his feet.

For the umpteenth time lately, Matt and I doubled back over the bridge to extend our walk and spend a few more minutes together before getting back to Grandma.

As we reached the place opposite my dad's restaurant, I slipped my hand out of Matt's. "Shhh!" I put my finger against my lips and ducked behind the electric pole. I motioned for him to join me. He gave me a curious look but came anyway.

Behind the restaurant someone had called out, "Kitty, kitty, kitty." And it sounded like my dad.

"He's back there behind the restaurant," I whispered.

We peeked around to catch him leading a whole passel of kittens toward the shed like the pied piper.

"Cute," I said.

One corner of his building jutted close to the road, so we had a view of the parking lot on the left and the entire back side. My ever-present decorating instincts kicked in, imagining a privacy fence across the back, while others chimed in hoping nobody came out to the parking lot and saw us acting strange.

"Act natural," I said, tightening my stance and trying not to spill Grandma's tea.

Matt choked back a laugh and set Grandma's food carton on the sidewalk. "Right, like stalking and spying are completely natural."

Up on one shoulder my dad carried a big foil pan. Over his other shoulder hung a pink cloth about the size of a baby blanket. Cats mewed, leaped and reared, eyeing the pan. They were loud enough to hear across the road, though passing cars drowned them out. "Here kitty, kitty, kitty!"

The longer he delayed setting the pan down, the more the little fan club begged and danced. He stepped carefully between them and laid it in front of the shed. In one instant the mewing ceased, as fuzz balls, with tails held high, dove like magnets for the pan.

He leaned down and stroked each one in turn. I couldn't hear, but he seemed to be talking to them. It was clear he enjoyed the little critters.

After a minute, he walked over to a picnic table that was shoved up against the restaurant's back wall. On top sat a wooden doghouse painted green, blue, yellow and pink.

He parked the pink blankie on its roof, then reached inside to pull out a handful of towels, which he used to brush out the insides. Then, as carefully as could be, he folded the pink blanket and laid it inside, straightening and patting it smooth.

"What's he doing?" Matt said.

"Fixing it up, I guess."

Then he pitched the old cloths into the dumpster by the shed and went back inside the restaurant.

He never once glanced across the street.

I squinted and tried to read the carved sign above the doghouse door. But I couldn't.

Matt stepped across the highway to get a look and laughed as he returned.

"Well, it's not a doghouse," he said as he crossed back over to me.

"What'd it say?"

"*Cats Only, Dogs Not Welcome.*"

I couldn't help but smile. "I wonder if my dad made that."

As I stood by Matt watching the kitten scene across the road, I glanced down at Grandma's cup of tea.

Matt caught the look. "We'd better get back," we both said at the same time. We laughed. "Coke!" I said quick, remembering that old game Grandma had taught me.

We did an about face and retraced our steps, double-time. "What do you mean, *Coke?*" Matt asked.

"Don't you know? When two people say the same words at the same time, the first one to say *Coke* wins. The other person has to buy them the drink."

"Okay, shortie," he said, reaching back for my hand, "keep up, now!" His legs were longer than mine, and he was a whole head taller.

This part of the walk was uphill. "No fair," I said. "I'm walking as fast as I can."

At the crest of the bridge, he stopped and pulled me up beside him. We paused long enough to watch a fishing boat pass under the bridge and then headed down the other side.

With the B&B only a block away, Matt spoke. "Don't you worry, Coral. I'll buy you all the Cokes you want."

"Aww, c'mon, now. Don't take all the fun out of it." I adjusted the now slippery cup of tea. "Competition is good for the soul."

He laughed and winked. "For real, though…penny for your thoughts about the cat scene back there."

"Yeah…" I said.

My dad Ralph had shown us some positive signs. He might actually be a nice guy. But it was a little too risky to jump to conclusions just yet.

I scrunched up my face. "Let's not rush things. I want to wait and see."

As he and Coral walked back to the B&B, Matt frowned at the real estate sign just ahead. It had caught his eye before, and no, he hadn't been seeing things. It clearly said *Sandy Beach*. But real estate? This was the same name he'd thought up for his girl back at college before he learned that her real name was Coral.

The beautiful name, Sandy Beach, had come to his mind like a divine flash. An inspiration that struck as fast as that first sight of her, the moment he was smitten.

The sheer romance of the name—*Sandy Beach*.

The very words described her essence, the sun in her eyes, her freckles, and those waves of long sandy hair.

A name he'd never forget.

But now, here it was displayed on a wooden sign.

One they passed daily.

He signed. As perfect as her nickname was, if she spotted the words on a local real estate sign it would ruin the romance of it. And destroy his plan.

No offense, Sandy Beach people, but Matt couldn't let his girlfriend think he picked her name off a billboard.

Dog it! What a pickle this was.

He scowled at the sign. Nothing like words painted on a sign to degrade the poetry of his thoughts.

And now he had to come up with a new and equally good name.

Matt held my hand as we approached the B&B. Sunlight fluttered across the sidewalk and porch. A light breeze rustled the oaks. He brought my hand to the rail and let go.

"You know," he said, "I've been thinking. And, if you don't mind, I've come up with a few ideas for us."

I tipped my head to look up at him.

He looked into my eyes, seemed to falter, and then regathered his thoughts. "First of all, your dad—he seems to be checking you out. Right? Like he thinks he might know you. At least that's how it appears. What if he can somehow identify you?"

I set Grandma's cup on the steps and leaned against the rail waiting for more.

"If it comes down to it," Matt said, "we could mix him up, throw him a curve ball."

"Okaaay. Sounds fun. Like what?"

His dimples creased. "We'll simply plant a fake name for you."

I laughed. "You sound like a spy."

"I am. And so are you, watching him feed his cats like that."

"Ha! Touché!"

"Remember, we're in this together. And now—idea two—we all knew this Carrabelle thing could take a while, right?"

"Yeahhh," I said, dragging out the word and wondering what else he had up his sleeve. His first idea was big enough.

"Well, since you're going to need more time, and you're not sure when you want to meet your dad…" He waved his arm at the B&B. "Maybe we should find some short-term rentals or apartments of some type. One for you ladies and another for me."

"Hmm."

"We know Grandma's able and willing to foot the bill, but I can't stand idly and not do my share as her money flies out the window. And maybe I could find some useful employment."

"That's three ideas."

"So, what do you think?"

I liked his willingness to contribute. That was great, very macho actually, but I hated the idea of him taking off and leaving all this to me. Maybe he'd put that off. But yes, we'd be in a fix soon, because the B&B's calendar had reservations coming up for other people.

"I do like the way you're taking charge. And these are all good ideas. Think we can find apartments in this little town?"

He shrugged. "Maybe."

"What about that fake name?"

"It just came to me, and I think you'll like it."

I grinned and crossed my arms. "Do tell."

He stepped across the porch, opened the door with a twinkle in his eye, and then motioned me inside. "After you, Miss Sandy Shore."

"Ah, Sandy Shore." I picked up the tea and passed him with a chuckle. "Very nice. I do like it."

Matt saw me to my room and greeted Grandma, still in her flannel gown. She wore her pretty white one and was propped in bed reading a book. He handed me the lunch carton, gave her a hug and a kiss, and then headed upstairs to his room.

"Lunch and iced tea, Grandma. I'll set it on your bedside table."

"I hope you brought me crab cakes," she said as she climbed out. I helped her into the chair and fluffed a pillow behind her so she could eat in comfort.

"Sure did, and they're still warm," I said, opening her catsup and utensils. It was important to get her up and moving, and I looked forward to the afternoon when we could all take a short walk.

"Eat as much as you can, "I said and gave her arm a pat. "We need to put some weight on you so you can get your strength back." These days she wore out quickly, and her bird-like appetite remained our biggest concern. At least she loved this seafood.

I turned on the television. "Want to watch the weather?" She enjoyed that channel, and even though it was repetitive, we both liked to know if there was any bad weather looming out in the Gulf of Mexico. Hurricanes move pretty slow, and this way she could keep us posted. So far so good.

"After you eat, I'll help you get a shower," I told her.

While she ate, I studied our calendar and compared it to the B&B's other reservations for this room. Matt was right to start working on the problem. This was a precious place, and I sure hated to leave. Unless we took a room upstairs, which was out of the question for Grandma, we only had a couple of days left.

We needed a Plan B. And soon.

After Grandma ate half her lunch, she inched forward to stand.

"Let me help you, Grandma."

"No, give me a chance first." She persisted, rose all by herself, and gripped the walker. "I'll let you know when I need a hand. The more I do, the stronger I'll get."

Way to go, Grandma. "Just don't get too frisky if we're out. I don't want you falling."

"No, we don't need that, do we?" She laughed.

Independence was her middle name. I made sure she was safely in the shower and cracked the door to keep an ear open. A few days before, Jessica, the home health nurse, had managed to get us a shower seat.

When her shower was done, Grandma called, and I guided her out of the shower.

"Good job," I told her. "You hardly needed me."

She was able to pull the garment over her head and straighten it out. "I'll let you zip it up," she said.

"There you go."

"I couldn't do that when we first got here, you know."

"Jessica, Matt, and I, we're all impressed with your progress." Especially considering the slower prognosis her doctor in Ft. Myers offered.

"Prayer makes all the difference," she said.

"I bet you hated those hospital gowns."

"To tell the truth, I hardly remember them. But I do remember that disgusting hospital food."

"Food?"

"Tasted like plastic a la arsenic."

I smiled. "Well, nobody cooks like you do."

Those simple activities had nearly winded her. Yet I could tell that day by day, her strength was improving.

Fixing her long white hair was a trick. "I'll comb it out in a bit," she said.

I offered to help.

"No, it's good exercise. I should do it myself."

Up until her hospital stay, she wore it braided in a circle around her head. Her own particular style. Sort of like a halo. Right now, it was all over the place.

After she combed it out, I would braid it.

Grandma's custom was to wear a particular color outfit for each day of the week and a matching flower on her hat. I'd emulated this practice with matching flowers on my straw purses.

Loud tropical prints were her favorites. Today, on the wrong day of the week, she chose red. And instead of a matching flower, she kept the orange one from yesterday.

I said nothing about these details, but they helped inform me of her progress.

"Grandma, if you're up to it, we'll call Matt after a bit and take a walk. We'll go down to the boardwalk." It was across the street, and the sunshine would do her a world of good. "You can sit on the bench and check out all the handsome guys on the boats."

She chuckled and swatted the air. "Oh, pshaw!"

Regarding the dress and the colors, Jessica, her visiting nurse, assured me that Grandma's lapses were astoundingly minor and could still improve. She'd been through quite a bit with that sepsis.

I couldn't have been more thankful for Jessica and her experience with patients like this. I enjoyed her personality and actually wished we were neighbors.

Grandma was getting stronger, and I was sure God was listening to our prayers. I made up my mind to not worry. I'd just do my part and let it happen. I expected nothing but further improvement from here on out.

But we still needed a new place to stay.

I'd hate to have to leave town for the lack of it. Especially now.

Besides its scarce lodgings, the town had few restaurants as well. Once again, the next day, Matt and I found ourselves strolling up to the Captain's Table for supper. Our presence was becoming very obvious.

"With your permission, Miss Sandy Shore," Matt said. "I need to add an attachment to yesterday's idea."

"Mm hmm."

"It has to do with Ralph, in case he gets into a conversation with us, and starts asking questions."

"Go ahead."

"Could you, in that case, not say anything at all, at least for now, and just let me be the spokesperson?"

I raised my eyebrows and nodded. Why not? I'd freak out otherwise. "Oh, for sure. I'll be glad to keep my mouth shut. What would I even say to him?"

Matt laughed.

So far, I'd escaped having to speak with my dad, a thing I dreaded like a stick dreads fire.

"You not saying anything will help me squeeze in the fake name," he whispered, and swung open the Captain's Table door.

Matt's hunch was right. Our time to speak with Ralph came that very day.

After dinner, we stood at the register waiting on someone to check us out. Matt held cash in one hand and Grandma's hot lunch box in the other. Grandma was probably getting tired of restaurant food. I sure was. Very few veggies and plenty of fried stuff. A recipe for reflux.

Matt laid his ticket on the counter. We glanced around, but Millie, who usually checked us out, was nowhere to be seen, probably tending tables elsewhere in the back of the L-shaped dining rooms.

The kitchen door swung open behind me.

Matt glanced across my shoulder and cleared his throat. He smiled at whoever it was. "It's Ralph," he mumbled like a ventriloquist. "Remember, let me do the talking."

Sure. I shuddered. Within seconds I'd be right next to this man—my father. I eased away from the register space.

Ralph squeezed his broad shoulders in behind the counter and perched on the barstool. "Afternoon, you two. Nice to see y'all back again." He picked up the ticket and began to peck at the keys with one finger in an unpracticed way. He glanced up at me. Several times. "Glad to see you like my restaurant."

"Oh, sorry, I forgot," Matt said, drawing his attention away from me. He laid some cash down and pulled out his wallet to extract the courtesy meal discount from the B&B.

Ralph nodded. "So, where you kids from?" His eyes went from Matt to me, then back again to Matt.

I smiled and cleared my throat, grateful for Matt wanting to handle things. I reached in the jar for a mint and stuffed it in my mouth as fast as I could. If not for Matt, I could never have returned to this restaurant day after day like this to observe the man. Not alone, anyway. It simply wouldn't have worked.

Matt jumped right in. "Know anything about Charleston Galena University?"

Ralph shook his head, finished up, and presented the change to Matt. "Students on break from school, huh? That's great. I hope you're havin' a nice time. We don't get that many long-term visitors. They tend to head west of here along the coast."

Matt pocketed the change. "Carrabelle's a nice little town, a good place for my grandmother to get some fresh air and sunshine while she recovers."

Ralph nodded. "Hope it all works out for her. And she's better right away."

Matt picked up Grandma's food. "Thank you, and..." he raised a finger, "by the way, since we could be in town a while, I might be looking for a short-term job. Not too important what it is, just something productive to pass the time."

My father frowned and furrowed his brow. "Well right off the bat, you probably noticed my *help wanted* sign outside," he looked Matt up and down, "there's that—a wait-staff position. Millie's all by herself here lately. Works her legs off. But there's fishing boats all up and down these docks. I know a few captains, and if that suits you, somebody's always looking for help. Come back later, and we can talk about ideas."

"Thank you, I'll do that."

Matt took my elbow as if to go. I grabbed Grandma's tea.

But my father hadn't quite finished. He crossed his arms and leaned his elbows on the counter. "You both from Charleston?"

I wondered if Ralph was nosy, curious, or just friendly. Millie was clearly in the friendly category, and greeted us now with *Here come the kids. Come on in, y'all.* But concerning Ralph, I wasn't sure. For now, I'd give him the benefit of the doubt. Especially since he worked with Millie. And they were an item. I could tell that now.

Matt paused. "Well, not exactly. You've heard of Las Vegas. That's me." Then he grinned. "And my girlfriend, here…" He gave my hand a little squeeze. "…Miss Sandy Shore—she's from Fort Myers."

What a clever way to slip in that new name. A heat wave rose in my face. I recall very little beyond Matt's comment, just a blur of conversation between them, and Ralph saying something about Grandma getting well soon. We finally made it out the door.

And all I could think about was Matt's choice of words—*my girlfriend.*

Long after the sun set, Sol and Term emerged from the lobby and settled into their vehicle near the propane tank. Sol wondered why the owner hadn't made them move the car, but he wasn't about to give up the only scrap of shade around the place.

But now it was nighttime, and Sol lowered his window about half a foot and closed his eyes as the rhythmic tune of crickets and critters filled his ears. The background roar of the interstate added good white noise.

A nearby coyote howled, and Sol sat straight up. Term, already stretched out with his eyes closed and arms over his chest, didn't budge.

Sol raised the window a little more and leaned back again. He didn't want to smother, but then, he wasn't going to let some critter climb inside. "A coyote wouldn't stick his nose in the window, would he?"

Term's mumbled answer was barely discernible. It sounded like no.

Well, if Term wasn't worried, then Sol wouldn't be either. He eventually relaxed and then drifted off. It wasn't too hard with the pleasant outdoor sounds of crickets and such.

Tonight's dreams were uneventful. Sol awakened only once to the loud hoot of an owl. He turned and cracked his eyes just as the bird, with its six-foot wingspan flew across beneath the lights and scooped up a rat.

He opened his mouth to mention it to Term, but once again, Term's seat sat empty.

Hmmph.

Sol closed his eyes again. There seemed to be no accounting for some people.

The next morning Sol and Term re-situated themselves in the gas station lobby. Before long, the tire truck pulled in to make its long-awaited delivery. Within minutes Sol's retread was installed, and the owner came around with the bill.

Sol pulled out his wallet, but the gas station man wanted to talk. "I'm selling you this tire with a good bit of hesitation."

Sol crossed his arms. Yeah, sure, the guy wanted to hesitate. His back room was full of brand-new expensive tires. He wanted to sell Sol one of those.

"The reason we don't normally stock these is because they're not as strong as new tires. And in this desert heat…" He turned the ticket around for Sol to sign. "There's no guarantee. Please be careful out there."

The man tore off the ticket and handed Sol his copy.

Sol ignored the comment, stuffed the paper in his pocket, and motioned to Term. "Let's go."

In the car, they decided to skip breakfast at Aunt Susie's and get on down the road. They merged onto I-10 heading east. Sol rested his hands on the steering wheel and stared ahead. Same scenery, different day. "Let's see how far we get before something else happens."

When Term didn't respond, Sol glanced over. Dude was staring out his window again.

"What are you grinnin' about?" Sol said.

When he turned, Term's smile reached from ear to ear. "What makes you think I'm grinning?" he said.

Sol shook his head. No accounting for some people. No accounting.

About nine, Sol's phone rang. He looked down at the screen. "Oh, man. It's Paulette—my ex. What do I say?"

Term shrugged.

Sol stared at the phone as it rang again. "We haven't spoken for five years."

Two more rings.

"You'll figure it out," Term said. "Answer it."

"I-I-I don't know what to say."

Term shrugged. "Say hello, then."

Sol clicked the button. "Hello?"

But he didn't need to worry about what to say next, because Paulette said it all. And the content scorched his ears.

"I stopped by the store today," she started out. "Thought I'd see if anything had changed with you."

Sol glanced over at Term. Her voice was so loud, he could probably hear every word she said.

Paulette railed on about Sol's treatment of his young employee Eddie. She complained about how Sol tricked him into loaning him his car. And how he'd conveniently forgotten the key back at the house.

His fiery redhead. Bawling him out. A thrill rippled through Sol. She'd actually called him on the phone. And stopped by the shop to see him. To see about—whether he'd changed.

Changed?

Then she brought up that favorite evil word of hers again, *selfish*, and all the past came flooding back…

…his selfish ways—according to her—the reason for her leaving in the first place.

His mind tried to revisit that parting scene, but her voice interrupted and informed him that she was going to be taking charge at the shop for now, that Eddie was working himself ragged, and his mama needed him at home from time to time. And—by the way—Paulette didn't work for free, so don't be getting any ideas.

That was Paulette, always taking up for the little guys.

And then she topped off her news by reminding him she still had his house keys.

She further advised that she'd be getting those car keys and handing them over to Eddie to use. After all, Eddie and his mama needed to go to the grocery store on occasion. "For shame," she finally said.

But Paulette wasn't finished with him yet. "Say something, Sol. And don't you even think about hanging up on me."

Well, what could he say?

He looked over at Term who mouthed, "Do you miss her?"

Sol screwed up his face. Of course, he missed Paulette. Term deserved the frown.

Term threw up his hands. "So, tell her," he whispered.

Sol squinted his eyes at him. *Busybody.*

"What's all that whispering?" Paulette demanded. "Who are you talking to? Is that a woman in the car with you?"

Sol thrust an elbow in his passenger's direction. "It's this guy I call Term. I'm giving him a lift."

"And tell me this, are you taking good care of Eddie's car?"

Sol gripped the phone. Between the shock of her showing up out of nowhere after five years and her manifold accusations, Sol was struggling to interpret things.

He had no comebacks for her. Not like before. This—this was like an ambush—a good one, maybe—and he couldn't come up with even one sentence.

Sol glanced over at Term who shouldn't even be listening in, but which Sol couldn't do anything about. Term swiveled away discretely, and peered out the passenger window.

Finally, Sol managed a few words. "I—I've missed you, Paulette."

"What?"

There was a long pause on her end now. She didn't seem to know what to say.

But then she spoke again. "Don't think this gets you off the hook with Eddie. You'll be making this up to him."

Then she hung up. Didn't say good-bye and didn't give him a chance to say good-bye, either.

He laid the phone down, placed both hands on the wheel, and let the sting of her words reverberate.

Like a foreign coin, Sol needed to turn things over, to consider all aspects of what just happened.

Paulette still had the house key.

She stopped by the shop.

Then she called him.

But most of all, she'd come with intent.

To see if he'd changed.

But what kind of change was she talking about?

I stepped outside of the Captain's Table with Matt and realized he still had hold of my hand. As we stopped to read the help-wanted sign posted below the restaurant's carved wooden logo, my head still buzzed from him calling me his girlfriend in front of Ralph. Once I regained my equilibrium, I tried to offer a pertinent comment regarding the *help wanted* sign.

"So, have you ever waited tables?" I asked as he tugged me away toward the sidewalk.

"No way," he said, "Not if I can find something else. It's not me."

"Millie's nice. I bet she'd be great to work with."

"I'm sure. But it's too close to the center of action. What if things go south? Did you see Ralph's biceps?" He waggled Grandma's to-go box. "I don't want to end up like this ground beef."

I nodded, my brain darting back to his *girlfriend* comment.

"Before I do that, I'll go on down to the marina and see about working on a fishing boat. I can't just sit around."

He led the way across the road and stopped on the other side. Then he pointed out the top floor of the restaurant. "What do you see up there?"

I shrugged. "Dark windows. Two deserted floors."

"My point exactly. Question is, what's up there? A livable space? An apartment I could rent?"

"A penthouse?"

He laughed. "Not with those filmy windows. I've watched them at night, though. They're never lit up. Gotta be a junk-space. Maybe I should check it out?"

"Isn't that still the center of action?"

"Nah, not like all-day-every-day. Renting is mostly like a once-in-a-while encounter."

I shrugged. Matt's choice of living quarters wasn't my decision.

"If you like it, then so do I. I just appreciate how you're not trying to push me and my dad together, and that you're spending all this time up here with Grandma and me without complaint."

He squeezed my hand and winked. "I have a vested interest in your success."

"That up there—is a really good idea," I said. "All you can do is ask. But if he rents it, he should give you a discount for having to climb all those stairs."

He smiled. "We've got all the time in the world here, Miss Sandy Shore."

"But," I gripped the Styrofoam cup with both hands, "I can't talk—can't go eye-to-eye with Ralph yet." I shook my head. "I just can't."

Matt smiled, and wrapped an arm around my shoulders. "Nobody's pushing you, nobody at all."

We walked back to the Cozy Inn like that—and despite the summer heat, I couldn't help but shiver.

Back at the Cozy Inn, Grandma and I watched the weather on the TV while she ate her supper. Matt had circled back to Ralph's to explore his job options.

I was impressed that Grandma was so hungry. She enjoyed the cubed steak and mashed potatoes and took her time eating nearly all of it. We watched the weather until the reporters repeated their stories and then changed over to an old black-and-white cowboy show. Eventually, I tried to coax her into lying down.

But she would have none of it. "You know, Coral, I really want to take a ride. Why don't we get out and see a little of the countryside?"

"Yes, I've heard…"

Before I could finish, a light knock rattled the door.

"If that's Matt," Grandma said, "have him come in and sit down. We'll talk about that ride. And an ice-cream bar."

Wow, where did all that energy come from?

I opened the door, and Matt popped in. He greeted us both and gave Grandma a kiss on the forehead.

"Good news," he said and perched on the edge of Grandma's bed. "Ralph's gonna take a look upstairs to see if the deserted apartment is fit to rent."

Grandma nodded. "Good for you. That should get you closer to Ralph."

That wasn't the point, exactly. It was to save her some money. But how could we tell her that? Matt didn't want her to feel bad, I was sure.

"And… if Zeke, Ralph's friend comes by," Matt continued, "Ralph will be speaking with him. Zeke owns a charter fishing boat and might know of a job for me."

Oh, dear, I couldn't imagine Matt, from landlocked Nevada, going to work on some fishing boat. "What about…"

He nodded. "I know. I'd better plan ahead and get some sea-sick pills."

Matt seemed to have plenty of faith in his plan. He didn't even sound nervous.

Grandma inched forward and then rose up behind her walker. "Let's go get the car, kids. Time for a ride—before I get too tired."

I admired what Matt was doing, but how would I be able to observe Ralph if Matt was at work?

The summer sun sets late, about nine o'clock. So we still had plenty of daylight for our ride. I crawled into the tiny backseat of the Mustang while Matt helped Grandma into the front seat. She wore her yellow dress today and a sun hat with a mis-matched green flower. Her progress was encouraging.

With no legroom, I twisted my feet sideways, thankful now beyond measure that we'd had two cars driving up. I couldn't imagine ten crippling hours back here.

"Which way?" Matt asked Grandma as he turned the key.

"First off, pick up your sea sick pills," she said.

"Yes, ma'am."

I hoped this evening's ride wouldn't set her back.

It shouldn't. She'd ridden all the way up here, and even though it took the wind out of her sails for a day, she'd regained that ground. Jessica was a godsend, and Grandma really responded to her care as her home health nurse. Once again, I wished Jessica lived right here in Carrabelle.

After Matt located the seasick pills at the only grocery in town, he hopped back in the car. I couldn't wait to get going and get some air.

"I'm curious about the lighthouse," Matt said, "and it's not far down this way. According to a book I read, it used to be out on Dog Island but blew down twice and got moved up to the mainland. I really want to see the place."

Hmm. So Matt had been reading in his spare time. I was beyond impressed.

At this hour, traffic was sparse. He pulled out along Highway 98, the only road through town. We passed the carved wooden sign for the Captain's Table and then crossed over the Carrabelle River past my dad's restaurant on the left.

"There it is, the restaurant," I said, pointing it out to Grandma. Of course, she'd glimpsed it before on the day we first arrived.

She nodded.

I'm sure gray concrete struck her the same way it struck me. Boring. I wished my dad would decorate. The artist in me wanted to fancy things up.

But on the other hand, buildings along the coast did get battered by storms, and maybe that made it too expensive.

"When I'm stronger I'd like to see the museum that goes with it," Grandma said. "It's right there at the base, you know."

She was a reader too.

"And you are getting stronger, Grandma," I said. "Day by day."

"Don't forget, save your energy, you might want to climb the steps to the top," Matt teased. "I've heard that's an important part of the lighthouse experience as well."

She swatted at the air between them and laughed. "Aren't you the smarty britches? One thing at a time, young man."

His eyes crinkled as they met mine in the rearview mirror.

"Slow down here, Matt," Grandma said, pointing to a sign ahead on the right.

He stopped and then backed up and pulled over so we could read the words. "*Tate's Hell State Forest. Information here. Trails. Campsites.*"

From my spot in the backseat, I could barely make it out. "Sounds creepy to me," I said, twisting around and trying to figure out where the info center actually was. Must have been down the side road at the Forestry Service.

"Sure is creepy," Grandma said. "And there's a strange little story about Tate's Hell you might want to read…back at the Cozy Inn."

Matt pulled back onto the road. Within a minute Grandma tapped his arm. "Over there, it's the public beach. Go real slow now." She leaned back. "Aw, now, isn't that beautiful? We should come back for a picnic—once I'm up to it. You two could do that anytime, though. Just look at that horizon. You could view the sunset."

Funny, after Grandma's earlier comment about me taking things slow, it felt strange to hear her telling us to go check out the beach and have a picnic. Perhaps she wasn't matchmaking and simply wanted us to enjoy it.

Matt rolled down his window, and warm salt air flowed in. The Gulf's waters were as placid and calm as a lake. I couldn't imagine a hurricane stirring it up and destroying the coastline. But it had, so many times.

He kept us rolling, and we approached a curve. "There's the lighthouse," Matt said, pointing to the right.

The huge red and white metal skeleton was nothing like I'd imagined. No storm could blow that thing down.

We coasted by, made a U-turn, and headed back to town.

Grandma leaned back on her headrest. "Matt, honey, thank you so much. This was absolutely refreshing. You're a dear."

"Still want that ice cream?" I asked, wanting some myself, no matter what the flavor.

She laughed. "Wherever we can find some."

After a brief tour through town, we gave up on finding an ice-cream shop that was open. So, we returned to the grocery store and settled for a six-pack of fudgesicles and some bottled spring water.

Matt drove us back to the beach parking lot where we opened all the car windows and wolfed down the fudge bars before they could melt. Good thing we had a box of tissues.

Once again, as I swiped the chocolate off my fingers, I reflected on Matt's use of the term *girlfriend*.

I thought of Grandma's and Peter's advice to take it slow.

In fact, I probably should, since it might just be part of the act, a made-up thing to go with a made-up name.

Since Jessica's last visit with Aunt Allie where she'd learned about the elderly lady's bad vision, Jessica had determined to see if she could schedule her a visit with an eye doctor. Jessica would take her, of course. And her argument this morning with her awful boyfriend gave her some extra time and a good excuse to stop by for another visit.

Just like the other day, her boyfriend woke her out of a deep sleep to complain about things. Oh, he finally apologized, called it a misunderstanding, and then made it up to her with this cup of coffee. But she never could get back to sleep.

The lid was on tight this time. She'd made sure of it. And now Jessica questioned whether the other day's spill had just been an accident, as he claimed, or meanness. And after his latest heartfelt apology, she debated whether to keep him around or not.

She took a sip of her coffee as she neared the curve by the general store and tried to decide whether to see Aunt Allie first or her patient, Miss Rosella.

An almost imperceptible tug guided her wheel, and she found herself crunching to a stop in the limestone parking lot in front of the store.

It was as if the car had a mind of its own. She'd make a note to get that steering checked out—or maybe the alignment.

Coffee in hand, she climbed out and mounted the steps. She knocked and then pulled the door open. The bell in the back jingled like it had the other day. "Aunt Allie, I'm back!"

"Have a seat," came the frail but now familiar voice. "Be there in a minute." A whiff of coffee drifted in, and Jessica considered its distinct percolator scent—nothing like her weak stuff from home.

As she waited, Jessica took the opportunity to study things on the shelf she hadn't noticed before, like the lineup of Tupelo and Dog Island honey and below them a row of mayhaw and other jellies—local specialties. Wire baskets of fresh vegetables and fruits sat near the big double doors in the back—an old loading dock for sure.

Saws, hammers, and an odd assortment of tools covered with the patina of age—or perhaps salt air—hung against the back wall, and below them stood an ancient Frigidaire. Taped to its front was a handmade list of RC, Coke, Pepsi, and Nehi drinks for sale.

What a museum. She'd missed so much the last time.

On the east wall near the window hung yellowed calendars and curling newspaper articles—one in particular announcing *President Kennedy Assassinated.*

Aunt Allie shuffled through the kitchen door with a steaming coffee. She stopped off at the fridge to pour in some cream. "I like mine plenty pale," she said.

Jessica liked hers the same way. "It's good to see you, Aunt Allie."

"You too, Jessica. Didn't think I'd see you again so soon."

"I see your newspaper up there about President Kennedy. What a relic."

"A good man," she said as she took a seat by the old stove. She set her mug on top. "Very smart man."

"That was way before my time."

"Kind of forgot about those newspapers," she said. "My eyes. Can't really read 'em these days. Can't sew, can't cook. Aggravating state of affairs."

Maybe that's why she'd confused Jessica with her granddaughter. But Jessica could help with that. She felt a kinship to this old lady and was glad for an excuse to stop in. And she'd be glad to take Aunt Allie anywhere she liked. "You mentioned your eyes before. Could I take you to see an eye doctor?"

"If you know of one. It's been ten or twenty years now, and we don't have one here. I'd like to get these glasses fixed if I can."

Her glasses, with delicate silver flowers along their frame, were beautiful. "I bet they can do wonders with them."

"Thank you. I'm sure of it."

"Speaking of history, this must be a strong building. What I mean is, I'm amazed that this building has survived all the hurricanes." She'd heard of them flattening entire towns up the coast. "How old is this place?"

"If you've lived as long as I have, you begin to learn, there are helpers—angels. God sent them to help us through these things. Anytime I've had to face that kind of thing, I asked God to send me some. It's always worked. It's been here since the 1880s."

"How bad has it gotten?"

"Oh, we've all been evacuated before. And since then, all but ten of the old buildings have been busted to pieces. Right now, there's only three left standin' from the 1800s."

"Angels, huh?"

"You can always ask God to send angels." She took a few sips without speaking. "I've asked Him to put them around that grand-daughter of mine."

There had to be a story there. "I hope for your sake she comes home. Anybody'd be proud to have a grandma like you."

"My goal before I pass on. And just to let you know, I'm not suffering delusions. I've got all my faculties. I'm not mistaking you for her. Just thought you might be her the other day. In my dreams she came right through that door. Oh, she'll come. I know it. I'm just not sure what she'll look like now."

Aunt Allie was so sweet. She deserved a hug. But Jessica wasn't sure if the woman would appreciate it. She didn't seem to be the huggy type.

Allie took a few more sips and studied Jessica. "You're just a stray kitten, aren't you? Don't you have a family?"

Anybody else would have been offended at that. But not Jessica. "Not around here, just me and my boyfriend at home." She took her own sip and showed Allie the cup. "He fixed me my coffee this morning."

"Uh huh."

Sounded more like *yeah, right* to Jessica.

"You don't seem too keen on him," she said.

"Shame on that man! He's no provider. *You* are. And he's getting away with murder. And don't think he doesn't know it, honey. Suppose you get pregnant. He'll be gone in a flash. *Hmmph*. Has no more regard for you than a cricket on a hook."

Miss Allie spoke her mind. Jessica's friends would turn inside out at this conversation. They'd walk out.

But not Jessica. Somehow it tickled her. Somebody had the guts to speak the truth. Nobody else spoke out on her behalf.

"You need a room, Kitten? I've got rooms. There's one in the back. Next to mine. This used to be a rooming house you know. Got more upstairs too."

"Oh, I wasn't..." But as soon as she said it, Jessica recalled her previous decision—to keep her eye open for a rental. Truth was, here was a place to stay, and it had landed in her lap.

It seemed too easy.

Up to now, she'd only half-searched, but with everything so expensive, she'd let it slide.

"Thank you."

"Well, I don't care for this boyfriend of yours. He doesn't love you. He wants you. No kitten of mine's gonna live like that. You come move in here."

Wow, this conversation was overwhelming. Was Miss Allie actually confused and trying to make her into her granddaughter? Jessica should tread lightly. "I-I'll have to think it over. Thank you."

"You do that. I don't like my little friends taken advantage of."

This was too much to process. Jessica glanced at the time on her phone. "I'm going to need to get to work. But I'll be checking on that eye doctor for you." She stood. "Do you mind if I hug you?"

"I guess so, Kitten. I guess you can. C'mon over here."

Allie sat straight as Jessica gave her the hug. It felt like hugging a post. "I haven't had one of those in a long, long time," Aunt Allie said.

But even before Jessica loosened her hold, tears formed in her eyes. She blinked them back.

"I'll see you again soon," Jessica said. "Real soon."

Out in the car she turned on the ignition and wiped her eyes. Allie's words burned in her heart. Truth was, Jessica was just one in a series for that boyfriend. His eye was already roaming, and she saw no desire for permanency in anything he had to say. It was all about him and his convenience.

She gazed into the distance.

Maybe she should take Aunt Allie up on that offer.

Jessica made a few phone calls on break that day and then swung by Miss Allie's on the way home. She found her out back feeding the chickens in her old gray sweater. Sometimes the elderly felt chilled even in the heat.

"Aunt Allie, could I pick you up at nine in the morning and take you to the optometrist? I called mine, and he'll be glad to see you."

"You don't have to work?"

"Flexible schedule."

"Oh, my." Allie's voice carried the unmistakable note of surprise." How far are we going to go?"

"Just up the road to Crawfordville. Can you manage?"

"Well. I'd be much obliged. Much obliged."

Leaving Aunt Allie behind, Jessica turned and headed back toward the gate. She pushed it open and whirled around to wave. Aunt Allie, leaning ever so lightly against her gnarled cane, waved back.

As she turned and walked away, for some reason, Jessica's steps seemed lighter. Lighter than a cloud. For once, she felt she was heading in the right direction.

Bit by bit, Ralph's lunch crowd at the Captain's Table's filtered out with their toothpicks and to-go cups and headed back out to their vehicles or docked boats.

By mid-afternoon Ralph plugged in the vacuum cleaner to tidy up the floor while Millie took a break. But the door opened, and a familiar customer slipped back inside. That young fellow Matt who'd been asking about jobs and that upstairs room the day before.

Ralph flipped off the switch. He'd hoped the boy would just forget about the room. But here he was, back again today.

"So sorry to interrupt your work," the young man said.

Ralph waited for more.

"Yesterday, when I mentioned renting that short-term apartment idea—I should have mentioned the two ladies will be needing a place too, separate from me, of course. But not a job."

Ralph rested his palm against the handle and wrinkled his brow. "Lemme see now…" The rental. Course there were some nice expensive condos up the road. Plenty of those along the coast. And then Millie had a couple of cabins—one was storm-damaged, and one was full of junk.

"I was wondering about the idea I mentioned before," the kid said, "if you'd had time to think about that third floor up there, or to check it out."

A cold wave passed through Ralph. His hand twitched, a sudden and unexpected thing, wobbling against the handle of his machine. He grabbed the cord and flipped it around to make it look intentional. Yeah, he had promised to think about it—to go up there and check it out—just to get rid of the guy. Ralph hadn't twisted a key in that upstairs lock for twenty years. Not since Nadine.

He'd rather the kid just rent from Millie and leave that top floor alone.

The boy continued speaking, but not a word registered. Seconds passed before Ralph's ears tuned back in.

"…no lights on and it doesn't seem to be used," he brought up for the second time. "I'm not looking for fancy or even furniture—just a place to crash for a while."

Ralph sucked in a breath. Well, that shot down the fancy condo idea. Back to something practical. But naw, not his upstairs. He needed to find a way to squirm out of this—never should have told the kid he'd check it out.

"Well, now, I could speak to Millie. If mine's not suitable she might have a cabin you could rent. Not sure about the ladies." The cabin full of junk might work. But where would Millie put all her stuff? And lately she'd been actin' kind of funny. Like she was mad at 'im or had hurt feelings or something. Who knew if she'd be willing to rent. Ralph couldn't be sure.

"I appreciate you looking into it."

Ralph nodded. And now it seemed like he was stuck. For the second time, his ears zoned out. Okay, so the whole crew was staying awhile. This could buy Ralph some time to figure out who the girl was.

Ralph refocused. "Hah. Speakin' of that job you were askin' about," he said, "I happen to be lookin'…."

The young fellow shook his head. "No, I saw your sign out there. But I'm not really cut out for waiter work. I'm more of a hands-on kind of guy. Maybe if something else turns up…."

"Yeah," Ralph told him. "I'll try to help with at least one place to stay. You'd have to wait, though. Millie's on break right now."

Now if Millie would just say yes, he could get the kid off his back.

The boy nodded.

"Why don't you relax, go take a little walk, and I'll run it by her."

"Much obliged. Thank you, sir." The young man turned toward the door and paused. "I've learned one thing about this Forgotten

Coast…" He reached for the handle. "Everybody's so friendly and helpful. Haven't found a grumpy soul yet."

Ralph nodded. Friendly and helpful, huh. He gave the kid a wave. "I'll try and see what I can do."

"I appreciate it, I really do."

"Come back in a little bit. Just don't be gettin' your hopes up."

When Matt walked out, Ralph started up the vacuum cleaner. It sucked up crumbs and half a sandwich.

In the meantime, just in case Millie said no to renting a cabin, he'd given his word. He'd have to go up and check his top floor.

Enh. Ralph attacked another patch of crumbs. He couldn't let Millie and her problems distract him right now.

Where'd all this mess come from anyway? His contraption found another smashed crust and gobbled it up.

As soon as he could, he'd make things up to Millie.

In the meantime, he considered what he might find upstairs. After all these years it would be loaded with dust. Maybe even varmints. But guaranteed it would be in rough shape.

The door, the windows, the doorknob. Salt air did all kinds of damage. Had to be rusted shut. Better grab some WD-40 and take it along.

Reckon he'd figure out how he felt when he opened that apartment door. And that was the real deal.

He didn't want to let the kid down, but even if Millie said no, he didn't *have* to rent the thing out. He could just say no, like anyone else.

Ralph let out a puff of air. After all these years, though, maybe it was time he let things go—shake off his backstory.

Hmph. Yeah, right.

There were some things—permanent things—that time could not erase.

A hand tapped his shoulder, and he startled. Turned.

There stood Millie with a yellow legal pad and sharp pointed pencil. A big smile brightened her face. "Got a minute?"

Ralph couldn't believe his eyes. So now Millie was all chipper? He noted the stuff in her hand. What was this, some kind of planning session?

She stepped over and unplugged his machine.

"Hey, what the heck? I'm tryin' to work."

She laughed. "Sit down a minute, Ralph. I want to show you something. Something I know you're goin' to like."

Well, maybe he was out of the doghouse now, but considering that notebook and pencil, who knew? Millie's ideas always cost him money. But that wasn't as big a deal as…

He stepped over to the booth and sat down, pulled the salt and pepper shaker over in front of him to twiddle with, and wished for a customer to come through the door. "This ain't another decoratin' idea, is it?" His restaurant did fine without all that *décor* stuff she called it. Too *fru fru* for him.

She pressed the notebook against her heart, batted those long lashes, and gave him a sly smile. "Why don't you let me show you?"

"Oh, all right," he said, glancing toward the front door. "But just for a minute. I'm kinda in a rush right now."

"In a rush? This is important."

"Never you mind," he said. "I know it's something important, honey." His hands formed a square around the shakers. "What's up?"

She stood by the table and glanced down at his hands. "Please stop it. That's no way to act."

"I'm sorry, honey. It's just I don't have very much time. That boy and girl you've seen come in on a regular basis—he wants to rent a place upstairs …"

"He wants to? By himself?" She frowned. "They have a fight? I thought there was a grandmother involved. How's a grandma going to climb all those stairs?"

"Well, I don't know about a fight. But yes, for him alone."

"You've never rented that out before. Hmm. I bet they did have a fight."

He watched as she slid into the other side of the booth.

"But I didn't want to rent it," Ralph said.

"So, tell him no." She paused, smiled, and pressed her fingertips against the notebook. "All right now, back to the main topic," she said. "And hear me out, please, with no interruptions. I don't wanna lose my train of thought." She waved an arm. "And this other story has already distracted me."

He leaned forward, intent on her face. Those big brown eyes. They took him to another place. Always did. But he forced his gaze away, and down to the table.

"Here." She turned the yellow pad toward him. "Let's take a look at this." She leaned back with the pencil between her fingers. "I worked on it for a long time. A few little ideas for the Captain's Table. I've drawn pictures to show how we can make it look more *captain-ish*, or *ocean-ish*. Things to boost your business, maybe make people wanna stop on in." She opened her fingers wide, her face full of enthusiasm. "People adore atmosphere. They really do. And this could be the ticket."

So people adored atmosphere. Well, he adored his Millie. She propped her chin on her fist and smiled across the pretty garnet ring he'd bought her for her last birthday. Boy, had she loved that thing. Made a fuss over it. At first. But then, boom, she never mentioned it again. It seemed to make her sad somehow.

And for some reason, in the back of his mind, that fact nagged at him.

"Look at this." She turned to the second page and pointed to a drawing of the main dining room. "We could put a few old mileage arrows up here, you know, like Apalachicola so many miles… Panama City so many miles, etc. etc. We could string fishing nets and corks around the mirror like this, maybe hang some paddles and buoys. Prop a cut-down skiff over here. Get some fake sea-oats. The lunch bar, that's what grabs a person's eye. We could start there."

Her drawings were gorgeous. "You drew this?"

She seemed pleased. "Larry helped me."

"Larry? You guys ganging up on me?"

She turned another page and showed him more. Then a few more pages. She'd even drawn ideas for the outside.

He glanced toward the door. This little presentation could take all day. "Millie. Honey. These are all good ideas—even great ones.

And beautiful pictures. Gorgeous. But we'd have to go out and find truckloads of things," he said. "Then we'd have to install it all. Clean it, paint it, wax it…"

"Ralph, you, of all people, are not among the lazy. And you're not a cheapskate. What's really bugging you?"

"Shoot. How would we find all that decoratin' stuff?"

"Now, Ralph. You know these things are a cinch to find if you know the right people. Especially along this coast. And you know everybody."

Yeah, the poor old commercial fishing industry had about been regulated out of existence. The coast was packed with stuff. Broke fishermen would be glad to sell things off. Earn a little survival money.

Shame. What a shame.

Maybe she'd forget about all her decorating if she had to hunt the decorations down. "You'll never come up with all that stuff."

She raised her eyebrows as if to tell him otherwise. Millie always met a challenge head-on. Stubbornest woman he'd ever met.

And she wanted a ring on that finger. A diamond…

Then it hit him.

Oh, golly. That had to be it.

He laid both palms on the table.

He'd bought her a garnet instead.

And now, if he let Millie decorate this restaurant, that would shove him one giant step closer to marriage. And no matter how he felt toward her, or even loved her, that idea scared the willies out of him. Then with all her input, Millie would think she owned the restaurant, owned him, and then next thing up, she'd want babies and kids, and…oh, criminy, what had she said lately, her *body-clock was running out?* A wave of heat washed over Ralph. No, there wasn't anybody else in his life. But he wasn't ready for all that hullabaloo.

He crossed his arms and leaned back. "Too much money," he said, though money had nothing to do with it. "And think of all the work. People shouldn't try to fix what ain't broke."

But right now, as proud as he was of his fortitude, Millie's downcast eyes told him he'd delivered a low blow and snuffed out her sunshine. He'd crossed a line.

A thing he hadn't intended.

Millie slid out of the booth and closed the pages of her yellow notebook as she stood.

Ralph stood too. "Wait, Millie. There's something else. An important request."

He'd better talk fast. "You know that young man Matt and his girlfriend?"

Millie stared him down with that serious expression of hers.

His words came tumbling out. "The young man, Matt, like I said, when he said he needed a rental—I—I took the liberty of telling him about your cabin."

She laid a hand on the table and leaned forward. Her face said what her words did not, "You volunteered my ca—I can't believe what I'm hearing."

"I thought you'd be willing to rent it out."

Her lips formed the word *no.*

Of course not. He thought back to his questions about the girl. The way Millie had resented them. Was she jealous? Suspicious?

Ralph placed his hand on the vacuum. His body felt suspended in time. This was growing worse by the minute.

Millie finally spoke. She gathered her pencils and then jammed the notebook into her purse. "You should have asked me first."

He shouldn't have shoved away her heartfelt work and then asked for favors. Guilt attacked him as he glanced down at the notebook sticking out of her purse. Millie had spent time and effort coming up with ideas, and he didn't even have the courtesy to finish looking at.

How would he ever dig his way out of this?

She crossed her arms. "Well, I'm sorry, Ralph. It won't work. You don't want me to help you decorate, and all I wanted was to help you prosper. And now you turn around and ask me favors?"

"Think about it, honey," Ralph said. "If you rent it, you'll have money in your pocket."

Millie snorted and pranced toward the hall. "It's not my job to babysit every person that comes through town, is it?"

He stared after her.

"Phooey on you, Ralph. And don't be surprised if I go home early again."

Ralph's arms hung limp. After what seemed like forever, he wrapped the cord around the vacuum again. What a mess. Maybe he could look at those plans with her again tonight. Ask her about them, and make her feel better.

He glanced up as the back door slammed. His heart wanted to holler out, "I'm sorry, Millie…"

But his mouth would not allow it.

I took one of Grandma's elbows, and Matt took the other. This would be the shortest and quickest stroll ever. "You sure you don't want the walker?"

"No, ma'am," she told me. Her voice was precise and crisp. "I hate that hideous thing, especially when my grandchildren have me by the elbows. Let's just go."

Matt winked at me across the top of Grandma's hat. I grinned back as we headed across the highway. This late in the day, traffic always slowed and was an ideal time of day to be walking her across Highway 98—which sounds like a bigger road than just two small lanes. On the other side we'd dogleg left to reach the boardwalk. But today for the first time, she'd asked to go beyond that, past the marina.

"I want to check on those cute fishermen that hang around down there," Grandma said. "And I thought I saw some nice-looking rocking chairs up on that porch."

I hadn't noticed the chairs. But I had to discourage the whim this time. "Maybe tomorrow," I said. "Matt has to get back to the restaurant in a few minutes." He was in the middle of chasing down that third-floor apartment to see whether Ralph would rent it.

And I certainly didn't want to be left with Grandma by myself, especially without her walker. She wasn't that steady yet, and I couldn't lift her if she fell.

Matt pointed at the rocky ground ahead. "Be careful on this limestone gravel, Grandma," he said, always hyper-aware of anything that would trip her up.

We didn't want to wear her out, either. At the boardwalk,

we had her rest on one of the many benches provided for the boat-owners.

She turned her face to the breeze. "I could sit here all day like this watching the sun glitter off those ripples."

"So could I, Grandma," I said, gazing with her across the masts and flags of sailboats and fishing craft that bobbed in the slips. An occasional voice floated up through their open hatches. I could only imagine the solitude and adventuresome life these people lived, and then in contrast, the extreme comfort they must appreciate at finding neon signs, friendly faces, and good hot food along the boardwalk.

As I daydreamed, Matt took the opportunity to stretch his arm across the back of the bench. He brushed a finger along my cheek and tucked a strand of hair behind my ear. I smiled and leaned into his hand.

He hadn't found a job yet but had already made inquiries. He seemed to be quick and willing to tackle whatever problem came up—a go-getter—and I liked that. Very much.

The sun felt pleasant and warm at first, but after about ten minutes Grandma spoke up.

"My thin skin is getting baked now. So, I think I'm ready to go back. But let's at least walk down the boardwalk and around the building that way."

"Absolutely," Matt said.

I was ready too.

Sure enough, there on the porch behind the marina sat about a dozen rocking chairs, and behind them, the store's big glass doors. From the highway I had no idea the store even existed, and based on what I saw through the doors, I knew it would be fun to explore. Funny, all this time I'd mistaken the place for just another restaurant we hadn't tried.

Grandma craned her neck, exploring what she could from the boardwalk. "We can always come back," I reminded her.

As we passed by the slips, we encountered a gravel slope.

"We've gotcha," Matt said, and we practically lifted her over to the sidewalk.

"Whooee," Grandma said, fanning her face with her hat. "Let's just stand here and rest a spell." She leaned against a light pole.

It took her a minute to catch her breath. But as we took off again, she replaced her hat and pointed across the highway. "You know, I wonder why I never noticed that old store before."

"I guess all our attention's been in the opposite direction," Matt said.

Situated across the street stood an old wooden building with a limestone parking lot. Rusted soda pop ads covered its gray board and batten sides. I read the carved wooden sign suspended from the edge of its front stoop. **Bentley's Store**. Sagging planks on concrete blocks led up to double screen doors with a corroded metal *Merita Bread* sign covering its twin cross-sections.

"Well, it's unique," Matt said. "We can come back soon if you like."

Grandma stood still. She couldn't take her eyes off it. "It's got to be a hundred years old."

"Then we'll make a point of it," Matt said and gave her arm a gentle nudge in the direction of the B&B.

We guided her past its limestone parking lot. "I agree with you, Grandma. There's simply no way it's not the oldest building in town."

"Bentley's Store," Matt said. "I hope we can find out something about its history."

And just like Grandma, I wondered why I hadn't paid much attention to it before. Maybe it was all the other gray buildings around it, the store at the marina, my dad's restaurant. Gray, the color of storm-weathered wood.

Yet somehow as we passed it by, I felt a draw. There had to be more to this place than met the eye.

When the young fella Matt turned back up at the restaurant, Ralph surprised him. "Hold out your arms," he said. Millie refused to cooperate, so he'd have to keep his word and do his part. He loaded the kid up with a dustpan and a caddy full of cleaning supplies, paper bags, and small tools. "Don't go fallin' up the stairs with that stuff."

Matt grinned and nodded as he shifted his load. "I guess this means I'll be renting."

Ralph gripped a bouquet of mops and brooms under one arm. "First, we'll see what we find. But no need for you to choke to death on the dust up there. This place hasn't been tended for twenty years." With the other hand, Ralph grabbed up a bucket and led the way out the back door. To their right, a rusted metal staircase extended up the gray wall. "Haven't paid much attention lately, but seems like I need to give these stairs a little maintenance," Ralph said. "Things like that sneak up on you."

The young man followed behind without comment. Ralph was proud of himself for not prying into the young man's personal business. However, he did wonder. Had lots of questions. This wasn't the usual situation. Not by a long shot.

And he did like the kid.

"Today's sweat equity can be a down payment on your first month's rent. No deposit."

"Thank you," Matt said. "I don't mind work."

"Long ago, my dad—this was his place—had plans for an elevator. "Funny, I came with him the day he bought the place. But he's never once set foot on the second or third floors. He sent me up there—a teenager—to report back."

"Oh?"

Ralph reached an arm around his mops and brooms and patted his chest. "Heart problems."

They climbed the first set of stairs in silence, and Ralph paused, glanced around at the view from where he stood. He cleared his throat. The memories seemed like yesterday. For his own sake he shouldn't have mentioned them. Felt like picking scabs.

"I'm real sorry to hear that," Matt finally said from two steps below.

"So," Ralph said, moving once again, "solely based on my limited experience and opinion—Mom was already gone—he up and bought the place."

Matt kept pace behind him. "Sure seems like a lot of confidence to place in a teen."

Ralph grappled with his load and pushed ahead. "Dad had a lot of hopes for this place. The old father-and-son dream."

"I appreciate you helping me, Ralph. The discount and all... I really do. We both know you could have said no or charged me an arm and a leg."

Yeah. The kid didn't know how lucky he was.

Truth was, the history of this place would mean nothing to Matt. The only person this place mattered to in this whole wide world was Ralph himself. To the kid behind him it would just be an apartment. Wasn't there a Bible verse somewhere about no man can meddle with another's grief? Or was that Ralph's imagination?

At the third-floor landing, Ralph set down his stuff to search through his keys. He hunted for the one he hadn't used since the day Nadine left—the one he'd used to lock the apartment. He lifted an arm and peered down at Matt. The landing only accommodated one. "Grab me that WD-40 from the caddy," he said.

Matt handed it up.

Ralph applied a few drops to the lock and worked the key until it twisted freely. "Ocean air rusts everything." He squirted more liquid around the doorknob, freeing it up as well. Then he forced open the door. Its hinges groaned out a loud complaint.

"Like you said, it rusts everything," Matt said.

Ralph stepped in, dropped his things and oiled the hinges inside.

Then he flicked on the single overhead bulb, illuminating the entire third floor. "Come on in," he said. It was a wonder the bulbs still worked. Tongue and groove pine paneling covered the walls—early sixties, and their woody fragrance brought back yesterday's memories.

"Drop your stuff over here," he said, turning his face away from Matt. He gazed toward the large salt-filmed windows that lined the opposite wall above the river and marinas—the same view Nadine had—until he could gather himself.

While Matt distracted himself, Ralph returned to the center of the room and ran his hand across the simple pine table—the one he'd built for the girl. And there was the knothole—right where he'd laid the money that morning. He rubbed his thumb across it and then his fingers—twenty years-worth of dust. Motes fluttered away in every direction. He wiped the dust on his pants and sneezed.

He wiped his nose and then gazed at the knothole, imagining the small stack of money, and the way she must have gathered it up. And then she was gone.

Gone.

Idiot. What else had he expected?

If only she'd waited.

He stepped back to observe the floor beneath the table. Scraps of yellowed paper plate, rodent-nibbled with no trace of its long-ago breakfast, lay scattered across it. The very plate he'd left on the table with her breakfast. After realizing he was too late.

The rustlings of Matt, organizing their supplies near the door brought Ralph's attention back. He turned. "That's fine right there."

"Floor first?" the kid said.

Ralph tipped his head toward the far-right corner. "Sure. Sweep, then mop. Sounds good. I'll dust." In reality, there was little to dust besides the table, the windowsills, and the bed. He'd toss that mattress over the rails and bring one up later along with linens.

He couldn't bring himself to chitchat right now, and those tasks ought to keep Matt busy awhile.

This afternoon, after he'd sent Matt away, Millie had distracted him with those plans of hers, then new customers came along, and Ralph never did find time to check the place out by himself.

And then, of all things, when Millie up and disappeared on him he ended up waiting her tables.

Then she'd reappeared.

She never did explain where she'd gone.

"Fill your bucket in there," Ralph said, pointing out the bathroom on the left. "Flush the lines. Better hope the pipes work. That alone could be a deal breaker."

Right now, Ralph wanted to be alone.

But here he was, doing this. Face to face with his past.

Ralph took a brown bag and stepped across the room to Nadine's old coral collection in the windowsill.

He lifted up one of its three pieces and blew off its coating of gray dust, dead flies, and moths. Ralph had wanted to bag her things in solitude, not like this. He opened a brown bag and placed them in the bottom.

When Nadine first laid eyes on their delicate form she had cried.

Ralph always wondered, though, whether her tears fell because he'd given her a gift, a thing she never had, or because she liked the coral so much.

He stared into space and thought back to their talk that day—about what they were going to do. Ralph shouldn't have brought up the idea. Shouldn't have left her the money.

Nadine.

If only she had waited.

Matt dumped another bucket of nasty mop water down the toilet. The floor, thick with dust, had been filthy. He and Ralph had just finished up when Larry appeared, out of breath, and red-faced at the top of the stairs. He stuck his head in. "Found you."

"What now," Ralph grumbled.

"Ralph, we've all been looking for you."

"Who's *we?*"

"Millie said to tell you she was going home. She took off and left. Now it's just me and that new part-time waitress."

Ralph shook his head. Not again. "And I was just gettin' some things done." He turned to Matt, "That's the thing about the restaurant business. You work dawn to dusk and can't get a minute to yourself."

"And Zeke's looking for you," Larry said.

"Zeke? All right. Go on. Get outta here. And send Zeke on up. You two handle the restaurant as best you can until I can get down there. Show me what you're made of."

Larry saluted, "Yes, sir!" and whirled around. He scrambled back downstairs, while Ralph stepped to the door, held out his cell phone, and yelled after him. "Hey, Larry. See this?" He waited as Larry gripped the rail and looked straight up. "Next time, instead of runnin' all over the place, just call me on it. It's called a *phone.*"

Matt chuckled as Larry gave Ralph another salute and bounded down the stairs. Probably just wanted to see what was up here.

Ralph stuffed the phone in his pocket and turned to Matt. "I hope he didn't burn up the dang kitchen while he was out huntin' me down."

Matt laughed.

Quite soon, the mysterious Zeke appeared at the door, big and tough, and somewhat less out of breath than Larry. He was around Ralph's age.

"Ralph."

"Zeke."

Zeke stepped in. "We brought you a shark today."

"Yeah? Thanks, buddy, I appreciate it. You make sure and get a hot shrimp dinner from Larry."

Zeke nodded his appreciation.

"Matt, this here is Zeke. We go way back. Been good buddies since kindergarten. He's got a charter fishing boat, and takes people out. Big groups, little groups, whatever comes along. Every now and then they bring in a shark. Then we add it to our menu for the night. Won't never let me pay 'im, though. A better buddy you can't find. And all he wants is a fried shrimp dinner in return."

Matt nodded. "Nice to meet you, Zeke."

"Tell you what, though. That shark was hard-earned this time."

Ralph frowned. "Whatcha mean?"

"My deck hand," Zeke shook his head and held up an arm. "All sliced up. Blood all over the deck."

"You're kiddin'."

"Scared me. At first, I thought he'd lost his hand."

"Yeah?"

"Honest truth. We called and found his wife. She raced him up to Crawfordville to get stitched up."

"Wow. Sorry to hear it, Zeke. He'll live, I guess?"

"Sure of it. But I'm out of help. He'll be gone a while. No idea how long."

Ralph tipped his chin toward Matt. "There's your new helper."

Matt pointed at himself. "Me?" Gee, that was quick. "I have no idea what a deck hand does."

"Been watchin' this fellow. He works hard, Zeke. Like a machine. Fast, too."

"If you want the job, I'll teach you what to do. It's not hard at all," Zeke said. "Oh, it's work, all right. But it's not bad."

"Ain't that the truth," Ralph said.

Zeke explained a few of the duties involved. He seemed to be a patient, subdued man. "I'd expect you at five in the morning. The *Gulf Princess* is berthed right out there in front of Ralph's."

"All right. Thank you. I...I guess I'll be there."

"Have you been out on the ocean before?"

"Not to speak of."

Zeke slapped the doorframe and stepped out. "Better get you some seasick pills—least till you get used to things."

Matt nodded as the man disappeared. "Yes, sir."

That base was covered.

Ralph wrung out his mop and poured the final bucket down the drain. "Sure wish I was goin' out on the boat instead of you, Matt. Nothin' like bein' out on the open water. Anyway, looks like you're all set here." He unhooked the key and handed it over. "Tonight, or tomorrow, whichever is convenient. I hope the place suits you. And again, nice job cleaning. I like the way you get down to business and don't waste your time flappin' your gums."

"Thank you."

Truth was, Matt was a nice kid. But now for that bit of bad news. Ralph propped a hand on the mop handle. "That cabin of Millie's. I spoke too soon. Looks like your ladies will need someplace else to rent."

The kid's shoulders slumped. "Well," he said and then pulled up his chin. "Something will turn up."

Ralph dragged the mop and broom into the bathroom and leaned them against the wall. "Keep these handy in case you need 'em again."

"So, about the ladies," Matt said, "is there another rental around here that you'd recommend for them?"

Ralph hesitated and then turned over a mop bucket to sit on, and shoved another one over to Matt. "Well… maybe," he said, taking a seat and motioning for him to sit too. "I'll tell you about one other possibility. Could be good for your girls and the landlord too."

Matt sat and leaned forward on his elbows.

"A long, long time ago—have you noticed that really old wooden store up the street—Bentley's Store? Very gray, a million years old?"

"Just happened by there today, but we didn't go in."

"Well, that's Aunt Allie's place. She's been here practically since the town was founded, the store too, of course. Her husband, back when he was alive, worked for the railroad. And that building of theirs was once a boarding house."

"Looks like a store to me."

"Take a walk around the side. There's rooms back there."

Matt nodded, listening.

"Well, she's a fine Christian lady. Elderly of course. And very opinionated. Won't put up with baloney out of anybody. In other words, she ain't no Liberal Lulu."

"No worries there."

"Didn't figure."

Matt nodded.

"So, check it out if you want. Go ahead, but I don't think she'll want to cook. What I do know is she might enjoy some guests."

"Grandma would love the company of someone her age, I can tell you already. I bet the ladies'll both be interested. I'll be glad to check it out."

Ralph laughed and slapped his knees. "Now, just how do you think you're goin' to check it out?" He cuffed Matt lightly on the shoulder and stood. "Aunt Allie goes to bed with the chickens. And you'll be up and gone by the crack of dawn."

Matt laughed. "Guess I can't, can I?"

"What a day," Ralph said. "Listen, Matt, I've got to get downstairs and get that shark fileted and start it marinating in milk or it won't be ready to serve later."

Ralph slid his bucket into the bathroom beside the mop and broom and then paused. "It's usually going to be late when you get off work."

Matt laughed. "Well, the girls can handle it."

"One more thing," Ralph said, crossing and then uncrossing his massive arms and then settling them on his hips. "And I'm dead serious about this. Do not under any circumstances mention my name or let on about who sent you."

A gentle tap rattled our B&B door, and I opened it to find Matt grinning from ear to ear. I smiled, too. He always swept me away with those dimples.

"Shh," I whispered, stepping outside and closing the door behind me. "Grandma's asleep."

He placed his finger over his lips, nodded, and then took me by the hand. We stepped outside and settled in the shade on the front porch loveseat. It was nice to feel the breeze and be out in the fresh air.

"What would you like first?" he said, throwing his arm across the back of the pillows. "The good news or the bad?" That persistent grin told me the so-called bad news couldn't be all that severe.

I hesitated. Shrugged.

"Great," he said, "let's start with the good news. Ralph seems to be an all-right guy, at least on this apartment issue. We scrubbed the third floor—it's one gigantic room—and since I helped, Ralph reduced the first month's rent."

Matt pulled a key out of his pocket and held it up. "Tonight he'll bring up some fresh linens, and I can move in as soon as I want."

Maybe the apartment was good news for him. He had to be proud of himself for finding a place so fast, but I would sorely miss having him close by. I'd grown accustomed to his popping in at all hours to check on us. But then, of course, mine and Grandma's world would soon be shifting as well. And I had no idea what form that would take.

"You're not smiling." He held up his palms. "This is supposed to be good news."

"It is good, Matt. And Ralph was good to step up so quick and help you."

"The whole town is like that," he said. "We're both benefiting. He had a second rental idea, but it didn't pan out. No problem, though. Then he gave me a third. Something very interesting. And that's what I wanted to talk to you about. It could be a good thing, or bad, depending on how you look at it."

He'd hardly taken a breath, so I listened without interrupting. I had no desire to burst his balloon. But the comment about it being good or bad, depending on how you look at, it gave me pause.

"But let me circle back to that good or bad thing," he said.

I couldn't help but smile at Matt's unabashed enthusiasm.

"And can you believe it? There's a job already. A job."

"You're kidding." So much had happened.

"On a charter fishing boat, too. Can you believe it, Coral? It just landed in my lap."

"A fishing boat?" Though we had already discussed the possibility of a job on a boat, my thoughts scattered like dropped marbles. There could be storms, sharks, and boats could even sink. And I couldn't imagine Matt, a landlubber from Las Vegas, on one. "Wow, you are just chock full of news. What kind of work would you do?"

He laughed. "Ordinary deck hand work. Zeke explained it while he was up at Ralph's. Waiting on the clients, helping them land their fish, serving up soda pop and frying up hot dogs, making change. Whatever it takes to make them happy. Then once we get back to port, I'll be cleaning their fish at the cleaning station and then back to the boat to sweep and swab the decks."

"Oooh, sounds like fun," I said, "I wanna go." And I wasn't being sarcastic. I spent many summer camps on such boats. They were a total blast.

"You betcha. What I don't know how to do, Zeke will teach me. And who knows? I might even learn something. Like names of fish—and *how* to fish. The bottom line is I do whatever jobs he wants me to do."

Matt was practically bubbling over.

We laughed.

"There's so much I want to know—and number one is learning how to navigate."

I appreciated Matt's sincerity—his desire to absorb all he could. His bravery. His grandfather Eduardo would have been so proud of him.

Matt kept right on chattering.

I realized then that excitement was a hundred times more desirable than fear when approaching a new hurdle in life. Here he was, inexperienced, didn't know a thing about the duties of his job, a complete novice out on the water, and he wasn't a bit afraid. He was invigorated.

Had I been afraid of those boats as a child? Of course not. I'd enjoyed my adventures.

And I wanted him to enjoy this. He was fearless, and I was so proud of him.

Sitting there in the shade, I took in a long slow breath as I felt the strength of Matt's attitude taking hold of me. It only reinforced my resolve to meet my father.

Why fear it? Why debilitate myself?

Then Matt told me about the former deck hand's gruesome injury. "The boat job only lasts until he's able to return. With three young kids at his home, I think he'll be in a hurry to get back and earn his pay. In the meantime, I'm happy to not be useless…"

I interrupted. "Matt, you've never been useless."

This brought a smile.

"I'll be contributing to the rent and meeting people. The best of which…." He paused. "Coral, for your sake, and back to the purpose of you being here, there may be a divine purpose for this meet-up. Zeke and Ralph go way back. To kindergarten."

Kindergarten. Hmm. I nodded. Zeke could be a wealth of information.

A gust of wind blew a strand of hair across my face, and Matt rescued it, sliding it behind my ear. "Coral, I know you've been having some pretty positive feelings about your dad. For that reason, and that alone, I was able right away to say yes to the offer. Zeke was at wit's end. He needs the help."

"So it…"

"I made no promises. But I know he needs me. Tomorrow, without a deck hand, would be a total failure."

"I just don't want…"

"I know. You don't want to be stuck here if things go south." He took my hands in his. "But you're my first consideration. If this whole thing with your dad breaks down, and you decide you want to leave, I'll just have to tell Zeke good-bye."

I nodded.

"Whatever you want," he said. "I'd never force you to stay if you want to leave."

I took a deep breath. "And that boy's hand—the other deck hand—it's just deep cuts? Not a broken bone or tendon? Some injuries take longer to heal than others."

"Not that I know of."

I nodded. "What about your work hours?"

He checked the time on his phone. "It's getting late. We'd better go grab some supper, don't you think?"

Okay, so what was his bad news?

Matt opened the door for me at the Captain's Table, and we made our way inside. He'd been telling me about the shark-steak—courtesy of Zeke—that was posted on tonight's special menu board, and wanted to try it. The restaurant seemed busier than usual, as if there existed a fan club for shark-steaks.

"You go ahead and order it," I said as we took our seats. "I'll taste yours. A very tiny piece. Grandma and I like our crab cakes."

He laughed. "Final offer. I learned today that Captain Ralph only serves shark when Zeke accidentally snags one and drops it off—in honor of their life-long friendship."

"Well, thank you anyway. The very thought of chowing down on a man-eating monster makes me shudder."

Once our steaming plates arrived, he forked a tidbit of meat and held it out to me. I shook my head. "Never mind, Matt. I can't. You eat it. Sorry to disappoint you."

"It's okay," he said and pulled it back. To his credit he didn't try to force the issue. Instead, he surprised me by changing the subject entirely. "So, are you ready for the bad news now?"

I leaned back. "Not really."

He chuckled, and plunged in anyway. "You were asking about my hours. Dark to early evening. And after we scale the customers' fish and clean up the boat, probably close to dark."

I frowned. My fork with its piece of crab-cake hung in mid-air. Then I shrugged. "At least the sun sets late in the summer."

"That's not every day, though. Sometimes I'd come back before that. Remember, his boat was back at dock by mid-afternoon today. Depends on the guests we take out and what they want."

I nodded. This could be bad. What did I expect, though, with charter fishing trips?

But then, I didn't want to ruin Matt's day. So much good had happened for him. And here he was helping Zeke through a bad time. Grandma had always said to put others before yourself.

He laid his open hand on the table, and I took it. "We can make it work. For Zeke's sake. Who knows? Maybe he'll let you tag along. Would you like to go out on the water?"

I leaned forward. "I love it on the water."

"I probably did agree too soon about taking the job. I'm sorry. I didn't realize the crazy hours. But like I said, this might afford us an inside track on Ralph."

I refused to think of these things in negative terms.

"We can't visit the Captain's Table as much. But this new opportunity gives us a way to be more creative in our research. Via the Zeke angle."

"That's true," I said, "But I hope the guy's hand gets well quick," I said. "'Cause I'm gonna miss you."

After supper Matt picked up Grandma's take-out box and grabbed my hand. Grandma didn't drink tea at night, so I had nothing to carry.

"I'd like to see Zeke's boat," he said as we stepped outside. He led the way down a narrow gravel path around the side of the restaurant.

As we rounded the corner on the river side which we'd never visited, he stopped in his tracks, and I nearly slammed into him.

There, lined up in slips along the boardwalk, bobbed a half-dozen sailboats and other craft. Ralph had his own little marina back here. We'd seen the marina on the other side of the bridge, but not this one. And since we'd never used his back dining room, we'd never even seen it through the windows.

And there at the far end sat the beautiful *Gulf Princess*, her gleaming white surface aglow in the waning sun and framed against the palmettos and cabbage palms. It could have been a painting.

Matt whistled in awe, and I gaped at the two-deck boat, all battened-down tight and as big as a small house.

"That's Zeke's?"

He nodded and raised his eyebrows. "Now that's a boat."

We studied the scene in silence.

"Fantastic," he said.

"I don't believe in luck, Matt. But as the saying goes, you are so lucky. And yes, I certainly would like to go out on that."

We eventually tore our eyes away from Zeke's fancy boat and left it behind as we passed back over the bridge on our return to the B&B. Matt, always the proper gentleman, stayed to the outside. At the far end of the bridge, he cleared his throat. "Now, for the rest of the news."

I'd almost forgotten. "Well, with all that other, I can't begin to imagine what it would be."

"*Meh.* Could be good. Could be bad, depending on how you look at it. But if I know you and Grandma, it will turn out fine. It's a possible rental for you."

Nothing could beat our B&B. I glanced up at him, determined to tolerate this news with the same courage he'd shown earlier about his new job. "As long as it's not some dirty old dump."

He laughed. "No, no. I'd never do that to either one of you. We'd leave town before that. But it is historic."

I grinned. "Some shacks are quite historic."

He tugged on my hand. "No. Truly historic. Like historic-register or the-founding-of-Carrabelle historic. So…" he said, jutting his chin straight ahead, past our B&B. "Look up there. It's Bentley's Store. Wanna take a look?"

My mouth flew open. "The store? You're kidding. We were just talking about it today."

He led the way, and we passed our current accommodations and struck out for the board-and-batten building. Its planks were ablaze in the lowered sun. A rusty ten-by-twenty overhang protected its two multi-paned windows and twin screen doors—already closed tight for the evening. Up close it was huge.

Our feet crunched over the limestone rocks. "Is it two stories or just extremely tall?" I asked.

"Not sure. Let's check around back. But first…" Matt stopped beside one of its simple concrete block pillars and placed a hand on one of the blocks above my head.

For a split second my heart leaped. I thought he was going to kiss me out here, by the highway, in front of the whole world. But he turned his face toward the bridge.

"All right, now check out the restaurant," he said.

I followed his eyes and looked across the bridge.

"See? If you and Grandma stay here, I'm just up the street. All you have to do is wave your arms and holler, and I'll be there."

I smiled. True. I guess he sensed my feelings, because I really would miss having him upstairs.

We moved on past the old store-front windows. Very little could surprise me, but this store didn't seem so bad. Up until I turned twelve and met Grandma Rosella, Mom and I stayed in the worst roach and rat-infested places anyone could imagine. Matt would probably pull out his hair and run the other way if he knew the truth about my early years.

At the corner, we passed a huge tree and turned left down a side-street. Bentley's Store and its property took up the whole block.

"I wonder if people ever run this stop sign because of these low branches," I said.

Matt, who hadn't noticed it, turned to look. "Yeah, that could be bad." He took out his pocketknife, and trimmed enough branches to reveal the faded word *stop* and dropped them around the base of the tree. He gave me a wink as he stepped back to check it again and broke off one more branch.

I smiled as he slipped the knife back into his pocket. A good man will take charge like that and see that things are done.

He laughed at my expression and took my hand. "What? We can't have unsafe conditions, can we?"

A fence led around the side of the store, and we followed it around to where it met an ancient metal gate with curlicue parts. Its latch lifted up like Grandma Rosella's.

Set back about ten feet from the fence was a covered porch with rockers, with another huge section of building behind it, clearly a two-story residence.

"I bet Grandma would love to sit and rock on that porch," Matt said as we moved on. We passed the building's large backyard with its fruit trees and chicken coop.

At the opposite fence stood an old lady with a cane, her hair as white as snow, chatting with another lady. "I bet that's Aunt Allie back there," Matt said as we passed. "Allie Bentley."

Aunt Allie had her back to us, but the other person waved. It was Millie.

We waved back and then circled the next block and returned to the B&B.

Matt paused at the door and smiled down at me. "So, here's the bad news," he said, brushing the hair out of my eye. "If you do decide to check out the old historic place, I'll be gone all day, maybe till dark. Aunt Allie goes to bed early. So you'd have to make all the arrangements yourself."

I laughed. "Is that all?" What a relief. I'd rented before. "That's not so bad."

"Well, of course, it is for me. I would have enjoyed impressing you—by making all the arrangements."

I smiled. "Thank you, though. You did find it, and that counts for everything."

Matt needn't worry about impressing me. He was doing just fine.

After lunch I helped Grandma dress. The day felt strange—empty—without Matt around. He had left before the crack of dawn for his new job on the boat.

I wondered if he felt the same way.

"Grandma, I'd like you to come visit one of the native ladies of Carrabelle with me," I said. "Remember Bentley's Store?"

Grandma brightened and reached for her hat on the dresser. "I'm ready when you are."

"Matt told me she used to rent out her rooms," I said. "Not so sure she still does, but I know you miss having Grandpa's buddies come around every day. And you might enjoy this lady's company."

Before Grandpa Eduardo died, and up until Grandma's hospitalization, his friends came down daily to play Cuban card games and smoke cigars at their patio table. I've always called them my uncles. And there was always Grandma, with her coffee and cookies. Their house was the center of fellowship.

She placed a wrinkled hand over her heart, that big diamond still sparkling. "Oh, honey, you don't know how I miss them."

"I can only imagine," I said. "Inch by inch, with the Lord's help, we'll get you back to health."

She touched my arm. "I've almost forgotten what that feels like."

In the end, those friends' daily visits saved her life when they arrived and found her windows dark and the door locked.

She moved to stand. "Let's go on up there," she said.

"Only if you use your walker." I pulled it toward her.

She mumbled something about hating it but took hold anyway. Good thing Aunt Allie's place wasn't far.

Grandma's bones felt delicate under my touch. The nurse Jessica mentioned it a priority we get her weight back up. She was still hovering at about a hundred pounds.

"No need to hold onto me," Grandma said, "I'm doing fine."

Maybe so, but I wasn't taking chances.

Today she wore a yellow and white Hawaiian print and a green flower on her sun hat. It matched okay, but in the past, she would have worn a yellow silk flower.

"I understand you want to get along on your own," I said. "But Matt's not here to help. Let me at least keep a hand on you, okay? Just in case. Because it is a little rocky."

Her independence, evidence of improvement, was nice, but having her out on the street by myself was a big responsibility.

She straightened and lifted her chin. I nearly chuckled aloud. Grandma never fussed when Matt held her elbow.

At the store, we cut across Bentley's limestone parking lot. The store's doors were closed up tight today. "Wait right here," I said. "There's a note taped to the window. I'll have to get close to read it." I stepped up and pulled open the screen door. "Okay," I said, shutting it back. "It just says she's around back on her porch."

I realized then we should have stuck to the sidewalk. "You doing okay, Grandma?"

"Don't you worry about me," she said as we rounded the corner. "I'm holding up just fine. Just fine."

She did have a little pep in her step.

I hoped for both our sakes that Matt's rental idea worked and we didn't have to hunt for another new place. The very idea of this store being historic intrigued me. Another week or so in this quaint town with its quiet streets and laid-back people wouldn't hurt my feelings.

In the meantime, while my doubts about meeting my father were fading, I still wasn't ready to rush in and introduce myself.

"Oh, wait." I stopped before the gate. "I forgot something, Grandma. Listen, if I give her a different name for myself, if I call myself Sandy, don't let on. Okay? Matt and I are…I'll explain it later."

Grandma frowned, opened her mouth, and shut it again. She nodded. "Okay. But you've got some explaining to do, young lady."

I grinned and hugged her shoulders. "Just please—it's important—so don't let on."

Millie glanced up from her rocking chair up on Aunt Allie's porch. "Well, I'll be. Looks like the girl from the restaurant. You've got company."

The girl and a tiny elderly woman in a bright yellow and white dress approached the fence and stopped at the gate.

Aunt Allie uncrossed her knees and eyed the visitors. "Land's sakes. Sure looks like it." She shifted her cane to her left side. "Afternoon, neighbors. Come on up and sit a spell. Can you make it up?"

Millie stepped off the porch and opened the gate for the newcomers. She took the tiny lady by the elbow and walked her up the steps. The girl brought up the walker. "Come on in. We were just havin' a little visit."

"Thank you," they said together.

"Millie, how are you doing?" the girl said. "Missed you at the restaurant lately."

She nodded back. "Afternoon." So, this was the little grandma they'd been taking all the plates of food to. Cute little thing. But, goodness, frail as a bird. "Got plenty of rocking chairs," Millie said, "just pick one out."

The little old lady settled in beside Aunt Allie. "We saw your note in the front window," she said. "It's nice to make your acquaintance." She motioned toward the girl. "This is…"

The girl leaned over and shook hands with Aunt Allie. "Pleased to meet you, ma'am. I'm Sandy Shore. And this is my Grandma Rosella."

Millie pulled up another rocking chair so the girl, Sandy Shore, had a seat and then took her own.

"Well, it's a pleasure," Aunt Allie said. "Name's Allie Bentley, but everybody in town calls me Aunt Allie. And this is Millie, my neighbor. It looks like you've already met her, though."

Millie jumped in, "And this young lady…"

"Sandy," the girl chimed in.

"…is one of my regular customers. And that handsome fella you seen her with last evenin', well, he ain't usually far away." Millie turned to the girl and nodded.

Aunt Allie rubbed her thumbs along the arms of her rocker. "Millie here just got back from Tallahassee. Had her hair and nails done."

Millie stuck out her hands and modeled her fingertips. "This is why you haven't seen me lately, I took a little time off for myself."

"Good for you, and that's very pretty," Grandma said.

"Nice color," Sandy added.

Millie wondered how Ralph had handled her job and his. She hoped he'd missed her and given that part-time waitress a few extra hours for once.

"Grandma Rosella," Aunt Allie said, as if committing the name to memory. "You mind if I just call you Rosella? Is that all right?"

Rosella waved the question away with a smile. "Of course."

"How are you and your granddaughter enjoying our little town?" Allie asked.

Rosella held up one finger. "And my grandson."

Millie frowned and pondered this a minute. She pointed at the girl. "But I thought…"

The girl laughed and crossed her knees. "Grandma Rosella's not my flesh and blood grandma. But she's as good a grandma as I'll ever have." She smiled at her grandmother. "All…well, most of my real family is gone."

"So sorry to hear that," Millie said. "But I'm happy you have your grandma."

Millie gripped the rocker's arms with both hands and stood. She figured it was about time to leave them to their visit. She leaned over to shake Rosella's hand. "It was nice meetin' you, ma'am," she said. "Time to get back home and put my supper on."

"The pleasure's mine," Rosella said. "I hope to see you again."

Millie stood beside the rock post where Aunt Allie liked to prop her feet. She pointed toward her own place. "I live right around the backyard there on the next block. Come on by and visit if you like." She leaned her hand against the top of the post and…*Click!* She jerked it away. There on the post sat a toy metal frog. She picked it up and held it between her thumb and finger.

"This thing. It scared me to death! What are you doin' with this?" she asked Aunt Allie.

"That's my clicker. You asked about it the other day."

"The one you call your chickens with…" She laughed. "Good thing it wasn't alive. I'd a' squished it."

Allie laughed and turned toward Rosella. "They used those in WWII you know. My husband had one during the Normandy Invasion. The real one's in the house. This one's just a toy."

"Oh, really?" Rosella asked. "Your husband trained for that? We love heroes, don't we Cor… honey?"

Sandy Shore nodded, all ears. "We'd love to hear the whole story."

"Well," Allie said, "Millie says she needs to go, so I'll keep it short. But seeing's how you've asked…." She waved her cane left to right in the direction of the highway. "All along the coast out here, these twenty miles, the water's extra deep. The perfect spot for our military to train for the Normandy Invasion. Thousands of troops came in. And this clicker was one of the things they used."

"What does a clicker have to do with an invasion?" Millie asked.

"Well," Allie smoothed her cotton dress, "over at Normandy they'd be landing on the beach on a coal black night. They wouldn't be able to see a thing. So orders were, if a soldier heard you rustlin' nearby and clicked their clicker, you'd better click twice real fast, or they'd shoot you dead. That way they could tell who was friend or foe."

Millie turned the clicker in her hand. "And this is what they used."

"Well, the real clicker was a square little thing. A toy, actually, but I'm not bringing my husband's real clicker out to ruin, though I do wear it around my neck sometimes when I call the chickens. But this one's been sittin' around my store shelf for many a year. I just brought it out in case I forget the other one."

Sandy Shore held out her hand to see the clicker and then showed it to her grandma. "Fascinating," she said.

When Sandy clicked the frog-clicker, Millie pointed, "See?" She slapped her knee and turned to Aunt Allie, "Didn't I tell you the other day? Didn't I? That little clicker sounds just like cockin' a gun." She looked to the two guests and nodded. "Don't y'all think it sounds like a gun?"

"Yes, it does," Miss Rosella said. "Do it again."

"It does," the girl repeated and pressed on the metal toy to click it again. Everyone laughed. "I love this thing, but I'm putting it back right now before I accidentally carry it off," she said, handing it up to Millie.

"Well, there you go." Millie replaced it on top of the post.

Aunt Allie laid her cane across her lap. "Oh, there's a lot more World War II and Civil War history up along this coast. In the 1800s they made salt right up the way there. That was for preserving meat. And up at Lanark they held German and Italian prisoners. We've had pirates, smugglers, you name it, all up and down here."

"Matt would love to hear all this," Sandy said.

"The officers' barracks," Aunt Allie said. "They're still up there."

"You're kidding," Sandy said.

"They're repurposed as apartments now." Millie added.

Somehow that reminded Millie of a question she had for Aunt Allie. "Before I forget, Aunt Allie, what was that you started to say about Ralph the other day, that he just loved…*something*, but you never finished."

Sandy turned and focused on Aunt Allie.

"Let's see." Allie puckered up her lips and gave it some thought. "I told you to bring him by to visit, I remember that…Oh, he loved the Bible. That's it. Loved things about the Bible and the Lord."

"Really?" Millie said. Pretty interesting. Couldn't tell it now.

"Just before school, he waited inside the store for the bus. We'd sit around the wood stove. And we'd talk. Didn't talk about it all the time, but many times. He just ate it up. Guess he had the theologian in his blood."

That's all Millie needed. She straightened. "Okay. I'm headed home now, this time for real. Got to get home and put supper on. See you soon, Aunt Allie, maybe I'll stop by next Wednesday if this taking-a-day-off thing works out for me." She waved at the others. "Nice to meet you. Bye, now."

As she walked away, Millie raised her brows.

Wow. Her Ralph was full of surprises.

I waved good-bye as Millie stepped through the gate and disappeared down the left fence line.

"Sweetest thing you'll ever get to know," Aunt Allie said, turning back to us, her visitors. "Her family has all passed away, and she inherited those three cabins back there that her aunt used to own. Came from Tallahassee 'bout three years ago."

"So that's why she drives all the way up there to get her hair done," I said.

"Strong ties up there, for sure," Aunt Allie said. "Now do tell me about yourselves and what brings you to this tiny town of Carrabelle. I love to hear accounts of the outside world."

We shared stories about ourselves and how we came to know each other. How Grandma Rosella stepped in and became so important in my life. Grandma contributed some, but allowed me to tell most of the story.

"And your grandson, how does he fit into all this?" Aunt Allie asked.

That's when Grandma spoke up. "He's a college student, too, and he's helping our family friend with a little research."

I gaped at her, impressed with such a clever answer. Never would I have thought up such a thing. Yet it was true.

Aunt Allie nodded, accepting her vague answer. "You ladies are pretty special. The Lord has blessed you both."

"What about your family?" I asked.

"I've mentioned my husband," she said. "After the war, he took up a job with the railroad. We had one daughter…and well, it's just me now. Not much to tell." She waved her cane, indicating the building. "My roots, like those of an old weathered tree, grow straight down in this very spot."

Seemed to me Aunt Allie had just skirted a painful topic of her own—her daughter.

We mentioned our desire to find an alternative living place for a week or two. As she listened to our story, her clear blue eyes and erect posture radiated an intense sharpness. The term *sharp as a tack* came to mind. She reminded me of Grandma Rosella before her illness. As a storekeeper I bet she tolerated no malarkey from tricksters.

Aunt Allie explained the history of her boarding house, stories of interesting characters that had stayed there, and how she used to cook big meals every day.

"I do very little now. My eyes. Wish I could enjoy books like before, too. It's past time to get my eyes checked."

Once again, Grandma chimed in. "You poor thing. I'd hate to give up reading. It's one of my greatest pleasures. We've got to help you get that appointment."

"Believe it or not, I've had an appointment and am just waiting on the new prescription."

So far, I didn't think Aunt Allie considered us as potential renters. So, I came right out with it. "Do you mind if we ask you about an important matter?"

Grandma leaned back and let me talk.

"Would you consider renting us a room and allow us to cook—a menu of your choice—for all of us?"

Aunt Allie's face brightened. "Oh, my, that would be delightful. To have you here as guests and enjoy good food. And you two would make excellent company. When can you come?"

Millie strode down Aunt Allie's fence line. Of course, her rush to get supper going was more of a pretense than anything. She didn't want to be stuck conversing for a long time. Not with new people. Let Aunt Allie do that.

And the girl—Sandy—didn't seem so bad. That was more on Ralph. The girl had her grandmother to tend to, a very nice lady. The boyfriend was fine, of course.

Millie mainly wanted to get away and think. To think about Ralph and what Aunt Allie said about him back there.

Based on her history, maybe Aunt Allie could do a study with her. On Wednesdays. Millie liked the Bible, too. Just didn't know much about it.

Anyway, Ralph had his carving hobby. And his kitties. Why shouldn't she have some things of her own?

Yeah. She needed a day off each week and her own things to do.

Inside the B&B parlor, I found a good book on the history of pirates around Carrabelle and took it out to the side porch loveseat where I could stretch out and read until Matt came back from work.

Grandma, tired but excited, had crawled in bed as soon as we got back and had fallen asleep way before sunset.

As things turned out, she adored Aunt Allie and Millie, and she couldn't wait to move in tomorrow.

By this time tomorrow, we'd be moved into the downstairs bedroom next to Aunt Allie's and share her bathroom. Part of our payment would be cooking and dishes, which to me was not a big deal.

I hadn't even finished chapter one before I spotted Matt crossing the bridge. Apparently deep in thought, his head was down as he plodded across the road into the parking area and up the front steps.

"Hey there," I said.

He looked up. "Hey, yourself!" He threw me his million-dollar smile.

"Your clothes are wet."

He came around to the side. "I didn't see you up there."

"Been watching you, though," I teased, "from all the way over the bridge." I shut my book and gripped it on my lap. "Penny for your thoughts."

He plopped down beside me, smelling of bleach and fish and fried shrimp.

"Just thinking about my first day on the boat and that hot dinner Zeke treated me to up at your dad's place. He's a good guy, and I think we'll hit things off just fine."

"That was nice of him. How was the first day?"

"Long. Very long."

I nodded waiting for more.

"The Dramamine worked. No problems there. The work's not hard. Two families. Not their first trip. The dads were pretty independent. Wanted to bait their own hooks. The mamas were a different story. More chatting than fishing. And the kids. More eating and playing than fishing." He pulled out a couple of large bills. "They tipped me good."

"Oh, my. Did you cook for them?"

He nodded, and we sat in silence for a bit. I could tell Matt didn't feel much like talking. He probably wanted to head upstairs and hit the shower.

"Did you have to clean fish?"

"That stinky, huh?"

I grinned. "Doesn't bother me."

He studied my face. "How'd it go for you today?"

I summed it up as quickly as I could, feeling guilty for keeping him from his needed rest but wanting to keep him close just the same.

As I started in on how Aunt Allie wanted us to move in and that Grandma just adored her, Matt's eyes began to droop. I didn't have the heart to keep yacking. But I did want to let him in on one more thing. "I stayed away from the restaurant today. It felt funny going alone."

He nodded and closed his eyes. "I understand," he whispered. "We're not going to let that slide, though. It's too important." He rested his hand on top of mine. "We'll figure it out. We will."

"That's not a guilt trip I'm trying to put on you."

"Never crossed my mind."

More silence. I wondered if he would drop off and begin snoring. But somehow, he didn't.

"This is our last night here," I said. This obvious fact went without saying. But in my heart, I knew it had to be spoken—marked in some way. Tonight was a turning point.

"I'll run my bag up to the penthouse in the morning," he mumbled, eyes still closed.

I laughed, stretched my legs, and scooted down on the seat. I'd sure miss Matt.

He moved his arm around behind me on the loveseat and leaned in close to give me a warm, weary kiss. Then he stood and pulled me to his side as he opened the front door and guided me in. "And all the time I'm out on that water, Sandy Shore, I'll be thinking only of you."

He walked me to my room, opened the door a crack for me, and then whispered, "I don't know how this job—taking me away from you and your dad—is in the least bit logical. But in here, "he pressed a fist against his chest, "I know it's going to be just fine. Like part of a bigger plan. It's the right thing to do despite what my brain is telling me."

I nodded. No, it didn't make much sense. But in my heart, too, despite feeling sad, it just seemed right.

"Tell Grandma g'night, now," he said and touched me on the nose. "And before you know it, we'll be warming up the rocking chairs on that other porch."

I'd hoped for another kiss, but instead, he turned and trudged up the stairs.

Zeke stepped into the cabin of the *Gulf Princess* to check the weather radio. In a few minutes, he'd be firing up her engines and moving to a new spot.

He chuckled. Matt, his new landlubber deck hand, was portside untangling clients' hooks and helping them with slippery bait.

Two days ago, Zeke hadn't known how he'd make it without his old deck hand, and then thanks to that shark he brought in, he'd bumped into Matt up at Ralph's.

He glanced through the porthole at Matt who seemed to be doing a pretty good job. Lots of patience, as needed. Good with the kids and sharp in the galley, too.

But one thing Zeke regretted was mentioning his old friendship with Ralph, and how the two of them went way back. That was two days ago. And now Matt was slipping in questions like some undercover PI. What the heck?

If it hadn't been for that shark they'd taken up to Ralph's place, the topic would never have come up. And what business was it of Matt's, anyway, what kind of person Ralph was?

Zeke leaned his head out. "Pull up the lines up, Matt. We're weighing anchor and moving locations."

The boy grinned back. "Yes, sir" and hopped right to it.

Zeke had no complaints about the kid. But all those questions… Heck, Zeke didn't even know all the answers.

Zeke wondered himself what had changed Ralph. Always had. The war? His dad's funeral? Inheriting the restaurant? He couldn't even corner Ralph and get him to talk. What happened to all their plans?

Thing was, Ralph wasn't even mad at Zeke. Nothing like that. He just backed off. Gave him the stiff-arm.

Zeke would for sure like to know what it was all about.

A few minutes later, Matt stepped through the pilothouse door. "We're set, Captain. All the lines are up."

"Weigh anchor."

Zeke fired up the engines. It took several minutes for him and Matt to wench up the anchors. When Matt re-entered, Zeke handed him several bags of cheesy puffs—treats for the clients to toss at the gulls while the boat moved. They would soar along at arms-length hoping for a handout. "Pass 'em out," he yelled over the racket.

Matt left to distribute them. This and the engine noise would give Zeke a nice break from any questions.

Ten minutes later at the new location, the engines ceased, and the boat settled and rocked. And now the slapping of the water against the hull and the rusty shriek of the gulls were the only sounds.

Fishermen stowed the rest of the cheesy puffs and set out their freshly baited hooks. Time to concentrate on their lines. Fish were hungry, and it kept Matt busy pulling them off hooks and re-attaching bait.

Eventually, Matt came around to the bait box where Zeke leaned against the gunnel.

"You haven't asked me any questions lately. You run out?" Zeke said.

Matt laughed. "I was just trying to establish the lay of the land. I've got some big news to present to Ralph. Not sure how he'll receive it."

Zeke crossed his arms. "How he'll receive it, huh?" So, now they were getting down to the meat of things. The first thing to cross Zeke's mind was a negative—like a subpoena. "Not so sure I like the sound of that." Just what kind of setup did Matt have up his sleeve? Zeke, regardless of how clammed up Ralph was these days, didn't plan to let anyone broadside his friend. No, sir. "What kind of news?"

Matt loaded a small bucket of bait and closed the lid. "Life-changing."

"What the heck? Don't stop with that."

"Life changing and probably good, depending on how you look at it. Only thing is, I don't know what his mindset is."

"Don't leave me hanging like that. Come out with the rest of it."

"Hold on while I take this bucket of bait around here." Zeke had impressed on Matt that until the clients exit the parking lot, their needs come first. So, what choice did Zeke have?

Matt returned with another little bucket and scooped in some bait. He paused. "Do you think I could bring my girlfriend along and let her explain?"

"This better not be some…"

Matt held up his hands. "Nope. Nothin' like that," he said as he turned. "But bringing her would be a much simpler way to explain. It's her news, really."

Zeke dropped his gaze to the deck. What had he gotten himself—and Ralph—into?

This better be good.

I was eager to move us over to Aunt Allie's, but Jessica, the home health nurse, was due to arrive any minute. She would need to know about it. And for the moment, Grandma was enjoying her late breakfast.

Since I was still hesitant about stopping in at my dad's alone, I'd ordered us eggs and blueberry pancakes from a rustic little restaurant up the street.

I tossed away my trash, and then the front doorbell rang. Sure enough, like an old friend, there stood Jessica "Come on in," I said, opening the door wide.

She checked Grandma's pulse and blood pressure and declared her healthy and alive, and I blurted out our big news.

Jessica seemed unusually pleased, and the pitch of her voice rose. "You're moving to Bentley's Store? Aunt Allie's? No way. Me, too!"

"You're kidding!"

She stuffed her stethoscope back in its case while she told her story about Aunt Allie's invitation. "I made up my mind this morning," she said. "Just now, on the way back from Apalachicola."

For some reason, I wanted to grab her hands and jump up and down like a little kid. But I held back. She noticed our suitcases and snacks by the door.

"We're about to head over right now," I said.

"Let me put my equipment away, and I'll help you. I need to stop by and tell her my decision anyway," she said.

We gathered Grandma Rosella's things while Grandma cleaned her plate. I wrote the owners of the B&B a thank you note and left it on the bed with a tip. We locked the doors behind us.

Seated in the Mustang with Grandma beside me on the right, I was about to close the door as Jessica leaned in. She lowered her voice. "Did Aunt Allie, by any chance, ask you if you were her granddaughter?"

Peculiar question. "No. Why?"

"Just wondering. She's probably just lonely. She's waiting on her new glasses. I don't think she thinks I'm her granddaughter, either. But she did ask. And I wondered if she asked you too—like maybe she asks everyone."

"Nah, not really."

"'Kay. Don't worry about it. She's clearly not senile. It was something about a dream. Two dreams. She had the dream twice. Just be aware."

I nodded.

Jessica patted the door and laughed. "Wait till she tells you the story about the hole in her cane and those two guys. She's quite the feisty lady."

"Can't wait to hear it," I said as I started the engine. "Anyway, no, like I said, she hasn't asked me anything about that," I said. "Bet she'd make a good grandma, though."

T wilight darkened Aunt Allie's unlit porch, and I arranged the rockers so they wouldn't make noise and wake Grandma. We'd moved in this morning, and our open bedroom window was at the other end of the porch. After supper Grandma had gone to bed as early as Aunt Allie had—pretty much along with the chickens.

Inside, our room opened to the kitchen on one wall and connected to Aunt Allie's on the other. It held a double wrought-iron bed with an old-fashioned cotton mattress that Grandma was eager to try out. "Like old times," she said. Aunt Allie had fixed up our bed with an old quilt and laid a crocheted doily across the antique dresser. A single bulb hung overhead. There was no closet, and nails in the wall held our few clothes on either side of the dresser. Sheer curtains wafted alongside two open windows. The place was beautiful in its simplicity. I enjoyed the experience. It felt like a trip back in time.

Grandma and Aunt Allie, her newly discovered friend, had delighted in their day together, and one of them mentioned a pending Bible study.

Even Jessica commented on the two women's increased vitality. But at the end of the day, Grandma was worn out completely. It would be a shame for my chair to wake her.

This evening after work we'd taken the easy route and ordered take-out burgers from the Captain's Table. Cooking would have to wait until tomorrow when Jessica moved in.

Jessica's plan was to call in late to her job tomorrow and move out while her boyfriend was away in Tallahassee. "He might get physical or cause trouble if I'm there," she said. "But he won't care enough to come looking. He'll probably go home to his mom's." Like us, Jessica had few belongings—at least ones that she cared to bring.

That evening after our feast of burgers, Jessica departed and then Matt phoned.

He was just leaving the restaurant. "We pulled in another shark today so Ralph gave us both a shrimp dinner. Funny," he said as he made his way over the bridge. "I'm not as tired as last night."

"You're just getting used to it."

"*Psst!*"

I glanced up, and there stood Matt by the gate with a big smile. I clicked off my phone and grinned. Even by the light of his screen, I could tell his skin was darkening. Latin genes. Mine would have burned.

"Everybody's in bed," I whispered. "Come on up."

"Thought they might be." He stepped up on the porch and knelt beside my chair to kiss me.

"I'm sure glad to see you," I said.

"How's my Sandy Shore?" he whispered up close, sending chills along my arms. "And how'd all the moving go?"

"Great," I said.

He kept my hand in his and leaned back on his heels to hear more.

"It was quick," I said. "One tiny carload."

His eyes, dark in the twilight, studied mine.

"We had a little challenge," I said. "Grandma almost made it up the steps. Then Jessica and I had to lift her."

He laughed. "Glad you didn't drop her."

"Light as a feather."

He nodded. "She'll get there."

I pointed to the open window at the far end of the porch and whispered. "That's our room there."

He rose and pulled my hand. "Come on over here and join me."

I followed, and we sat side by side on the top step for ever so long, holding hands and gazing out across the vacant lot next door. Now and then the lights of a passing car would brighten it, but eventually its colors faded from gray to black, and crickets began to sing around us.

Matt slapped at a mosquito on his neck. "I realize you're getting closer to telling your dad about things, Coral. But don't let yourself be rushed by circumstances."

A mosquito landed on my arm, and I swatted it. "I know. But I'm feeling more positive as time goes on, especially after some things Aunt Allie told Millie yesterday."

Right now wasn't the time to go into that with him, but he nodded.

"I want you to be there when I tell him," I said.

"Oh, I plan to be." He cradled my hand in his. "Here's an idea—for later or whenever. Zeke could invite Ralph fishing—with you and me there. And we could approach your dad out on the water."

I laughed. "Well, he would certainly be cornered."

"Think about it, though, if he started yelling and cussing nobody would hear him."

I shook my head. "Better not. He'd feel trapped."

"Yeah, you're right. That could backfire."

"Let's not do anything tricky. It feels manipulative."

Matt stared into the darkness. "Excellent point."

Eventually, Matt said it was time to go. He had another big day tomorrow, and the mosquitoes were getting too aggressive.

"Listen," Matt said. "Get settled in here, and in a few days I'd like you to come out on the boat. But only when you're ready. Explain things to Zeke if you're okay with that. I gave him some hints."

"He's not going to…"

"No, no. He's fine. But it's your story, right? Besides, I want you out there with me. I miss you."

He wrapped me up in a hug and followed it with a meaningful kiss that sent a thrill down my arms. Then he stood. "There's no rush, Coral. None at all. But I will tell you, day after tomorrow would be a good day to go out on the boat, we have a light day."

I nodded, just to let him know I was paying attention.

"Whatever we work out here in Carrabelle has to be okay with you. We won't make any moves until you're sure. Even going on the boat. It's up to you."

We said our good-byes, and I wrapped my arms around my knees and watched as he shut the gate and disappeared around the corner.

Matt replayed the conversation from back there on the porch. He liked the way Coral refused to be tricky or manipulative.

An honest woman.

And now that Coral brought it up, he could see it her way. Clear as day. A set-up with Ralph on the boat would be wrong. What other girl would be bothered by that?

But how in the heck were they supposed to present the truth to her dad? Matt barely saw Coral these days, much less with Ralph around.

He sighed. Taking this job with Zeke might have been a stupid move. But he'd given his word. And now he'd have to give it his best shot. The situation with Ralph couldn't be rushed, but the last thing he wanted to do was let Coral down.

What had Grandma always told him? Do right in the small things, and you'll have no trouble doing right in the big things.

He wondered if Coral had written that in her book of wise sayings.

Then there was that fake name he gave her. He'd eventually have to straighten that out. That was his idea too. And she'd gone along with it. Maybe he was corrupting her.

At the top of the bridge Matt stopped and pulled out his phone. He should have told Coral about this evening's call from Peter. He lifted his phone and called her.

She picked up right away.

"You still on the porch?"

"Yes," she was still whispering.

"I heard from Peter today and forgot to tell you."

"Is everything okay?"

"Coral, I want you to know you're the most honest—the bravest girl I've ever met. And I admire that in you."

"Thank you." Silence.

She sounded a bit suspicious. He didn't blame her. That come-on probably did sound bad. "Well, I should have told you this back at the porch, I'm sorry. But I want you to be brave when I tell you now."

More silence.

"My dad. Just warning you. He's not the world's favorite person, and right now, he's had some slow-ups along the way, but he continues to make his way to Florida. Once he finds out we're here, it's only a matter of time. He'll be hot on our trail to Carrabelle."

I blinked back tears and climbed back into the rocking chair with the phone on my lap. I set it down on the floor beside me. A sigh of relief escaped my lips as I wrapped my arms around myself. Those words, "I want you to be brave," had scared me to death.

They'd sounded like a lead up to something awful.

Oh, sure, it was crummy news that Sol would boomerang back here soon. He could certainly *raise Cain* as they say. But compared to what I thought Matt was about to say—what he sounded like he was leading up to—something bad about our relationship or something bad about my dad—this news about Sol was nothing.

But was it?

I sat there with my heels on the rungs and pondered Sol's coming and what it would mean.

First off, there was a high likelihood that he would try to force Grandma back to Fort Myers. I couldn't imagine what that would do to her. Did Sol have the ability to carry it through? In his own self-righteous way, I knew he'd claim Grandma's trip to Carrabelle was too hard on her. Aside from kidnapping her, I wondered if he held some kind of legal sway over her, but I doubted it.

Peter would know.

And second, worse than that, would Sol try to chase me out of the picture? After all, I was just the *neighbor girl*. What right did I have to join Matt as co-executor of Grandma's estate when Sol had no say?

For Sol, this was, after all, more about his inheritance and not about protecting Grandma's health.

I'd heard him yelling and hollering over the phone with Grandma.

Not about me, because I'm not sure she ever told him I existed—but about other things. With Sol, she didn't even need to put her phone on speaker.

How would his bad behavior affect Grandma and Aunt Allie? Neither one of them needed that kind of trauma.

And then there was Matt.

Would his dad's arrival change things between us?

The next morning, Grandma and I sat in the kitchen enjoying our morning cup of coffee. We'd slept in.

Aunt Allie busied herself in the store sweeping and straightening. She came in and out of the kitchen where we sat and brought in a handful of speckled squash, shriveling beans, and speckled tomatoes from the store to the kitchen. She dropped them on the counter beside a thawing chicken. "I can't sell these now, so we'll use them for supper," she said and disappeared again.

Grandma and I spent some time washing and cutting up the produce. Aunt Allie came back in and sat with us for a few minutes.

"I was wondering," I said, "how do you get your produce? You have no car, so I know you can't pick it up. And I've never seen it delivered."

A bell rang from back inside the store. She stood. "Well, child. I have a theory about that," she set her coffee cup in the sink and took off for the store. But she never explained.

Theory? Didn't she *know* how she got her produce?

I was still pondering on her mystery veggies when we finished our task. Then Grandma dropped a bombshell.

"Why don't you get the keys to the Mustang," she told me. "And let's go have an early lunch at the Captain's Table. I want to get a good peek at that father of yours."

And before we knew it, there we sat, Grandma and I, across from each another at my dad's restaurant.

"I'd like another of those big juicy hamburgers," Grandma said. "Like the other night."

I didn't blame her. My dad's burgers were hard to beat. I opened up the menu but kept my eye on the happenings in the dining room. Millie wasn't here, apparently, and I suddenly recalled her wanting days off and wished I'd remembered it a little sooner. I closed the menu and laid it down. "Good idea. I need a break from seafood myself."

Grandma glanced toward the kitchen door, and my eyes followed hers.

Out came my dad with a little pad in his hand.

"Grandma, that's him," I said behind my hand. But I wasn't sure she could hear me.

She eyed him for a minute and nodded, but I couldn't discern her thoughts. The restaurant wasn't busy yet, and except for a couple in the far back, we were the only ones there.

"So, ladies, good afternoon," my dad said, stepping close. He acted as if he didn't even recognize me from before. He should realize that I was here with Matt's grandmother. But he didn't mention it, and I didn't either. Was he blind, forgetful, or just a good actor?

"Welcome to the Captain's Table," he said. "What can I bring you?"

It took only a minute to give him our orders and pass him our menus. "Back in a few minutes," he said and returned to the kitchen.

I turned to Grandma. Right now, my concern was for her. "So—Sol's coming soon. Are you worried?"

She waved the question away. "Oh, pshaw. Sol's a bunch of hot air."

"I'm glad you think so."

Maybe now, in the quiet restaurant, before Sol came busting into town, would be a good time to tell my dad about myself.

If he liked my news, I'd have my own personal ally when Sol arrived.

But then if Ralph wanted nothing to do with a daughter—I peeked at him behind the pickup window. He seemed nice. But what would the man really do?

People, I'd learned, can surprise you.

In really dreadful ways.

What if my dad got angry and flew off the handle?

Matt's advice came back to mind. And a warning bell clanged in my head. "Don't be rushed by circumstances."

I reminded myself of Matt's investment in this whole venture—adventure. He wanted to be there when it unfolded.

I turned my eyes to Grandma again and studied her pale skin and thin arms. She'd been through an awful lot.

I laid my forearms on the table.

No, today was not the day. It would wait.

She didn't deserve to have her dinner spoiled.

I opened my purse at the register and froze. Behind the register stood my dad waiting on me to pay. But my credit card! There was no way I could give it to him. It had my name on the front. I glanced back at Grandma, still seated at the table with her eyes on me. I needed cash. Did I even have any? I opened my wallet to thumb through.

My dad waited patiently. I'd leave Grandma sitting here and run back home to get cash if I had to, but I couldn't give him my name. Not after Matt told him my name was Sandy Shore.

Normally, Grandma carried cash, but she hadn't brought her purse.

"Listen," my dad said, "You're one of my regulars. Let this meal be on me. My treat."

I breathed a sigh of relief. "Oh, thank you. Are you sure? I left my cash back at the rental. I could go get it real quick."

He reached for the ticket and slid it near the register. "Never you mind. It's my place, and I can do as I please. You ladies have a nice day and come back again soon."

Then things took a chilling turn.

Grandma, who hadn't heard my dad, called out my name. "Coral."

I gulped. There behind the register stood my dad, probably wondering why Grandma called me Coral. What could I say that would make any sense without spilling the whole pot of beans right here and now?

I turned. "I don't think so, Grandma. I think it's pink." Whew. "Her hat's pink, don't you agree?" At least Grandma wore that color today. Her dress, her hat, all of it.

He glanced at me and then back at her, still a little puzzled. At this point, I'm sure Grandma didn't know what I was talking about. Then she put her fingers over her mouth.

My dad nodded. "I guess."

I put my purse away and headed over to Grandma. "Thank you again for the lunch, and I'm sorry to hold you up."

He leaned his forearms on the register as we left. Who knew what he was thinking?

I couldn't wait to get out of there. "Bye, now," I said, "I'd better get her home."

The door shut behind us. "Goshhh!" The word gusted from my mouth. I couldn't blame Grandma, and I hated lies to begin with.

How stupid I must have sounded.

Matt and I needed to get this lie straightened out right away.

After lunch I felt like such a dirt-bag, a total liar. Which I was. The lie crackled all over me.

"Let's get you back to the store, Grandma."

She didn't ask me to explain my *pink* comment back at the restaurant. All she said was, "A lie has a way of growing, you know."

Of course, she'd figured it out.

I took a deep breath. "I know. I know, Grandma. Matt and I are going to get that straightened out. I'm sorry."

"Tell the Lord about it, not me."

Now I had another wise saying—learned the hard way—to write in my little book.

I was glad when Jessica moved in. Her upstairs room was similar to ours. Her stairs came down beside the bathroom on the far side of the kitchen.

After supper we decided to tackle a small pile of mending for Aunt Allie. Grandma Rosella helped us with the old treadle sewing machine, and we joked about how glad we were that Jessica's boyfriend was so awful.

"If it hadn't been for him," Jessica said, "I never would have been here with y'all. I guess this is what it's like to have a sister."

"Right," I said. "And I love it."

She laughed. "Wanna go with us to pick up Aunt Allie's glasses tomorrow?"

I stopped to think. "Hmm, wish I could. But I've decided to go out on the boat with Matt."

T he *Gulf Princess* rose and settled as Matt scooped a final bucket of bait. In a few minutes, ahead of the storm to the west, they'd weigh anchor and head back to Carrabelle for the night.

Coral, with her rod over the rail, stood around the other side of the boat. At least she was out of earshot. Matt cast another glimpse at Zeke where he leaned against the gunwale, a toothpick twirling in his mouth. Matt's initial excitement had deflated when Zeke reacted with suspicion at their account of Coral being Ralph's daughter. And over the past several hours his doubt-filled expression hadn't changed.

Oh, Zeke hadn't let on to Coral, and Matt was grateful for that.

But what a tragedy. Today could have been a joyful time of revelation for this long-time friend of Ralph's. Matt could only hope Coral's encounter with Ralph turned out better than this one with Zeke. In the meantime, Matt hoped he hadn't messed everything up today.

Back on topic, Zeke shook his head. "So this Coral Smith, this girlfriend of yours, is Ralph's daughter? And after all these years, I've never heard a word about it."

Matt nodded, "Yep. She sure is." He lifted the bucket. "Back in a minute." Matt delivered the bait to the lone male fisherman over on portside. The man seemed eager to squeeze every last minute out of his trip—and, unlike Matt, said he "couldn't care less" about a little storm. Two family parties with young children waited inside near the galley, all sunburned and packed up. Long since ready to go home, they rested or napped along the benches and tables.

Coral, portside as well, was catching her own share of fish. She'd stuck with it most of the day except for lunchtime when she helped him in the galley. "Gotta earn my keep," she'd said, and Matt was only too glad to have her by him. "And I don't want you getting in trouble on the job."

He wondered if the man standing near Coral was trying to impress her. Or flirt with her.

Sorry, buddy, she's taken.

Coral winced as Matt touched her shoulder on his way by. "Oh, I'm sorry, Coral. We'll have to get something to treat that." Her skin had turned pink in spite of the sunscreen. He didn't linger, because she'd be able to read the let-down on his face after his talk with Zeke. Instead, he kissed her and headed back to the bow where Zeke was.

He rounded the corner, and Zeke hadn't budged.

"Please promise me you won't discuss this with Ralph," Matt said.

"And once again, why can't I discuss it with him?"

A knot formed in the pit of Matt's stomach. Today was a total failure. And he didn't know how to fix it. "She wants to tell him in her own way."

"Here's the problem Matt. Here's the deal…"

Matt braced as a strong gust of wind rocked the boat. Dark clouds had now piled higher.

As was Zeke's custom, by this point in the fishing trip, they'd relocated the *Gulf Princess* closer and closer to port. But Matt knew it was time to weigh anchor and get back, and this conversation was holding things up. Neither he nor Coral wanted to be bobbing around in a storm.

"Look, you're a good kid," Zeke said. "You do good work. You're smart. You're helping me out here. Coral is a lovely girl. That's all fine and dandy. But…" He shook his head again.

Matt stared at Zeke as the sound of the wind whipped up. Ropes slapped against metal. Around them, little white curls rippled the darkening water.

He'd ruined this day for Coral and endangered her experience with Ralph. And now there was no guarantee Zeke would keep quiet.

Matt could only blame himself. Above all, he wished he could figure out where he'd steered things wrong.

"Weigh anchor," Zeke said. "And never mind about the girl," he said above the increasing noise. "I do like her. And she's welcome here anytime you like."

Matt stared at the man. One minute he was dumping cold water on Matt, and the next he was inviting Coral to return.

If Matt could only understand what the issue was.

Zeke paused at the wheelhouse door. "And I always honor my word. I won't talk to Ralph about it. Don't expect me to help you, though. I can't. Truthfully, if things are like you say—I can't see how—then, absolutely. More power to you."

Then a scream. "Matt! Help! Help me!"

Zeke bolted around to port, with Matt just ahead.

Matt's girl, Coral, lay sideways on the deck clutching the middle of her rod as the line reeled out. The handle lay between her feet. She had no control over the reel. Good thing the line was above her fingers and not under them.

"Something huge on there!" Zeke yelled. He grabbed the rod's handle and locked her line. "Hold it here, kiddo, and hang on. Hang on. This is your fish. You're going to pull it in. Just don't let go! And don't touch that line, it will cut you to the bone."

"Where's the other fisherman?" Matt yelled.

Coral gripped the handle like Zeke said and braced her tennis shoe against the bottom rail. "I almost went over!" she said.

An icy blast chilled his veins. Zeke turned to Matt. "Other fisherman?" Matt pointed to the man's rod still clamped in its holder. "He was right there!"

They turned toward Coral. "Where's that other fisherman?" they yelled together.

Coral stabbed her finger through the rails. "I can see it. It's a shark!"

Matt knelt beside her and took her by the chin. He turned her face to him. "Coral. Where's that other fisherman?"

Her hyperventilating eased, and her gaze shifted to the space behind Matt. "Up there. In back of you."

Matt turned, and there stood the missing man with a cigarette in his hand.

The man grinned, amused with himself. "See? All heck breaks loose when you turn your back and go to the head." He laughed.

Matt turned back to Coral. "Try to calm down," he said.

Zeke, muscles taut from the force of the fish, turned back to the water. He blew out a breath as the prickles left his chest. "Oh, God, thank you. Thank you. Thank you."

He pulled against the spinning, flipping shark and tipped his face toward the man. "Better step back."

Zeke cast a glance at Matt as they reeled in the six-foot creature. "At least a hundred pounds," he said. "Take this rod, Matt. Pull it close. Coral, keep your hands on the grip." Matt did just as he said, and Zeke reached to the wall for a long-handled hook. He handed one to Matt and took one for himself. "It's a black fin," Zeke said. "Copy me." He swung the rod around behind and gaffed it. Matt did the same and together they lifted the flipping, fighting creature up and over the rail. Blood poured from the wound and smeared across the deck.

Coral stepped back. "Oh, my gosh. Oh, my gosh."

Finally, the man with the cigarette tossed the butt into the water and took the rod from Coral. "It's OK. It's OK. People catch sharks all the time."

Matt stepped between them. "You did good, Coral. Nice catch. I'm proud of you."

Zeke just smiled. It wasn't unusual for his fishermen to get excited. He turned to cigarette man. "Better reel yours in, too. We've got to go."

Skies were darkening, and the families inside had roused and were plastered along the windows watching the show with wide eyes. Zeke studied the shark. Ralph would be pleased. He could get a lot of meals out of this one. And Coral would have a forever story. So would Matt. He'd better remind Matt to take pictures back at port.

And port is where they needed to be a full ten minutes ago.

"Good job, Coral," Zeke said. "Let Matt and me handle it now, and you can step inside with everybody else."

He leaned back and grabbed Matt's arm. "Just make sure you keep your hands away from those teeth."

Truth was, he and Matt would have to tase this shark, make

sure it was dead, and drag it up to the bow to get it on ice. They'd gut it real quick before the urine in the guts spoiled the meat. The sooner the better.

Legally they weren't allowed to cut the fins off out here, so they couldn't dress it. Wouldn't take long, but Ralph had to do that in the kitchen.

Matt guided a trembling Coral through the door and gave her a tight squeeze. "It's okay."

Zeke stood behind him and addressed the clients at the window.

"Sorry for the delay, folks, but we hope you enjoyed the show courtesy of this young lady. Stay inside, and hold onto your hats. We'll be firing up the engines momentarily."

He stepped back out with Matt and sent him to the bridge for the taser so they could quiet the still-flopping beast.

Matt was a dependable helper. He'd handled this well. And Zeke was blessed to have him as a sub. But Zeke was no fool. All that talk about the girl being Ralph's daughter—baloney. Ralph had never had a girlfriend such as the one Matt and Coral described. Not before Ralph went into the Army.

Or Zeke would have heard about it.

Either they were innocently confusing Ralph with somebody else, or they were running a scam.

Engines hummed as Zeke's boat headed back to Carrabelle. Matt left Zeke in the wheelhouse to catch a minute with Coral. He found her seated on a bench in the stern.

Though dark skies reached high in the west and southwest, golden sunrays slanted across the deck and the churn of the boat's wake. The effect was mesmerizing. He settled in beside his girl and leaned in to kiss her. But she leaned away.

He studied the blue of her eyes, her lashes, the sunburn over her freckles. "What?"

"We should talk."

He smiled and tweaked her chin. "It wasn't the shark encounter, was it? I had to yell at you. You were getting hysterical."

She smiled. Reddened. Shook her head.

He shook his head. "Don't be ashamed. Everybody gets hysterical about something. And you did it beautifully."

"No, not that. It's that cute name you gave me. Sandy Shore. It's nice and all. But…"

He'd been bothered and was glad she brought it up. He took her by the hand. "But it's a lie. Right?"

She opened up then and told Matt about yesterday's encounter with Ralph and her near exposure with the credit card. "I felt so, so awful. And I don't ever want to do that again."

"It's all my fault, and I'm sorry to put you in that position. Besides, the lie was beginning to bother me too. But did you notice today? Tell me you're proud of me. I did not tell Zeke your name was Sandy. I used your real name."

She nodded. "We'll have to straighten this out. Somehow."

Matt drew her close, but she flinched. Her sunburn was stinging. "Hold on. Maybe Zeke has something for that."

He headed for the bridge and within a minute returned with a can of sunburn spray. "I'll have to go back to work in a minute. But hold your breath and close your eyes."

Matt and Coral waved away the medicinal cloud, and he put the lid back on. Coral lifted her shoulder and grinned up at him.

"Wait." She tapped her lips. "Don't forget that kiss."

Back at the restaurant Zeke heaved the shark's heavy carcass onto the stainless-steel kitchen table. "Better get this thing fileted and cut up right away."

Larry's eyes grew large as he looked at the shark. "Nice one."

"We're still cleaning out the boat, but I'll let you know when to throw on the shrimp. There'll be three of us today."

Larry nodded.

Then Ralph, like a bull out of the chute, burst in from the dining room. "Hi, Zeke." His eyes lighted on the shark, and he grinned. "Well, would you look at that."

"Third one this week." Zeke grinned and took Ralph by the arm. "I may just get tired of shrimp." He led Ralph toward the back hallway. "While I'm here, buddy. Got a question for you. I'm just tryin' to solve a riddle."

In hushed tones, he asked Ralph about the girlfriend.

Ralph swallowed. "Why are you askin' me all this? And whaddya mean, did I have a girlfriend before the Army? What's that got to do with anything?"

Zeke crossed his arms and waited.

"Where'd you ever hear such a thing?"

"Well?"

Zeke watched his friend's face. He knew the man wouldn't lie.

"Did you ever see a girl? Where would I hide one? You and me, we spent all our time out on the boat. Or helping my dad in here. You know it, and I know it. Neither one of us had time for a girlfriend."

"You haven't answered."

Ralph crossed his arms. "Do I keep secrets? Don't you think I'd have told you? Or you would have seen her? I mean, c'mon. And why all the fifty questions?"

Zeke stood there for a minute drumming his fingers on his arm. He turned away from his old friend and walked down the hall. "Didn't think so. We'll be back in a little bit."

Ralph hadn't out right said no, but he might as well have. He didn't claim to have a girlfriend before the Army, and he'd made good points.

The result was just as Zeke had suspected. There was no way Coral could be Ralph's daughter. There was simply no girlfriend.

So, as he suspected before, either Coral and Matt were confusing him with someone else, or they were running a scam.

Millie invited herself to the Bible study and fish fry, courtesy of Sandy's deep-sea adventure yesterday. When she first learned of the event at Aunt Allie's, she knew she had to attend.

The young girl, Sandy, took a bite of the fried fish and turned to Aunt Allie. "When are you going to tell me your theory about that basket of vegetables?"

Millie had never heard tell of such. She leaned in to hear what it was all about.

"Ah," Aunt Allie nodded. "The basket theory. Soon, maybe. But I think everyone would like to hear about your boat adventure yesterday."

Sandy seemed a little disappointed in not getting her answer about the vegetables, and so was Millie.

But the girl went ahead and told her story about the shark she caught on Zeke's boat. Millie already knew about it from Ralph, so she wouldn't dare spoil it for the girl.

"A frightful event if you asked me," Sandy said.

Everyone nodded.

"But I'll definitely go out fishing again," the girl said. "I love it out there!"

Millie wondered about the young girl's common sense but kept it to herself. "Sharks? Most people want nothing to do with those demon-possessed fish."

Jessica giggled and chimed in, "I think what you really love about the boat is that special someone."

Sandy blushed and smiled, and everyone laughed.

After lunch, Aunt Allie placed her hands in her lap and looked around at her guests. "Well, bless you all for this feast. You've out-done yourselves. And it's such a pleasure to have y'all in my home. I hope we can do this again next Wednesday."

"I'll sure be here." Millie never had time for lunch breaks when she worked at the restaurant, but a few times lately, she'd taken time off. She'd made up her mind. Wednesdays would now be her designated day off at the Captain's Table.

She had every right.

Aunt Allie opened her Bible. Today's verse was James 1:27. After she read it, they all gave it some thought then discussed its appli-cation in their lives. *Pure religion and undefiled before God and the Father is to visit the fatherless and widows in their affliction, and to keep himself unspotted from the world.*

But after they finished, Jessica brought up an item that made an even bigger impact on Millie. Not that the other verse wasn't great, but this one applied directly to her own situation.

"Aunt Allie what did you want to say about my live-in boyfriend?" Jessica asked. "You started to tell me about it the day I met you. Remember the day I spilled coffee all over my scrubs?"

"Well, honey," Aunt Allie said, "living together like that is wrong. It's the freebies that make it so. And you know what I mean. Think about the ten commandments."

"The ten what?"

A silence settled and Jessica turned a bright red.

"Really, I never heard…"

The older woman's voice had weakened. "Rosella, would you mind helping me out here?"

Millie guessed her voice wasn't used to this much exertion.

So Miss Rosella explained God's ten rules for right living. "And this is what God expects from those who are truly His."

Jessica nodded.

"Now remember, they're not suggestions. They're commandments."

In the meantime, Aunt Allie looked it up in Exodus, the twen-tieth chapter, and asked Millie to read them out loud.

Millie had not heard these since she was a child, and it was a good refresher.

"Oh, I thought that was the way you were supposed to do it—move in together," Jessica said. "Then get married if you like each other."

"A lot of people think that. They're breaking the no-adultery commandment," Aunt Allie said. "If you serve God, you need to repent of it. You don't want hell-fire, do you?"

Wow. Millie stared at Aunt Allie. Hell-fire. What a statement. The lady didn't mince words. Miss Rosella nodded.

This news bothered Jessica. "Y'all, I've never had any church at all. I don't even know what you're talking about with hell-fire and repent."

Sandy placed her hand over Jessica's, but the girl was already in tears. "You mean I'd go to hell? But what can I do?"

"Shall I finish for you, Allie?" Miss Rosella offered. "I know you're tired."

"If you're up to it, Rosella," the older woman said, folding the corner of her napkin. "I appreciate it."

Both ladies were tired.

Miss Rosella turned back to Jessica. "When you know you've done wrong, you repent. That means you tell God you're sorry and then you turn away from the wrong. In your heart. And in your actions. And believe about Jesus being the Son of God and that there is no other way to be saved."

Jessica wiped her eyes with her napkin. "Can you show me how?"

And they prayed right there. She repeated after Rosella, "Lord, forgive me for all your commandments I've broken. Help me know right from wrong and teach me. I believe Jesus is your Son and He paid for my sins on the cross."

"Now you go out and do right," Miss Rosella said.

Millie knew one thing for sure. She had to repent and get right, too.

Jessica glanced at her watch and stood. She wiped her eyes. "Thank, y'all. Thank, y'all so much. But right now, I've got to get back to work."

"See you tonight, kitten," Aunt Allie said, and Jessica leaned over and gave her a good long hug.

Millie rose, and along with the others said, "See you later, Jessica." She collected the paper plates and her empty dish. "I need to get home as well. And thank you for everything, Aunt Allie. I'll see you next Wednesday, for sure." She laughed. "I'd stay and wash dishes, but I think I'll just toss 'em in the trash on the way out."

In the meantime, Millie had some packing to do. Ralph would have to move out.

Right away.

My eyes adjusted to the darkness as I eased my rocker toward the column, or chest-high rock post, of Aunt Allie's porch so it wouldn't *clickety clack* over the boards and wake up Grandma. With one arm pressed against my cotton night gown, I swiped a towel over the damp chair and then settled in, dropping the towel beside me. The chair's surface cooled my legs, and I pressed my heels against the rungs.

I'd die if anybody saw me like this, but I planned to go back inside before the sun came up. At 5:00 AM, out on the highway, a thick fog hid most everything around, except for the glow of the round yellow streetlights.

The screen door creaked, and I jumped, turning to see who would be up at this hour.

"*Psst*, everything okay?" It was only Jessica.

"Couldn't sleep," I whispered. "What are you doing out here?"

"Came down to go to the restroom and found the percolator plugged in," she said. "You sick or something?"

"No, just things on my mind." Everything, actually. "But thanks. Stay and talk if you like."

"No, I'm heading back to bed. This is way too early for me."

The screen door shut behind Jessica and then the solid door. Now I'd have to guess when the percolator was done.

I turned away. Somewhere in the distance, a songbird awoke. And then another. Clatters and clunks and voices of distant dock-workers carried over the water.

But then a closer sound perked my ears. The slow crunch of gravel near our stop sign.

I squinted, leaned forward and held my breath. I stared past our wall where it severed my view of the highway.

Workers always walk toward the water, never this direction.

Then out of the fogged stepped the shadow of a man—with a load in his arms. I swallowed hard and straightened as he turned onto our street.

Crunnnnch. Slow and heavy. *Crunnnnch.* I held my breath. Willed him past.

I backed against the chair.

Why sneak? Unless he was up to something.

Slow crunnnnch. Slow crunnnnch, closer and closer he stole.

I wrapped my arms around myself. Surely, he couldn't see me back here behind this post. Thank the Lord, I'd adjusted the chair. Moving only my eyes, I glanced down at my nightgown. It stood out like a full moon.

A bass drum pounded between my ears and flashes of Mom's old boyfriends pulsed like fire alarms. *Dear God. Don't let him come through our gate.*

But the sound of his footsteps changed as they left gravel and touched grass near our fence.

I ducked and gripped the rocker as the latch clanked, metal against metal. Squeeak.

There was no place to flee.

I leaned left. Surely, he couldn't see me behind this rock post.

Two quiet steps. Then thump, scrape. His load hit the porch. Then quick steps, another squeak, and a click. No delays now. A retreat.

Thank God. I sucked in a breath and leaned around to watch as his shadow came back into view near the highway again. The slamming of my heart rocked my whole body.

I could finally breathe again.

But then he turned to face an approaching car.

And my jaw dropped.

The man was my dad.

I waited a good long time after my dad was gone before I moved. Or looked in the box. In my heart, I saw no reason to fear what might be in there. Had it been left by someone else—I might be afraid. But not one left by him.

However, I didn't want him to backtrack and catch me snooping.

Once again, I wrapped my arms around myself and wedged my heels against the chair's rungs. I stared into the fog considering all that had just happened and all the things I'd seen over the past several days. And then, bit by bit the fog began to dissolve. The black outline of sabal palms and buildings began to show. The eastern sky brightened. And I, in my nightgown, would soon be in full view. It was time to get inside and off the porch.

And as I returned my gaze to the box, I could tell it was only vegetables. Bell peppers, onions, squash, tomatoes—things Aunt Allie sold in her store and used in her kitchen.

I wondered why Aunt Allie wasn't sharing her theory with me, and why my dad had to sneak those vegetables to her.

Yet these thoughts only served to bolster my reassurance about the man. He was human, but for whatever reason he did this, I couldn't imagine it being anything sinister. I'd always admired good deeds done in secret. Maybe like the Bible verse he was caring for the widows and orphans.

All in all, I was pretty sure the man was not to be feared.

At the Captain's Table, Millie glanced through the order-pickup window at Ralph's pouting face above the fryer. Larry and Jack the dishwasher had shown good sense all morning and steered clear, casting sideways glances at him to see how long the glum mood would last. So far, he'd kept it up all morning.

First thing this morning, she'd called Ralph back into the hallway and explained about the Bible study and the Ten Commandments and what she'd decided about him moving out. She'd intended to tell him about it the night before, but he'd come home so late. Today would be better.

At first, he'd shown disbelief. Then he'd crossed his arms and hung his head, "You don't love me anymore?"

"Not true, Ralph. I still love you."

"Is that what you've been doin' with those days off? Findin' another man. And now you're lettin' me down?"

"Of course not. We're not breakin' anything off, honey." Heaven only knew Millie wished he would ask her hand. There was nothing she'd like more than to be his wife. Tie the knot. Share a commitment. Have a real family.

Ralph turned his face to the side.

She touched his arm. "Those days off are for me. Nobody needs to work seven days a week. But back to the subject, Ralph." She pulled his stubbled face back to her. "Look at me. You, of all people, as a boy who loved the Bible—you should understand what I'm tellin' you."

He puffed up. "What do you know about me and the Bible? Huh?"

"I know things, dear. And I love you all the more for it."

That seemed to calm him.

"I'll box up your things with love, and you can run them up to your apartment when you get off tonight."

"Tonight? But sweetheart…"

"Tonight, Ralph. I've done made up my mind. I'm makin' things right between me and the Lord. And I want you to do the same."

He had no comeback for that. Just dropped his head.

"I can't move upstairs with that kid up there. There's only one bed, and besides—people will think things."

Millie laughed and gripped his biceps. "You big thing. Nobody's goin' to think that." She reached around his neck and gave him a smack on the lips. "But if it'll make you feel better, you tell—his name is Matt, by the way, not *the kid*—he can rent that broken down cabin from me. I've got lots of work needs doin' and might cut the rent waaaay back if he can get it done."

"How come you didn't offer me that deal?"

"It ain't the same, and you know it."

"He'll think I tricked him into cleanin' the apartment."

"I'm sure he'll understand. You just do your part." She gave him another kiss and let go. "I'll take off a little early tonight."

Ralph's head swung around. "Again?"

She stopped him. "I'll take off a little early and get a cabin ready. Now all you have to do is tell Matt about it and get him to bring his things over. Cabin Two. I'll leave it open with a key on the kitchen table. With clean sheets and everything else."

Ralph sighed and slumped back to the kitchen.

He'd cooperate but not without a grumble.

Millie turned away from the pickup window and the gloominess beyond. Given time, Ralph would work through it and mellow out.

As long as she left him alone.

Ralph dumped the frozen fries into the basket. Shook it. This whole dang situation was lousy. Millie up and takin' her days off like she was the boss—and then turning around and kicking him out.

What was she doing? Letting him off easy? Had to be. He knew the signs.

He was about to lose her.

Unless…

He lowered the fries into the grease and crossed his arms.

The image of her unwrapping that un-diamond ring he bought her flashed through his mind. And the hint, just the tiniest hint of disappointment in her eye. Oh, she hid it well.

But he caught it.

He knew.

That one thing she wanted was marriage. And kids. She'd practically written it on paper and taped it to his forehead.

But after the gift, he figured if she could hide her feelings like that, then he could let it slide. So he shoved it like a hidden wad of gum into the back recesses of his heart. She'd think he hadn't figured things out, that marriage hadn't occurred to him, and eventually she'd get over it.

He gazed into the vat of boiling oil.

Yeah, what a laugh. *How's that workin' for you, Ralph?* he told himself.

Truth was, he didn't want Millie to leave him. Didn't want to be without her.

And now it might be too late. But if he did ask her—and surprise her with a diamond….

He shook his head. Scowled. Played back her words, "I know things, dear. And I love you all the more for it."

Get real, Ralph, he told himself. *She only loves who she thinks you are. Not the real Ralph. And she definitely doesn't know the worst things. And those things make you a louse.*

A crummy reprobate.

Even if they did get hitched, once she figured him out, she'd ditch him anyhow. So why even bother?

He lifted the basket from the vat.

What a fine kettle of fish this was. Fine, indeed.

I finished our few supper dishes and headed out to Aunt Allie's porch for some rocking and daydreaming. Aunt Allie and Grandma Rosella remained at the kitchen table comparing stories of old times.

As usual, I'd grabbed up Aunt Allie's chicken-clicker from the top of the porch column—that fun little gadget—and settled back into the old rocker. And just like a kid, I pressed my thumb against the plaything's smooth metal to enjoy its delightful noise.

I wondered how confident the soldiers felt as they trained with a dinky little toy for the Normandy Invasion.

I clicked in rhythm with the rocker as it *bobbledy-clacked* over the boards. Then I placed it back on the smooth concrete on top of the post.

Next to it stood Aunt Allie's antique milk bottle, and I picked it up to study its mossy green interior. Half full of water from the faucet, Aunt Allie kept it handy for rinsing off the "calling cards" that wayward chickens dropped. She didn't allow the yard-fowls on her porch, but occasionally, one flapped its way up, and she'd have to chase it off. She'd douse any deposits with water from the bottle and sweep them away with her hundred-year-old broom-nub that leaned against the wall.

As I slid it back into place, my thoughts returned to the soldiers and their bravery—and my dad and what bravery he might have shown. My *dad*. Not from the same war, but an army veteran, just the same. One of the brave ones. It took guts just to sign up.

The screen door creaked, and I turned. Grandma poked her head out. Even in the twilight, her color was returning. Likewise, her strength and independence. Aunt Allie and the little town of

Carrabelle were doing her a world of good. "Good night, honey," she said. "I'm going to bed now, and so is Aunt Allie."

I started to rise. "Let me help you."

"Nope. Nope. Don't get up. And Jessica's in there taking a bubble bath. Say good night to Matt when he comes in."

"G'night, Grandma. I love you."

I closed my eyes and considered the people around me. I could imagine a real sister like Jessica and a wise old aunt like Aunt Allie. Life felt so good with everyone around. And here I was finding out that my dad might not be so bad.

Mom had been wrong about one thing. He wasn't a mess. Maybe he had been at one time. But I didn't see it.

I just hoped when the time came, he would want me for a daughter.

My thoughts turned to Matt. He ought to be calling soon. I missed him bad and couldn't wait until he asked me out on the boat again. But that depended on Zeke and whatever business he had going.

Just then my phone buzzed from up on the post, and I reach up and tipped the screen. Yay. Matt himself.

"Ralph fed us again," he said. They'd brought in some sharks."

"You're becoming well nourished, I have to say."

"And you won't believe what I have to tell you. I'll be over in a minute." He whistled and waved from around the corner on the left, near the chicken pen, then trudged on up through the gate.

What was he doing coming from that direction?

"How are my girls?" he asked, bending over me to give me a kiss that smelled of sun, work, and fried seafood. But I didn't mind. "I couldn't wait to see you," he said.

He took me by the hand, and we sat together on the top step. I snuggled close.

He wrapped an arm around me. I marveled that after all those hours on the boat, his skin had only tanned and not burned. "Tell me your news first," he said, "how you and Grandma are doing." He twisted around to glance at her bedroom window.

I knew what he was thinking. "She's already in bed."

"Shoot. I haven't spoken to her in several days."

I explained how much better she was doing and how buddy-buddy she and Aunt Allie had become. "She's like a fish in the water here," I said. "But what about your news?"

"Oh, before I forget. Day after tomorrow looks like a slow day for Zeke, and he says you might want to come out on the boat again."

I grinned. Best news ever. "But that's not what you were going to tell me, is it?"

"Turns out Millie kicked your dad out, and your dad kicked me out. All very amiably, mind you. He's already moved into my apartment, and my stuff's over at Millie's now in Cabin Two. Rent free if I do some repairs."

"Ooooh, that's better," I said, leaning into him. "You'll be closer to us."

He smiled and gave me a squeeze. "I'll do some scraping and painting, a little plumbing. Fix a few boards. Nothing much. How difficult could it possibly be? The place is tiny."

I nodded. Millie had said her vacation rentals were little more than one-room cabins. "Millie hinted something like that was coming. I wondered what my dad would do when she gave him the boot. Good deal."

"Well, there's that. But, Coral, I want you to know, I'm not blind to the fact that these commitments are all adding up, and that translates into time. You could decide to leave before I'm done. I'd hate…"

"I could help you."

"I'd hate to bail on anyone if I gave them my word. But you come first. If it comes down to it, I can offer her money in place of the work. Not sure about Zeke. That would leave him in a lurch. But I figure, if I have to, I could take you home and then come back until Zeke's deck hand returns."

"Zeke does need you."

"The only reason I could commit like this is because you're feeling pretty okay about Ralph. For now, anyway. And I get it. That could change."

"That's true," I said. "But I like my dad more and more every day."

I told Matt about my scare and the vegetable basket on the porch. "He's an okay guy, I think."

"Oh, man. Wow," was all Matt could say. I guessed he was talking about the scare. Then he gave me another squeeze.

"You should keep your commitments," I told him.

"I plan to. But I won't add a thing more."

I laughed. "Well, there is one teeny-weenie thing. Aunt Allie mentioned it yesterday—that chair in that corner." I pointed behind me. "It squeaks and everyone avoids it."

"You tell Aunt Allie I'll be glad to fix whatever she needs."

My dad wasn't the only person I felt okay about.

Matt was a good man.

And so was my dad. But not one of us knew that he was about to face his devils.

Millie's feet were screaming. She was overworked, but lucky for her the pace at the Captain's Table was slowing down.

She pulled out her order pad. It was the end of the lunch shift, and she found herself in the middle of a large order at the rear corner of the dining room. It was far away and out of sight of the pick-up window. This hefty group of eight were the restaurant's only customers.

Then the front door opened. Light poured in, and she peeked around the corner. *Oh, drat.* A wife and husband, and she looked pregnant. Ralph would probably stay in the kitchen and leave them to Millie.

"Good afternoon," she called out as the couple entered. "Be with you in just a minute." She turned her attention back to her order pad but couldn't help but wish Ralph would step up and get the couple seated while she finished her order.

Unless he was forced to, Ralph simply refused to wait on pregnant women or couples with babies.

And right now he was still pouting about his ouster from her cabin.

She wrapped up her order and raced it over to Ralph's window. And there he stood beside the empty fryer, studiously ignoring the new customers.

Thanks a bunch, Ralphie. Time to grow up. Millie understood how people had their idiosyncrasies—more like idiotic-sync-crazies for Ralph—and his were on full ugly display today.

Millie threw up her palms in a *what's up with you, anyway* gesture.

And he returned his bug-eyed waggle chin look that said, *too bad, you know I don't wait on pregnant people.*

She served back her clamped lips and squinty eyes that told him *you ought to be horse-whipped.*

Dadgum-it, Ralph. She hoped the new customers hadn't noticed their silent communications or been put off by having to wait.

She ripped off her order page, placed it in the clip, and then whirled around.

The couple had ignored the *wait to be seated* sign and had already seated themselves. They picked the same table Matt and his girl-friend always chose.

Didn't matter where they sat anyway, since she was the only waitress. She approached their table.

"Afternoon." She handed them menus.

"I'm really sorry," the young man said. "We weren't trying to ignore the sign. My wife—it's our anniversary—she's been having some twinges, and she needed to sit down—and this is where we sat on our first date—at this table—and, and…"

"Slow down, honey," Millie said. "It's all right. It's all right. Don'tchu worry none."

The girl caressed her side, and Millie wondered if it pained her.

"You okay, honey? How far along are you?"

She smiled. "Five months."

The man took his wife's hand.

"I'll be fine. This happened before," the woman said. "And the doctor said I was fine."

The young man gave the drink orders and without opening the menus, ordered grouper sandwiches. "Grouper. Just like we had on our first date. I was a little worried, but she insisted on coming today."

The man kept chattering. "But…but, I think we'll just eat real quick and head back to Crawfordville to get her checked out. I know she says she's okay, but it's a big deal, our first baby and all." He squeezed the woman's hand. "We'll just eat real quick, for old time's sake, and go on up to Crawfordville."

Millie felt sorry for the man, and she'd for sure get Ralph to hurry things up. "Good idea, honey. And the treat's on us today. In honor of your baby."

The man thanked her several times and turned back to his wife beside him.

She smiled and patted his arm. "Like I said, I'll be fine. This happened once before, and the doctor told me I'd be just fine."

Millie took the slip to the window and waited. She watched Ralph as he prepared the other order for the big table in the back. In the meantime, she made another trip to the big group in the back corner and refilled some glasses.

Back at the window, as soon as the big group's order was up and Ralph had the pregnant couple's food going, she brought the steaming plates around the corner to the gang in the back. The group wanted to chitchat with her and talk about the town. She tried to be helpful by mentioning a few sites of interest. Then she returned to Ralph's window for the pregnant couple's meal.

Ralph wasn't quite ready. Then fries and sandwiches appeared on the plates, now pickles. She took the dishes from the window and turned. But the young man now stood by his table. His wife was gone.

His face appeared gray. Serious. He pointed to the restroom door. "Can you check on my wife? As soon as you left, she went in there and hasn't come out. It's been too long."

Millie slid their plates back onto the windowsill and hustled over to where the faded women's bathroom sign hung on the door. She rattled the knob. "You okay in there?" She pressed her ear to the door. Not a sound.

The man, wringing his hands, stood by Millie's side. "Have you got a key?"

She stepped over to the register and reached underneath to a small box, took out the key and spoke through the door, "Are you all right?" Once more she knocked—and no answer. She turned the key.

"Sarah?" the man said, taking the knob. His voice wavered. "Sarah, honey. Are you okay?" No answer. He shouldered the door. It opened a crack but met resistance. He squeezed a leg through, then his body. "Oh, dear God!" he yelled. "Sarah!"

Millie's blood ran cold. She poked her head in. And there,

surrounded by paper towels, bloody smears and fingerprints, lay the unconscious woman. "Oh, dear Lord."

She backed away and gripped the doorframe. Her breath came short, and her voice barely worked. "Raaaaaalph! Call 911!"

Ralph stood in front of the restaurant. He watched as the ambulance rushed the woman away with the husband weaving behind them like a drunk in his own vehicle.

"Oh, that poor man. That poor man," Millie kept wailing. "They should have put him in the ambulance with her. He's gonna blame himself for this. I just know. For not makin' her go on up there to Crawfordville in the first place."

Ralph wrapped his arms around Millie and let her sob against his shoulder. "It's all right, Millie. Don't you go fallin' to pieces on me now." He ran his fingers through her hair. "He's gonna be strong. They all will. You'll see." After a bit she settled down, backed away, and dried her face with a handful of restaurant napkins from her apron pocket.

"You okay now?" he asked.

She nodded. "I'm okay," she whispered.

He led her back inside and then re-entered the restroom. He stood in the middle and gazed around.

By the looks of the carnage, it seemed the woman had tried to be a good citizen and clean up. And then she'd keeled over.

Why'd she even wait? Modesty? Embarrassment? Some folks were just too hard to figure out.

The ambulance workers had mentioned, based on the evidence, that she'd probably lost the baby. "Just save my wife," the man had moaned. "Just save my wife."

So far, they hadn't found the baby or the placenta.

"It would have helped if she were conscious," one had commented. They could've asked questions. But now they couldn't be sure of anything until they got her back to the hospital. All in all, they didn't offer much encouragement for her or the baby—if the baby was even still inside her. If the woman lived, it would be a miracle.

Ralph hoped for one.

Miracles did happen.

Millie stood outside the door watching Ralph.

"Put out the closed sign," he told her. "I can handle this."

She nodded, rubbed the tears off her cheeks.

"Take to-go boxes to the big table of customers and tell them not to bother about the bill."

"They left a long time ago," she whispered.

He'd forgotten all about them.

"I didn't charge them, though."

He nodded. Gave her a thumbs up. Millie knew how he handled this kind of thing. "Tell Larry and Jack to clean up and go home, and then you can go too."

"No," Millie said, blowing her nose, "I'll getcher mop-bucket. I'm not leavin' you with all this."

Ralph set to work spritzing down and cleaning all the surfaces. When Millie dropped off the mop bucket, he set to work on the floor.

But when he reached the small trash basket, he paused. How'd he miss that? Here were more fingerprints—and there behind the basket—lay a hidden wad of bloody paper towels, the corners folded in like flower petals.

He pulled the wad toward him. Then numbness seized his arms. His fingers trembled as he lifted apart its corners. The very thing they'd searched for while they were here and hadn't found. The very thing he knew they'd be looking for at the hospital.

There, clumsily wrapped and nestled inside a nest of papers, lay the woman's tiny but lifeless baby girl.

Ralph's mop dropped away, and he settled on his knees. He lifted the little baby and her paper wrap and cradled it like a butterfly in his hands. Studied her tiny chin, her beautiful nose and lips, her delicate fingers. "Your mommy and daddy loved you," he whispered. He sank against the door with the little bundle cupped against his heart.

And then all those worthless years—the ones since Nadine left—compressed into nothing. No amount of running had erased his sins. And now they'd met him face to face.

His face drew up. And great silent sobs wracked his body.

"Oh, God, how can You forgive me?" he whispered. His head slumped. "What have I done?"

By the time Sol and Term exited I-10 at Las Cruces, New Mexico, it was lunchtime.

Term suggested they eat at a nice two-story adobe restaurant not far away. "See, it overlooks those stunning Organ Mountains."

Sol eyed the restaurant. The place looked expensive. "We can see the mountains from the road," he said. "I don't need to spend a bunch of money just to—"

"Come on. Humor me," Term said, smoothing the sleeves of that same old shirt he'd had on for what—three days—as if prepping himself to go inside. Sol couldn't believe the shirt didn't stink by now, but it ought to soon. The guy hadn't brought a thing else with him.

Sol considered the fat wad he'd stuffed into his wallet before he left, barely touched. He also had a credit card. One look at the expression on Term's face and he gave in. "Oh, I guess."

"Think of it as something you'd do for Paulette," Term said.

Another frown. Sol was getting tired of this dude reading his mind.

They pulled into the parking place near a giant cactus, and then, as if he already knew the way, Term led them through an adobe archway, past a large splashing fountain, and into its dark air-conditioned interior. At Term's request, the waiter, with a napkin over his arm, escorted them upstairs.

What a way to break up a road trip.

Term was right. Paulette had always enjoyed this kind of thing. He thought back to how they'd started out. Yeah. Somewhere in the relationship they'd gotten away from what Paulette enjoyed.

The waiter seated them next to a plate glass window, and they ordered. Once again, Term copied Sol's order exactly, broiled *comida del mar* lunch on a crisp green salad with fried plantains, and flan for dessert.

Once it was served, the men dug in. Term raised his *café con leche* and took a sip. "How does this compare to Aunt Susie's restaurant?"

"This is fancy, but then Aunt Susie's was good on its own merits." Only it wasn't the food that made an impression. What stuck in Sol's mind was the little boy with the pie and his mother and their scrimpy situation.

"How did it feel?"

There was that intrusive question again. As if the man could read Sol's thoughts. "Like I said, the food was A-plus." He continued to fork through the steaming flesh of his broiled fish.

Term snorted. "You know what I meant."

Sol nodded toward the spectacular mountains outside. "Nice place, here," he said. "Good suggestion."

"And Angie? How'd she strike you?"

Sol had to hand it to the man. Term was persistent if nothing else.

Sol looked across at him. "The mother? Hard working. Heroic. Working double shifts and raising a boy while her husband is in the hospital. Pretty special, I'd say."

Term nodded.

"Like your own mom?"

His mom? Sol leaned back and stared at the giant. This guy seemed to know everything about him. He dropped his gaze to the discarded scraps on his plate and considered the question. This was new to consider his mom in such terms.

She did have to work when Dad had that stroke. That little boy back there at that lunch counter could have been Sol himself. Only, his mom worked at the casino.

Sol kept his thoughts to himself, and Term asked him no more questions. When it was time to pay, Sol reached for his wallet.

Term stopped him. "I'll get it, Sol. I know I twisted your arm to come in here, but I appreciate the ride to Florida."

"Thank you," Sol said. "The food was the best." As they retraced their steps past the fountain and through the arch to the parking lot, he imagined Paulette saying, "What a lovely time, dear. Thank you so much." Like when they were first dating. He imagined her beside him and her long red hair in the sunlight.

As they approached the car, Term spoke up. "Texas is next, and we need to fill up the tank. But would you like me to drive for a while?"

"Absolutely," Sol said, fishing out the keys and handing them over. "You seem to know your way around."

Term waved it off. "It won't take us long to get through there."

Sol didn't care about that, but El Paso with its knot of highways was coming up, and the map he'd seen looked plain scary. "Glad you like city driving."

Sol climbed into the passenger seat. Texas, yeah. State by state they were making headway.

Term adjusted the seats and turned over the engine. As he pulled out of the parking lot and paused at the stop sign, he looked over at Sol. "Your mom didn't really ignore you. How can you hold that against her? She worked hard and was a good mother."

Sol stared back at Term. Dadgummit, who was this man, and how did he know all Sol's business? As he turned away, three words flashed like neon lights inside Sol's head.

Forgive your mother.

At the Captain's Table, Millie wondered how cleaning the bathroom could take this long. Larry and Jack had cleaned up and left, and it was time for her to go. "Ralph, you okay in there?" she asked through the door.

She stuck her ear to the door only to hear the mop bucket rattle. "You need any help in there?"

"I'm fine. You go on home," Ralph said, his voice oddly rusty— hoarse, maybe. Millie couldn't tell.

Didn't seem so strange, though, for what they'd been through today.

Millie and Ralph were shocked by the incident, but that poor mother and father…

"You gonna be all right, Ralph?"

"I'm fine, I told you."

"See you tomorrow then," she said. "I'll lock the front door."

Ralph made his way through the dark restaurant and to the back door with his little bundle. The stale cooking smells and utter silence pressed down on him. Made him want to hurry.

Outside, though, in the afternoon sunlight, he took a deep breath. Kitties meowed at his feet and leaped up on the table to purr with all their might to earn a scratch on the head or under the chin.

Ralph nudged them aside. Not today.

Instead, he reached in the kitty house and pulled out the pink baby blanket. Gave it a good snap and a shake with one hand. Cat fur drifted through sunrays and floated toward the highway.

Ralph unlocked the shed and stepped in. Along the back wall hung tools and shelves of wood for projects. He pulled the light string and shut the door behind him.

No cats today.

He set the paper-clad infant down and used a knife to cut the pink blanket into four pieces. Tears ran down his cheeks as he lifted the tiny baby and laid her diagonally along one piece and then folded the huge corners around her. "Just like your mommy would have done. That's better, now, isn't it, little one?" He swiped away a tear with the back of his hand. "Old Ralph won't have you wrapped in them ol' paper towels. No way."

He lifted the pink bundle like a treasure and once again admired her tiny features. "Oh, God, forgive me," he whispered and then laid the small bundle gently in the cushion of the blanket's remnants. He leaned across and gave her a kiss. "Now you wait right here till old Ralph makes you a little bed," he said and turned toward his collection of wood and tools.

He drew out a plan for a simple pine box and cedar lid. As he sawed the wood, he planned the tiny carvings he'd make on the lid. Words maybe. And a cross. A rosebud. He had all the right tools.

With the basic box and lid assembled, he gathered his kit of carving tools and settled on the floor into his favorite spot on an old broken chair bottom down on the concrete, behind a rack of canned foods, where he could lean on the wall and carve with his feet stretched out—in the quiet with nobody around.

He laid the velvet tool-holder down beside him and untied its ribbon, rolled it out, and pulled out the pencil. First things first.

Bang, bang, bang! A fist hammered on the door. He hadn't locked it.

"Ralph? Are you in here?" It was Millie. Hadn't she gone on home? "I'm working.'"

"The police are here. Can I come in?"

He scrambled up, covered the tiny body with a corner of blanket. "Come on in."

"What are you doin' in here, Ralph?" One look at his face and she leaned away. Studied his looks. "You okay? You don't look so good. Your eyes are red."

"Yours would be too, with all this sawdust," he said, and shrugged toward the lid he was carving. "Just working."

"The police are here to see if you found anything when you were cleaning up. They want to know if you found the...the *fetus.*"

Pressure rose in Ralph's neck and head. He squinted his eyes. "Fetus? She lost her baby. So have them call it what it is, a baby. And just what do you think they'd do with the baby if we'd found it? Huh?"

Millie glanced around, wide-eyed. "That…that's what they said. I told them I didn't think you'd found anything, but I'd check with you. You're the one that cleaned the bathroom. They're waiting out front."

Ralph was glad they hadn't run into him first. He might be in jail right now for assaulting an officer.

"Well, I ain't found no *fetus.* And I'm glad I ain't found one, because you and I know just what they'd do with such a thing. And it ain't pretty. They sure as heck wouldn't treat it like no baby, now, would they?"

Millie leaned her chin to the right and kept her eyes on Ralph as if she wasn't sure what he was talking about. "I'll go tell 'em." She stepped to the door. Paused.

She rubbed her arms, looked ready to cry. "The mother didn't make it, Ralph. She died."

He turned and slammed a palm down on the workbench.

"I'm sorry, Ralph. See you tomorrow."

But Ralph was already settling into the broken chair seat. "Just shut the door, please," he said. "And lock it," he yelled.

The door latch clicked, shutting off the daylight and all noise of the outdoors. A silence fell over the shed. He closed his eyes.

And then, "*Meow!*"

He glanced up to see a little gray head with big ears peeking around the cans.

"How'd you get in here?" He laid down his tool. "Come on, then. Come on." He reached out a hand. The kitten padded on little white feet, purring and rubbing against his hand, and then climbed onto his lap.

He cradled its silky head against his chest and once again closed his eyes.

Now what? Now what, God? Please help me.

At midnight, Ralph shut off his alarm. Still fresh on his mind was yesterday's sorrow. He had no way of knowing the man's name who lost his wife and child. But he hoped the fella would be comforted and recover from the loss.

He opened the upstairs door upon a slumbering world and climbed down the two flights of stairs to retrieve the little carved casket from his locked shed.

The least he could do was take care of the couple's little baby. Give her a proper resting place.

He crossed the bridge with the carved box in his hands, a camping spade under his arm, and a grocery bag filled with ferns, a big clump he'd pulled out of the palm thicket behind the restaurant. In the bag were several large, smooth stones chosen for their color and beauty from his driveway.

He crossed over to the highway at Aunt Allie's store, circled around to the side, listened and studied the place to make sure no one was up, and eased in through the gate.

And there, to the left, inside the corner of the fence, among the roots of the mulberry tree, he dug the tiny hole—good and deep so no varmint would bother it, which took a good while because of the roots.

He mostly worked by the faint glow of the streetlights across the way and by feel. He lowered the little casket into the hole and covered it with soil. On top of it, he situated the cluster of ferns, using his flashlight only once to check the roots and make sure they were all buried. He flicked it off and arranged the stones around the ferns.

Ralph brushed off his hands, closed the gate, and walked back to the restaurant.

All real nice for this situation.

But there was nothing he could really do to fix his past and what he'd done.

Nothing.

Millie showed up at work the next morning. Larry was already slamming around getting pans out and cookers warmed up and food out. The kitchen was ready for a breakfast crowd.

"Mornin', Larry. Mornin' Jack." She looked around. "Where's Ralph?"

"Well, Miss Millie, he said you and me we was in charge today. Said for us to take over."

"Yeah, right. That's not about to happen." After yesterday's disaster, nobody should be joking about anything. But Larry was a teen. She slid her apron off its hook expecting Larry to laugh and admit to the joke. When Larry remained serious, she turned his way. "Okay, spit it out. What are you talkin' about?"

Larry shrugged. "Tol' me this morning. Right after we got here."

Jack, over at the sink, stepped back with his hands up. "I don't know nothin' about it. I wasn't here yet."

"We? You mean he *was* here. But he left? Where'd he go then?" She didn't recall any appointments or anything. Kinda aggravatin' him stayin' clear over here at his apartment. When he stayed at her place at least they could talk things out every day and night. And now, here he was actin' all weird and such.

Larry shrugged again.

"Stop that shoulder thing," she snapped. "No shrugging. Now tell me. What was he actin' like?"

Larry spread his fingers as if to say *I don't know.*

"Don't you do that either, for goodness' sake." She wanted to wring his neck. "Talk to me, Larry. Was he acting normal?"

Larry and Jack looked at each other.

Millie doubled up the apron and slapped it hard against the stainless-steel cutting table. The boys jumped. "Oh, for goodness' sake, Larry. Do I have to slap a knot on your head to get an answer?"

"Okay, okay, Miss Millie. He left in a boat. Just took off."

An icy wave washed over Millie. She hoped he hadn't done what he might have done. Gone out in his dad's old boat. That old beat-up thing hadn't been touched in at least a year. Maybe a couple of years. Last time she saw it, it had water in the bottom. Old decrepit thing. Had to have rotten fuel. If he'd gone out in that, he'd be in danger of sinking, or stalling, or who knew what else.

"Come with me, Larry." She grabbed him by the sleeve and practically dragged him out the back door and around the short way past the shed to the slips along the boardwalk.

She crossed her arms. "Show me. Show me right now what boat he took. Surely, you saw him leave. I wanna know what boat he took."

Larry hung his head. Pointed an elbow to the slip where the old boat had sat for so long.

And Millie's heart sank.

The slip was empty.

Sol slept all the way through El Paso. But a sudden cacophony of scrubbing noises, rocking, and *blam, blam, blams!* beneath the car jarred him bolt upright.

He looked over at Term, who didn't seem at all worried. Then he looked around at the scrubby desert wasteland surrounding the car. Bad place to be stranded. He'd never heard such a ruckus.

"What's that racket? And where are we?" he asked as Term slowed their speed dramatically.

The slapping and rocking slowed, too, but Term still didn't seem bothered.

"All chaos is tearin' loose under there—and there you sit as cool as a cucumber! This will be money outta my pocket."

Term nodded. "Yes, it is," he finally said. "To answer your question, we just passed through Sparks. We're coming up on the little town of Fabens, Texas."

"And our car's fallin' apart." Sol was yelling now.

Term gave him an odd look and slowed even more. "It does sound pretty rough, Sol. Like maybe all the tires blew at once."

Sol didn't want to believe it. "A time bomb. No way. The odds of it don't make sense."

Term's voice held calm. "Let's pull over at…" He tipped his head. "I started to say Fabens, but I think we'd better pull over right here and see about it."

"Aw, I'm so glad somebody's thinking. How long's the noise been going on?" Sol needed to blame the thing on somebody. Maybe Term had been ignoring it.

"Since right about the time you woke up."

A car passed by, honking and flashing its lights. Term waved back a *thank you,* but who knew if the guy in the car could even see him.

With his right blinker clicking, Term pulled over onto the gravel. Low sandy hills with scattered weeds surrounded both sides of the highway. It was a desolate non-paradise if Sol had ever seen one. Oh, but wait, he had, miles and miles of it up to now. Term liked it, though. Nothing bothered that dude.

"You get out and look," Sol said, "I can't take it."

Term climbed out and studied each wheel as he circled the car and came around to Sol's door. He opened it. "Come on out and join me. You need to see this."

"Noooo," Sol groaned and slid out. "Not bad news." What else could it be?

Cars whizzed by as he followed Term's footsteps around the car.

The news was not just bad. It was dismal. "All four tires? Shredded?"

"By the looks of it, the tires were all retreads."

Sol hung his head. Here went a wad of money. "This is Eddie's fault, putting on cheap tires."

"Mm hmm. Seems to me you bought a cheap tire yourself."

"But then, it isn't my car, and you know it." Sol twisted around to verify whether the tire he'd bought had shredded too. It had.

"Yeah, that guy could have sold me a higher quality retread."

Term shook his head. "Better get out your phone, Sol. We're going to need a tow truck."

Sol kicked at the dangling strips with the end of his flip flop. "Dadgummit all!"

The sun was setting before the Fernandez Towing truck arrived. Its pleasant-dispositioned driver tipped his head at Term and Sol and hooked up the car.

Term offered to help, but the driver shook his head. "*Muchas gracias.*" He pointed to himself. "I do it." With no delay, he cranked the vehicle right up onto the back of the truck. The man, not even five feet tall, seemed to be all muscle.

Sol complained about his blisters as he and Term climbed up and scooted into the cab. Sol sat next to the driver. "Where are we heading with this vehicle?"

The little man's hand drew an imaginary line across the steering wheel. "*No ingles, senor. Lo siento.*"

But Term volunteered to translate. He spoke a few sentences with the driver and relayed it to Sol. "We're heading into Fabens, as we intended," he said. "And this gentleman has a room in back of his house he will rent us as long as we need. Twenty dollars a night. Not fancy, but clean. With a shower."

Sol didn't have to think long. "Oh yeah. A hot shower. For twenty bucks? Wish every room came that cheap."

Term leaned his elbow out the window of the battered cab. His hair tossed in the wind as they rolled down the highway. "Yes. Simple pleasures, huh?"

The Fabens exit appeared before Sol expected. The truck turned off and to the right. They passed a handful of businesses, all closed down for the night.

"Where are all the trees in this town?" he wondered aloud.

Term gave him a shrug. "It's Texas, remember?"

"I know, but I thought maybe in a town they'd have some."

The driver spoke up. "Tree. My house, I have tree. Very nice. Very tall. Big."

Sol turned. "I thought you didn't speak English."

"*Un poco*," the man said, indicating the smallness of his vocabulary with pinched forefinger and thumb. "No much."

Within a few blocks, the driver turned left and slowed in front of a house with a large tree in the corner of the lot. Sol couldn't tell what it was, but it marked the man's house as prime real estate.

"My house, see? Big tree."

Sol nodded. "Nice." Indeed, the man's house, lined along the front with a concrete wall and pillars of the same material, appeared to be one of the cleaner, neater homes they'd passed. "Nice," Sol repeated.

But the truck pulled on past it to the next lot and parked beside a small corrugated building. Its construction appeared to be a collection of salvaged materials. **Fernandez Towing and Auto Repair**, the sign's faded paint said.

Sol's red car, no longer very shiny, appeared to be one of only two cars in the lot. The only other vehicle was a rusted green Ford from the fifties. Grass grew around its flat tires.

The tow truck driver leaped down out of his truck and beckoned to Sol. "Come, come." He reached out his hand. Sol took it as Term exited the other side and slammed the door.

"Thank you," Sol said, grabbing the man's extended hand. He winced as he landed. The flip flops dug into his blisters. He needed a Band-Aid.

"*Manana*," the man said. "Manana we take the vehicle down and fix the tires. "But now," he brought his closed fingertips to his mouth, "*vamos a comer*."

"He's inviting you to eat," Term said.

Sol nodded. "Vamos a…."

"Vamos a comer," the man said, helping him with the rest. "*Si?*"

Sol nodded. Whatever the man offered would be good. All that for twenty bucks? This was a pretty good deal.

"Muchas gracias," Term said.

Sol copied him. Such a deal. "Yes, muchas gracias."

The lowering sun cast horizontal rays across Zeke's boat. Matt helped the retired couple on portside reel in their lines and put away their rods. He cleaned up their small area as they entered the cabin to put their feet up for some much-needed rest. The other two reservations hadn't shown up this morning and simply forfeited their fishing fees.

It made for an extra light day, and Zeke hadn't lost money on anyone. Now, Matt had some extra time to spend with Coral over on starboard side. He peered across the boat through the windows as she cast her line anew. Beneath her sunhat, the wind teased her long hair. He smiled. Even out fishing she was beautiful.

"I'll be over in a minute," he called to her.

She turned and smiled as the sun, now golden, backlit her silhouette. No painting could…

Matt tore his eyes away and stepped into the galley. He served the guests soda pop and potato chips, made them comfortable, and then headed up to the bow where Zeke hung out. "Need me for anything? I thought I'd spend a minute with my girl."

Zeke grinned. "Sure. We've got a minute before we head to port."

Matt started away, but Zeke stopped him. "I do like your girl," he said. "And if Ralph had a daughter, she'd be perfect…

"And yes," Zeke added. "I will keep my mouth shut about everything. But listen. She can't possibly be who she thinks she is. Ralph never had a girlfriend. Just because of that one fact, she couldn't be Ralph's daughter. I think you kids are confusing him with someone else. But like I said, if she actually was his daughter, I'm sure he'd be mighty proud of her."

"I appreciate that. I do. We're not in a hurry to break it to him. She doesn't need a rejection."

Matt couldn't help that Zeke didn't believe them, but he took the time to explain about the fake name situation.

"Lies are webs, aren't they?" Zeke said.

"Yes. Stupid decision." Matt asked Zeke not to call her by either name until they got it straightened out with Ralph.

"I do hope she finds her family," Zeke said. "Now go, be with your girl, Coral. We'll weigh anchor in a few."

Matt stepped around the boat to where Coral stood, rod in hand. He opened his sticky hands, "Sorry, better not hug you, I'm covered in bait-stink."

She laughed. "Oh, I don't care. I love this."

"You're getting pretty good with that bait, yourself, I noticed." She'd caught three fish of two pounds or more. "I'm proud of you."

"You going to fish?"

He shook his head and looked into her eyes.

Then the engines began to rumble. That was quicker than he'd expected. Zeke would be calling him any second. Now, Matt would have to yell over their noise. "Coral, listen. I want you to know something."

She smiled up at him, waiting.

"What I want to say is all that hooey about a made-up name— don't get that mixed up with the other part."

She wrinkled her brow, "What do you mean?"

"The girlfriend part." He cleared his throat. "I don't want you to think that's just part of an act to go with a made-up name."

She smiled and tipped her head for him to continue.

"It's—I'm not pretending. I really want you to be my girlfriend."

"Aw, Matt…"

"Weigh anchor!" Zeke called.

"Back in a few. Reel it in quick."

Matt's hands shook as they pulled up the anchor and locked it in place. He hadn't wanted to leave the conversation midway.

He raced back toward Coral as the boat circled to make its one-eighty. Port was behind them. The wind kicked up as velocity increased.

"So will you have me?"

Coral reached around his neck, her hair tossing all which-a-ways. She clamped her hat down to keep it from blowing away and nodded with a big smile.

He bent to kiss her, then froze as his eyes caught the horizon. He squinted into the distance. "Oh, boy." A small boat, nearly impossible to see, bobbed between their vessel and the sun. In it stood a man, waving his arms.

"What is it?" Coral asked. She turned. Gasped. Put her hand to her mouth.

"Someone's in trouble," he said.

He scrambled toward the wheelhouse.

"Zeke!"

Sol kicked a rock across the bare backyard of the Fernandez house. He punched the air. "Delay, delay, delay. What else can go wrong?"

"There has to be a reason," Term told him. "Sometimes we're not in control of the situation."

"Problems with the tire order, not enough of this kind, or that kind, or the size won't fit the car. Delivery problem." He punched the air again. "What else can go wrong? Huh? And then Fernandez himself has no inventory. None at all."

"They're scraping by. Let's just make the best of it," Term suggested.

What should have been one night in Fabens ended up being several. As long as they were stuck here, Term, suggested they might as well treat it like a vacation, take a walk every day and learn about all the unique scenery. This morning their walk took them past a Family Dollar. The stepped inside and found comfortable tennis shoes and some socks for Sol.

Sol managed to keep his mouth shut about the twenty-dollar-a-night accommodations, which turned out to be three unpainted block walls surrounding fresh air. And the same chicken and rice and peas meal every night, which Mrs. Fernandez insisted on feeding them, and the long prayer of blessing and holding hands around the table, and the hammocks they were sleeping in. How Sol longed to be able to turn over in bed—but he kept it to himself. When he thought it over, he was proud to keep his trap shut, because like Term said, the people were trying their best.

And Term and Sol, by renting the room and doing business with Fernandez, were doing their part to help them out. Term made sure

Sol chipped in an equal amount for the missus—another twenty a night for the food.

It was still a good deal in Sol's book.

On the other hand, the four little kids drove Sol crazy. Especially the four-year-old boy.

The baby stayed inside with its mom. But none of the other three communicated in English. The two older girls giggled about everything he did. And the four-year-old followed Sol everywhere, even hanging around waiting for him to come out of the outdoor shower—the cold-water-only shower with a foot-high gap under its wall—or the matching outdoor toilet housed inside another rickety stall.

Despite all that, Sol had to admit he was cleaner than before— but those kids, especially the boy, acted like old bald-headed Sol was some kind of rock-star. Hmph! Imagine that.

For some reason they didn't act that way with Term. Acted like they didn't even see him at times. Or hear him.

Just this morning Sol nearly jumped out of his skin when the four-year-old boy poked a stick under the gap of that shower door and touched his foot. Sol hollered out. Thought it was some kind of critter—and the boy ran away giggling. But Sol knew the sound of that little voice now. His mama called him Timoteo.

Later on, that same little squirt shoved a squawking chicken under Sol's shower door. Seems the hens used to roost in the same shower at times. But judging by this chicken's wild flapping and pooping all over the shower floor, a hen doesn't much like water.

The chicken escaped, and Sol chuckled as he watched the poop rinse off the floor and onto the dirt outside. He really should get some antibiotic and Band-Aids for those blisters. Especially now.

Ralph slumped against the dead motor of his stalled boat. But then his eye spotted the distant vessel. He roused. *Thank God.* A fishing boat. It seemed to be anchored. How had he missed it?

He raised both arms, yelled a few hoarse words that barely rose above a whisper. He hoped they spotted him. Stalled here the whole day with nobody in sight, his limbs now resembled cooked lobster.

The sudden motion of his raised arms wobbled the tiny craft. His empty water jug rolled across the deck. "Somebody, help." Despite the burn and sting, he kept waving. If he lived through this, he'd be sick with blisters and sun poisoning. He turned briefly to scan the distant shore. Where was home, anyway?

His thoughts had long since begun to fog. And now he focused on the waving shadows of his arms. They were stretched now, far across the green ripples. They seemed to mock as they pointed straight at the fishing vessel. The sun behind him would make him hard to see.

His skin screamed.

The hull of his boat cast a horizontal shadow beside him. Cool green shade. Just the size to lie down in.

But then there were sharks.

He wanted to close his eyes. To sleep. To wake up on that fishing boat. He did not wish for the sun to set or the black night to come. The sun was a blessing and a curse.

He couldn't hear it, but the large vessel began to move and then circled. He watched as it made a loop. "Come on now. Don't go back to shore," he whispered, his voice weak and pained from trying to get the boat's attention.

His arms stretched higher, waved wider.

He didn't want to die.

He lowered his arms. In the evening, the fishing captains headed back to port like horses to a barn. The horizon was otherwise empty. If this captain didn't see him, he might end up in the dark. Not his favorite thing to do in a broke-down boat like his.

He waved again, giving it another shot. "Help! Come help!" He glanced toward the console and its busted radio.

Shoulda brought a good radio.

Shoulda brought lunch.

Shoulda brought more water.

Shoulda been smart and done a lot of things.

Shoulda told someone where I was going.

Too late now. He tried to wet his cracked lips, but a dry tongue didn't help.

Wait. Was the…?

It was! The boat was turning his way.

He stood. Waved wide. "Oh, thank you," he whispered, salt rising up like acid in his eyes. "Thank You, God. Come on, baby. Come on and get me."

The boat drew near.

It was Zeke's *Gulf Princess.*

Matt stood back while Zeke pulled out his telescope to study the craft floating in the distance.

He reached out and gave Matt a high-five. "Good eye. I can't imagine how you saw the boat out there with the sun like it is. Guess my eyes aren't what they used to be."

"What can you tell about it?"

"Too far away. Whoever he is sat down. That's all I know."

They drew closer, and Zeke lifted his telescope again. "No way." He handed the telescope to Matt. "Take a look. Is that Ralph? Ralph Stone?"

Matt reached for the device and put it to his eye. "Unbelievable. What's he doing out here? Why isn't he at the restaurant?"

Zeke placed his hands on the wheel. "We're about to find out."

Matt nodded.

"What you've been learning about tying up a boat at the docks is getting ready to come in real handy in a few minutes," Zeke told him. Then he proceeded to give Matt a revised lesson on how to tie up a smaller boat to the back of the big one. "You'll use the anchor rope. It won't stretch. Give it whatever length we've got. I don't care if we have a hundred fifty feet. Use it all. He drew a picture of each boat and sketched where the cleats should be on both boats and a diagram of how to secure them safely together with rope.

"I'll check you when you're done. But if Ralph needs first aid, his welfare is my primary concern."

"Got it," Matt said. Then he hesitated. "Can you keep Coral a secret back there? Like don't mention her at all, so Ralph won't notice her. This might just weird her out."

"Absolutely," Zeke said with his hand on the throttle. "And don't forget to tell our clients what's going on. When you're done with the boat, serve them free food, hot dogs or hamburgers, or whatever they like for having to wait. It's going to cost us quite a bit of time as we have to go slow, but not too much since we're close to port anyway."

Matt found Coral as he reentered the galley. "That's your dad stranded out there."

Her face contorted into a picture of concern. "Is he all right?"

Matt clamped his lips and nodded. "He's alive. But listen. Stay out of sight in the galley. Zeke is going to steer Ralph away from you. I've got a job, and I'll be back in a little bit."

Matt headed around to detach the anchor rope. He gripped the rail as the *Gulf Princess's* bow lifted and she picked up speed.

S ol found his antibiotic and Band-Aids. But the days stretched
on in Fabens. For lack of entertainment, his and Term's daily walks
always led west to the medical clinic and generally ended up at
the sweet shop on Main Street. "I've had enough of this," Sol
complained as he finished off a second donut.

"Ready for a new adventure?" Term said.

Sol raised his eyebrows. "Like what?" Wasn't too much to be
had in this little town.

"Want to check out the Mexican border—or at least get close
to it? Enough to see the big fence, anyway?"

Sol leaned away. "The Mexican border?"

Term laughed. "It's only two miles."

"You kidding? I've heard about that fence, but never imagined
seeing it up close."

"And—you can see some real trees."

No way. This place was a wasteland. "This I gotta see."

As they took off south along the main road, it wasn't long before
green grass appeared on both sides of the road.

Sol waved his arms above the irrigated turf. "I can't get over it.
The town in back of us is brown as a parking lot, but we come out
here, and now we've got a green carpet. Look at it."

Term pointed out the ditches and drains that connected to the
Rio Grande along the border.

Before long, they were walking in the shade between groves of
green pecan trees. "I can't believe it," Sol said. "We shoulda been
staying out here."

Eventually the trees ended, and they emerged into a wide cleared area. A hundred yards or more beyond them stretched the long brown fence in both directions as far as the eye could see.

Sol stood there gaping. His mouth finally closed. "Well, I'll be a monkey's…there it is, the fence the President set up. Just look at that thing. It's really and truly there, isn't it?"

Term nodded.

"You've made my day," Sol said.

"Remember that old saying, make sure to stop and smell the roses."

Sol clamped his lips and nodded.

"You want to get up close?" Term asked.

Sol shook his head and turned around. "Nope. Nope. That would creep me out. This is close enough."

As they headed north again, a wind rustled through the pecan groves, and Sol couldn't help but think of Paulette. She'd probably like to see all this.

The return walk was brief, but as they came into town and opened the front gate of the Fernandez house, a child's pain-filled wailing pierced the air.

The men hurried on into the living room. Mrs. Fernandez sat on the sofa, the baby secured beside her and the two girls, six and eight, clustered around. On her lap huddled Sol's little buddy, Timoteo. The mother lifted a tear-filled face in Sol's direction. "It's his foot. He yost fall out of the tree."

Sol looked at the boy's oddly twisted leg and then down to the child's mud-stained cheeks. Tears rolled out of his big brown eyes.

Sol's heart wanted to break. He knelt beside him

"Timoteo, buddy, I think we've got a broken leg."

Matt raced along the deck to the *Gulf Princess's* bridge where he snatched up the first aid box. Wide-eyed, Coral followed right behind and nearly stumbled over him.

He pointed to the small women's restroom. "Hide there, in the women's head. Stay inside until I tap twice on the door."

She stepped in and down and just before shutting the door said, "Don't you forget me, now."

He grinned—no chance of that—and raced to drop one anchor as Zeke stopped the engines. Together they guided the smaller boat close to the stern. "Stay seated, Ralph," Zeke called to the man.

Ralph remained where he was, the picture of sunburned agony. Zeke threw him a short line which Ralph secured to a cleat on his boat. Then Matt climbed down, and they helped Ralph up the access ladder into the larger vessel.

"Matt, you take over with what I showed you," Zeke said, pulling Ralph's sunburned arm around one shoulder. "I'm headin' up front with him where he can lie down on one of the starboard benches near the wheelhouse. He'll get a breeze and be in the shade on the trip back."

Matt handed him the medical supplies and set to work securing the craft they'd be towing.

"Thank you, thank you, thank you," was all Ralph could croak out. He was somewhat fuzzy-tongued, but Matt couldn't tell if it was only the dried-out mouth or something worse.

When Matt was done, he headed back inside the cabin where the tired fishing guests had lain down along the benches with their feet up on life preservers. "Excuse me, sir, ma'am," he said. "We're going to be a little delayed getting back, and I'd like to know if anybody would care for complimentary burgers or hot dogs to ease your hunger? We apologize for the delay, but we've saved a man's life today."

This woke them up. They declined the offered food, and after all the expected questions, they said they'd rather go back to their naps for now and to wake them up when they got back to port. Then they'd find a nice seafood restaurant.

Good. Matt could get back to his girlfriend. But first he needed to check on Zeke and see if he needed anything for Ralph.

Up at starboard, the sun was still shining. But that would change when they turned the vessel around. Ralph, now stripped to his undershorts, lay flat on a bench while Zeke with a can of antiseptic and analgesic sprayed down his burns. A flattened hydrocortisone tube and two empty water bottles lay on the floor.

"Towels, Matt. You'll find them in the galley. And pull that hose with the nozzle around. Take the nozzle off. We'll lay them over him and wet them down to cool him off. And bring me an armload of bottled water."

Matt saluted. "Yes, sir," and was off.

When he returned Zeke thanked him. "And stay within earshot inside the wheelhouse in case I need anything else."

Matt nodded and darted back to the head to rap twice on its door for Coral.

She peeked out.

Matt put his finger to his lips. "You can come out, but don't make a sound. I have to stay in there." He pointed through the door in the direction of the captain's wheel. "I have to be ready in case Zeke needs anything."

Coral nodded and climbed out.

Sol glanced from the broken leg to Term. The man had to know
what to do about this. But instead of taking charge, the giant turned
a hand toward Sol as if leaving the situation up to him.

Sol swallowed. He turned back to the woman. "*Donde Senor
Fernandez?*" At least he knew the word *donde.* It meant where.

She shook her head and let out a sob.

He moved his hands like he was driving a car. "Out on the road?"

She nodded hard.

"Good job, Sol," Term said. "You can do this."

The family had no other vehicle. "We need to get him to the
clinic," Sol said. He and Term had walked past it every single day.
"It's just up the road."

Term gave him a thumbs up. "Just reach out and offer to carry
him. She can follow with the kids. I'll bring up the rear. If he gets
too heavy, I'll help."

Sol reached out, and the mother let him take the gasping child.

"Hang onto me, now. Just hang on." He didn't want to jostle
that leg.

So away the little group walked, Mrs. Fernandez with her purse
on her shoulder and a baby in her arms, two girls at her heels—and
Timoteo, his arms in a stranglehold around Sol's neck, yowling for
all he was worth in Sol's ear, and Sol whispering and consoling him.
"It's all right, Timoteo. Just hang in there. It's going to be all right."

Truth was, Sol couldn't have let go if he'd wanted to. Timoteo
clung to his neck throughout the whole procedure, while Mom
stood by with the baby and girls. Sol worried that all that bending
over Timoteo's bed might just give him a crick in his neck tomorrow.

On the table when he couldn't reach Sol's neck, Timoteo wouldn't let go of Sol's hand, and when Sol had to detach himself and back away during the X-rays, the boy yowled with all his might with both arms extended. His mama had to calm him. But Sol made sure to stay right there where the boy could see him. He couldn't even sneak away to the bathroom. After the cast was applied, and it was time to go, and Sol picked the boy up to carry him home, the boy nearly squeezed the breath out of him. Several times he had to loosen Timoteo's grip to keep from passing out.

Good thing Timoteo wasn't in a pool getting rescued, or Sol would have gone under and drowned by now.

As the little family trudged home behind Sol, and the worn-out child lay asleep in his arms, that same feeling raced through his heart again. This time he decided it wasn't a heart attack. No, if felt too good for that.

But he wasn't about to mention it to Term.

Ralph welcomed Zeke's wet towels against his burning skin and the ice water down his throat. His whole body was on fire. His eyes, his lips, everything. "Zeke, you're a godsend."

"Feelin' a little better?"

Ralph tipped the last of another bottle into his mouth. Dribbles poured off his swollen lips. "Water. Sweet, sweet water." His voice croaked but didn't hurt as much as before. "Oh, that's good. I feel it runnin' through me—all over, down my legs, my arms." He shifted, groaned, and sat up. "I can't take this lyin' down and talkin'. I gotta git up."

"If you hadn't had that shirt on. And those long shorts," Zeke said, "I can't imagine. He took a seat beside him and looked him up and down. "We need to run you up to Crawfordville and get you some IVs. Some treatment." He opened a new water bottle for Ralph. "Have another."

Ralph took it. Poured it past his lips. "Needle in a haystack out there. How'd you find me?"

"Matt spotted you, but like you said before, you better give the credit to God."

"About that…"

"Yeah, about that, old friend…"

Zeke gave him a hard stare.

Ralph hung his head. "I know it's a bad time to bring this up…"

"What in the heck you were doin' out here in the Gulf in that old tub? You know better than that."

"I don't even know where to start."

"Why don't we start twenty or so years ago when you…"

Ralph interrupted, his chin still low. "No. Let's start with the other day."

Zeke plowed on, "…*twenty years* ago when you pretty much quit talking to me, the one and only best and closest friend you ever had. Your best bud. The one you shared everything with and who shared everything with you. Your future business partner. You just up and walked away from that friendship. Just how did you think that felt to me, your friend? The one who's still there for you and always will be?"

After a long pause, Ralph shook his head. "I'm sorry," he whispered. "And I lied to you."

Zeke crossed his arms.

Ralph shifted, elbows on his knees and leaned his face against his fingertips. It burned like hellfire, but oh, God, he deserved it. Confess your sins one to another—he knew that was in the Bible. And it was a long time coming. He owed Zeke.

"I guess I did it to hide the truth. All these years—I was afraid you'd dig it out of me."

"You don't know how much I wanted to," Zeke said. "I wanted to slap some sense into you and make you tell me what was going on."

"There was a girl. I told you no. But there was a girl."

Zeke raised his eyebrows.

"Not a girlfriend girl. But a girl I was tryin' to help. To protect her."

Zeke listened, motionless.

"And I…" Ralph's face scrunched up.

"Ralph, you didn't."

"But there's more to the story. A whole lot more. Her father—oh, God, what a devil—she lost his baby. Then ran away. And ended up here. I found her in the shed behind the restaurant."

"Why didn't you tell me. We could have—"

"That's the thing. He was dangerous. I couldn't tell you, or my dad, or Aunt Allie. He'd have shot and killed anybody that knew anything about her. The man was insane. Killed his own wife, according to the girl."

"But I don't understand. Are you telling me you got her…"

Ralph cussed. "Yes. I got her pregnant. Me, the protector. I messed up."

"You could have talked to me."

"I was afraid. I panicked. I gave her money and told her if she wanted to, she could…"

Zeke opened his mouth to say something, but Ralph stuck up his hand.

Zeke gripped the sunburned wrist and swung around on one knee, face to face with Ralph. "You gave her money for an abortion? Ralph, how could you?" His tone wasn't condemning. It was pleading.

Ralph shook his head. He deserved condemning. And that grip on his burned arm. He glanced down at Zeke's hand and Zeke let go.

"You and I," Zeke said, "we both knew the Bible—went to church and Sunday school. You knew better, Ralph. You always knew better. Why?"

Ralph shook his head. "Fear. Panic. Stupidity."

Matt, with Coral at his side, sat cross-legged beneath the captain's wheel. The engines were silent, and this allowed every whisper to filter in through the open porthole.

"You gave her money for an abortion? Ralph, how could you?"

There was no hiding what had happened. Matt turned to Coral at the look of utter sorrow on her face. The pain she must have felt shot through Matt's own heart.

Before he could say anything, Coral leaped to her feet. She teetered with her hand on the doorway. Matt scrambled up behind her. But she exited portside, circumventing the sleeping clients in the cabin, and stumbled toward the stern with hands over her face.

Oh, boy. Matt was torn. Coral needed him. And Zeke wanted Matt close by.

What else could Matt do? He darted to the farthest starboard hatch to give the impression—mostly for Ralph's sake—of being farther away rather than close by and eavesdropping. "Zeke, excuse me." From this angle, Matt could only see Ralph's knees. "Sorry to interrupt. Is there anything you need?"

"Not really, Matt." Zeke seemed annoyed at being interrupted at such an intense time, and Matt understood.

Matt pointed with his thumb toward the back of the boat and applied facial expressions to indicate his own problem. "It's Coral," he mouthed and then pointed to his ear and back toward Ralph. "I'll be at the stern if anything comes up."

Zeke nodded and shooed him away.

At the opposite end of the boat, Matt found Coral seated with her back against the rear cabin, sobbing.

Matt sank to the bench and wrapped his arms around her. "It's going to be all right."

She turned to face him, her eyes hot and full of tears, a deeper blue than ever before. "No, it's never going to be all right. He wanted to get rid of me. Wanted to kill me."

Even in her anger, she was beautiful. But what she said was true. He tried to imagine how it would feel to learn that about one's father.

Coral interrupted his thoughts. "What? You think he'd like to see me prance into his life right now, all grown up—all *hi, Daddy, how are you?*" She leaned into her hands and sobbed. Matt couldn't be sure which emotion prevailed, her fury, her fear, or her disappointment.

She spat bitter words. "Ralph's just like all the rest of Mom's creeps."

Matt pulled her close and cradled her head against his chest. He had no advice. No wisdom. "Shhh, shhhh, now."

There was nothing to do but let her cry it out. She was right. Ralph, a coward, wanted to kill his own child. Had wanted to kill *her.* And Ralph's biggest regret seemed to only be the lie he'd told his friend. What about the bigger issue: his effort to kill his child?

But then Matt and Coral had missed out on the last part of the conversation.

Coral turned her head, long enough to murmur, "When I get off this boat, I don't want to see his face."

Matt smoothed her hair.

He pulled off his outer fishing tee. "Here wipe your nose on this," he said. "It probably stinks, but that's all I have."

She pinched it against her nose and then hugged it against her chest.

Matt pressed her close. He'd let her do the talking.

"Not ever," she added. "Forget all the nice things I said about him. I can't stand him."

She wiped her nose again and sat upright, her voice hoarse, "And he—he took advantage of my…" the pitch of her voice rose, "*mother!*" She burst into fresh tears and fell against Matt.

He closed his eyes. *Oh, God. Please. Give me the words.*

A nagging thought reminded him, *You haven't heard the rest of the story.*

He stared across the water at the distant town of Carrabelle. His inner voice argued back with force. *Yeah, well, we heard most of it. We heard enough. What else could have been said?*

To be fair, he should at least mention there had to be more. Before she tossed her dad completely away. "Coral, Coral. Sit up a minute." His speech was soft.

She complied, wiping her face with the shirt. It was getting a workout. "What?"

He tried to use his gentlest tone. "Listen, we only heard part of Ralph's account. Maybe we're missing something important."

She drew back in disbelief. "Are you on his side? You *heard* the man."

He reached for her hand. "But I'm only trying to…"

She yanked loose, shook her head, and turned away. "I'm done with him."

Matt sighed, unsure of what to do. He prayed silently.

She spoke with her back to him. "It's—he's—I just want to go back home."

"I've told you before, Coral, whatever your heart desires, that's what we'll do."

Silence, and then the rusty squawk of a gull and along with it the warning in Matt's head. *You haven't heard the rest of the story.*

And that was the problem.

How was he going to hear the rest of it?

On the *Gulf Princess,* Zeke crouched on the deck beside Ralph's bench. He stared up at his old friend. "So, that's your excuse? Fear, panic, and stupidity?"

"I should have gone back upstairs that night. I couldn't sleep. In my heart I knew I had to make things right. I spent all night settling in my mind how we could make it work."

"So, you waited?"

"You gotta remember, her dad had a shotgun, and he was goin' door to door. My dad had no idea she was upstairs."

"Go on."

"We could have gone to another town. Worked it out there." Ralph hung his head, shook it. "But the next morning when I got back up there, she was gone. Along with the money."

Zeke puckered up his lips and stared at the deck. The wind had died down, and with clients onboard, he needed to get moving.

"I cursed that money. And myself. For leaving it there. Shouldn't have mentioned anything about what she could do about things. I knew better as soon as the words came out of my mouth."

Zeke snorted. What could he say to Ralph? "So you ran away to the Army?"

"I'm a killer, Zeke. That's all it amoun…." He leaned back. "And then yesterday," he extended his hands, "when I held that little baby in my hands…just like the one I…"

Indeed, Zeke had heard about the miscarriage at the restaurant, but not about Ralph finding the baby.

Ralph continued, "I felt like God was laughing at me, saying, 'Now, see what you've done, you wicked guilty thing.'"

"You've got that backwards, buddy."

Ralph frowned. "Whaddya mean?"

"Haven't you repented after all these years?"

Ralph gazed into Zeke's face and shook his head, tears in his eyes. "Every day of my life. Even more now that I've seen…" His face screwed up into a knot. "Oh, God. I'm so sorry for my whole life. It's a mess. A mess." He closed his eyes and let his arms go limp. He opened a hand toward Zeke. "Pray for me, friend. I don't know what else to say."

Zeke took the hand. "Ralph. You've repented. It's not God that's saying *See what you've done, you wicked guilty thing.* That's Satan's lie. He comes to steal, kill, and destroy. And accuse. He'd like nothing more than to see you ruined."

Ralph shot him a mournful look and then shut his eyes again.

Zeke continued, "Jesus is sitting at the right hand of the Father making intercession for you."

"I know what that means. But lay it out for me. Lay it out. I need to hear it."

"He's the one telling the Father, 'Look, he's repented. Brush his dirt off and set him on his feet again.' God loves you, Ralph. Jesus paid with His blood for those sins. He's not condemning you."

Ralph hunched forward on his elbows and turned his head toward Zeke.

Zeke kept talking. "When you repent, God's merciful, Ralph. Not condemning. Think of all the time you've wasted, dodging me and everyone else."

Ralph started to run his hands down his face but winced at the sunburn and pulled them away.

"You know that story about the prodigal son returning to his father? He wronged his family left and right…but who was it that rushed down the road to meet him? His father. He'd been watching—for a long time—for that boy. On the lookout. Saw him coming from far away. Couldn't wait to bless him."

Ralph blew out a long, slow breath of air.

"That's you, Ralph. Now take it. Take the forgiveness. And yes, I'll pray for you."

And he did.

Ralph prayed too. He repented again and shed more tears, but with a new attitude.

Zeke asked God to help Ralph accept the forgiveness and move on with his life.

"But there's one thing," Zeke said. "How do you know a hundred percent that you killed your child? You can't be sure."

Ralph raised one palm. "After seeing what I saw at the restaurant, I now realize I might have killed my baby and her mother."

Zeke shook his head. It was all he could do to keep his mouth shut about Coral. "What if the mother and child did not die? What if she just took the money and left? What if she and the baby went on to live their lives?"

Ralph sat up. The expression on his face transformed. "That would be the best thing I ever heard."

But Zeke still couldn't tell him. It was Zeke's turn to let out a long slow breath. "Welcome back, buddy. Welcome back. Now let's get this big tug runnin' and get you up to Crawfordville."

"I don't need a doc…"

Zeke held up a hand. "*And* no arguin'!"

“Weigh anchor!”

Matt leaped to his feet. He leaned down and kissed Coral on top of the head as the engines kicked in. “Gotta get to work.”

Coral reached for his hand to pull her up. She stood beside him, swiped the shirt across her nose. “I’m sorry, Matt, for acting like a baby.”

He took her by the shoulders and pulled her close. He wrapped his arms around her. “No, no. Don’t mention it. Look at what you’ve been through. I’d be in shock, too.” He took a step back with her hands in his. “Look, you’ll probably need to stay back here for a while so Ralph doesn’t see you. And maybe sneak into the head again when we come to tie off his boat.” Matt’s fingers slid from hers as he backed away toward portside. He blew her a kiss. “Zeke’s calling. I’ve gotta go.”

He hustled to the stern and followed a series of moves and hand signals from Zeke behind the wheel as he winched up the heavy anchor. Secure and ready, the captain geared up the motor and began his long arc of one-eighty so they could get back to port. Matt stepped back in the wheelhouse. He had to yell over the motors. “Anything else?”

“Get back to the stern and watch that boat. I don’t want it floundering or running off course.”

“Absolutely.”

But Matt hesitated. “I need to ask a favor.”

Zeke stared at him, waiting.

There was no way he could yell his thoughts without Ralph overhearing them, so he held up a finger for Zeke to hang on. He darted into the galley and located a pen and a paper napkin to scribble out his message.

Fortunately for them, with the roar of the engines, the tired clients were fast asleep. They were still comfortable back there, and some of their easy breathing had evolved into loud snoring. He chuckled inwardly. Thank goodness. This sometimes happened with clients after a long day in the sun. All ages.

The seldom-used pen had to be primed before it would write. Eventually it did. *Coral is upset. Very. Very,* he wrote. *She heard what Ralph said. Could I see her home and clean the boat after I get back? Five to ten minutes is all.*

Zeke liked to have the boat cleaned immediately. But he nodded, tossed his chin toward the cabin, and their two guests. "Clients first, though."

"Absolutely."

Zeke lifted a finger. "You'll be on your own. I've got to bring Ralph up to Crawfordville. He needs IVs."

Now that Matt had gained some skills, the chore of cleaning the clients' fish had fallen to him. Unless there were a lot of clients or fish. "No worries. I'll take good care of them. And the boat will be ship-shape by the time you get back."

Zeke gave him a thumbs up.

Good. Maybe Matt could talk some patience into Coral.

At the marina, Zeke docked the *Gulf Princess* stern-first. He had assigned Matt to gather in the tow-ropes and bring the smaller boat around to its own slip and lash it to its rightful cleats. The girlfriend had disappeared inside the cabin somewhere, and now Matt was busy over at the scaling shed entertaining their two drowsy-headed clients with his new scaling skills.

He had to admit, the boy Matt was all right. But Zeke felt bad for the girl. The way she reacted to Ralph's story, she had to be the real deal. At least she thought she was.

The two kids seemed real enough, and now Zeke doubted they were running a scam. But he wondered how it would all end.

A woman's voice called out from over at the restaurant, and he glanced up.

It was Millie who must have been watching for their return. She came flying off the restaurant's front deck like a wet mother hen fit-to-be-tied. She spotted Ralph's empty boat and stopped short with her mouth agape. "Where's Ralph?"

Zeke climbed up the ladder to the dock and wrapped a rope around a cleat. He was not about to tell her what all the man had been through. "Nothing to worry about. He's fine, Millie."

A look of relief passed over her. "Oh, thank God. I can't believe he took off in that old thing."

He stepped close and touched her arm. "Millie, listen, you might want to take it easy on Ralph. He's going through some tough things."

She shook her head. "It was that miscarriage, wasn't it? I knew that messed him up. Really threw him for a loop."

She leaned around Zeke to see where Ralph was.

"He's lying down. I'll go get him in a minute when things settle down."

She leaned the other way, still trying to spot him. "He's okay, isn't he?"

"I'll be taking him up to the ER…"

"ER!"

Zeke held up one finger. "Let me finish, Millie. He might need some IVs."

"IVs!" Her voice rose in pitch.

"Now, Millie, calm down. I told you he's fine. He's a little dehydrated. And sunburned."

That quieted her. Sunburn and dehydration were common things along the coastline. "But Ralph's *my* man. I can take him to the ER myself." She took a breath. "Wait. I'm sorry, Zeke. That didn't sound too nice. It's not that I don't appreciate your willingness to take him up there, but it's my place, ain't it?"

"You want to run get your truck then?"

Millie turned around only to notice Larry peeking around the corner of the restaurant. She stomped her foot. "Get back in there, Larry," she squawked. "Who's mindin' the store?"

She swung back around to Zeke. "Every one of us has been worried sick all day. Larry too." She wiped her eyes. "Good thing that part-time girl come in this evenin'. It's been somethin' else around here."

He nodded and watched as she hustled toward the building. She'd have to put someone in charge and report she was leaving.

Zeke headed back to the boat to find Ralph still on the starboard bench where he left him. He scooped up another bottle of water, unscrewed the lid, and held it out. "Need another drink?"

Ralph eased up to a sitting position, his skin a deep red. Zeke cringed. Ralph would really feel that tomorrow. "Millie's coming right back with the truck. She insisted on taking you to the hospital herself."

Ralph nodded as he gulped down the water. "That's my woman. Truck's in the parkin' lot."

"Listen, Ralph. So, what if I told you everything would be okay?"

"What do you know about it?"

"That's all I can say. Would you trust me?"

Ralph stood but didn't answer the question. "I'll see you later, Zeke."

Zeke wanted to hug his friend, to pat him on the shoulder. But he didn't dare. Just had to stand there.

"Listen," Ralph said. "You're a good friend. Always have been. Always will be. And I thank you for the rescue. And the prayers. I truly do."

Zeke followed close behind his friend as he climbed off the boat. Millie had returned to walk Ralph to the truck, and he handed him two more water bottles. "Keep him hydrated," he told Millie. She nodded, and they headed for the parking lot.

He was still standing there as Ralph turned and waved from the parking lot.

Zeke hoped it was true, that all would be okay. He truly did. For Ralph's sake—and the girl's.

Still concealed on Zeke's boat, I leaned against the inside of the head's door until Matt gave the all-clear knock. I eased it open. How strange. There I was hiding from my own father. And to think, a few months back I didn't even know I had one. I'd heard others derisively call their fathers no more than a sperm donor. The baseness of that term bothered me—I'd never sink to calling mine that, though he deserved an even worse name. Murderer.

So glad that didn't work out.

Matt reached out his hand, and I took it.

"Coral."

"Matt."

His sober face revealed a newly developed uneasiness toward me, as if he didn't know how to act now or what to do. I glanced around just to make sure Ralph wasn't there.

"Don't worry," he said. "Ralph's gone. Millie took him away in the truck. He's pretty burnt."

The way I looked at it, he deserved whatever pain he was enduring.

"I'm glad we spotted him," Matt said. "It was a miracle with that sun behind him."

"I guess you saved his life."

Matt locked fingers with mine and helped me off the boat. We circled around to the other side of the restaurant, passing Zeke who was busy rinsing off the fish-cleaning table. I waved. At least Ralph was gone. I didn't have to worry about running into him. We reached the bridge and crossed over to the opposite side.

So far, Matt had only spoken a few words. But I had my own mismatched thoughts and unsorted feelings. I couldn't put anything into words. Matt didn't deserve a dose of my horrible feelings, but I couldn't bring myself to chitter-chatter just to make him feel more comfortable. So, I kept my mouth shut.

At the sidewalk, we started up the incline of the bridge. "I hate to rush you home," Matt said as we reached the crest, "but I gave my word I'd help Zeke." Still, he held onto my hand and paused there long enough for us to gaze at the river below, our new custom.

"I thought we had to hurry," I said, unwilling for him to get in trouble on account of me. But I could tell he had something to say.

He sighed and turned my palm against the rail with his on top. "Coral. Hear me out. Will you?"

Not this again. I cut him off. "Listen, I'll pray for Ralph. The Bible says to pray for your enemies. This man never met me. Never knew me. But he wanted to kill me. That's murder in my book."

Matt opened his mouth to speak and then stopped. We stood there looking upriver to the north and away from town. A breeze wafted over our shaded faces.

"Yes, I agree with what you say. I really do," he said. "But could we hold that thought for a minute and look," he said, tipping his chin toward the dark blue water. "Up that way, where the river starts— somewhere beyond those palms, those tall grasses and palmettoes, is the beginning of the river. The beginning. Like the beginning of the story we just heard." He turned me around. "Where things first began, Coral. But tell me. Where does it go?"

I sighed. This wasn't what I wanted to hear, Matt taking sides with my dad.

Then Matt brought my hand around once again, and I turned with him. He checked for traffic and led me across to the other side of the bridge and stood like before. We squinted into the lowering sun. On this side flowed the curve in the river lined with sun-drenched stores, restaurants, people, sails, and boats, and the Gulf a little way beyond. Such a contrast to the other side. He lifted his arm, amber in the light, and spread his fingers toward the scene. "And there lies the rest of it. The part we didn't hear." He turned his face to me. "Coral, don't you want to hear the rest of the story? Don't you want to know?"

How could the end be anything positive?

There we stood, hands on the rail, our faces awash in setting sun.

Matt stood strong beside me and said nothing. I wished at this moment that I could melt like wax into his arms—go along with his idea—and have everything turn out peachy. But I knew better. There was no way that listening to more of Ralph's awful confession could make things better. This whole trip was a waste. And I knew Matt was disappointed with me. But I couldn't help it.

My wires were bent, and I didn't know how to straighten them out. My own father had wanted to do away with me.

I turned. We needed to leave, so Matt could get back.

My action seemed to deflate him, but right now, I could not express my mixed thoughts.

So, I changed the topic. "I'm sorry I was such a baby back there on the boat."

He squeezed my hand as we walked in silence to the base of the bridge.

As we crossed the highway, I spoke again. "And I appreciate that you're wonderful and full of romantic poetry and wisdom. That was wise what you said back there. Very." I paused there, gazed up into those dark eyes, the face of the man who cared so much.

And I didn't want to ruin what we had.

"But please, Matt. Don't. Don't pressure me like this. If you have any feelings for me, please don't."

A swat against his hammock woke Sol out of his slumbers.

"Good news, Sol." It was Term.

He opened his eyes.

For the last half hour Sol had drifted in and out of sleep. The sounds of the outdoor shower, then Mrs. Fernandez letting the chickens out of their coop, their quiet sounds as she fed and talked to them, had all semi-wakened him. And then there was the hushed conversation between Term and Mr. Fernandez.

Sol pulled down the side of the hammock to see Term's big square face looking down at him. "Good news?"

"Your retreads should be in by tomorrow morning."

"Well, then, why doesn't your face look any happier?" Sol said.

Term stepped away into the sunlight. The little three-walled outdoor room had served them well over the last few days, and Sol was ready to go. But for some reason he didn't feel any better about the retreads arriving than Term seemed to.

He should…

Then he thought back to Mrs. Fernandez down there at the clinic. And that wallet when she pulled out her medical cards. Completely empty. Not one bill in there.

And here they were enjoying those Fernandez eggs every morning and those chicken and rice dinners every night. All these delays so Mr. Fernandez could get those retreads in stock for them.

The extra money they'd given her for meals didn't seem to be stretching very far.

Sol stuck a leg out and flipped out of the hammock. "Term," he called out. "Term."

Term came back under the shade. The smell of fried eggs already drifted out the back door.

"Term. I've got an idea."

The giant crossed his arms and tilted his head as if ready to listen.

"I bet—" Sol couldn't believe he was doing this, but it wasn't the same this time as with that dude down the highway. "—I bet we could change that retread order to name-brand tires. Besides, it wouldn't take nearly as long to get new ones. Wouldn't that surprise the little family?" *And look at how it would help them, too.* But Sol couldn't bring himself to say that.

"Surprise them?" Term said.

This time Sol grinned. "Let's do it. Whaddya say?"

Term gave him a thumbs up and ambled back into the sunshine. As he did, Sol could have sworn he heard Term mumble something about Eddie and about progress again.

With new tires on the little red car, Sol and Term said their good-byes, merged onto I-10, and headed east once more. The Fernandez family seemed genuinely sad to see them go.

Little Timoteo cried so pitifully, Sol had to pick him up and console him. Then he told him using the best sign language he could invent to be careful and not climb that tree for a while.

Timoteo eventually dried his tears and nodded. Sol gave him a dollar bill.

When the two sisters' mouths dropped open, he gave them one too. They ran off giggling with Timoteo watching after them.

With the good-byes wrapped up, they set out on the highway.

"Nice ride," Sol said, referring to the tires. "Smooth."

Term had one better. "I liked the way Mr. Fernandez washed your car for you."

Sol was glad he paid the man for that, and yes, Mr. Fernandez had outdone himself. "You know, I'm gonna miss my little buddy, Timoteo."

"Well, you can always stop by and see him on your way back, right?" Term said. "Check in on the family? Take them back some Florida fruit?"

Sol hadn't considered that. What kind of fruit? It certainly wasn't orange season. "Seven hours to San Antonio," Term said. "You want me to drive us through the city?"

Sol nodded, eyebrows up.

The hours flew by. Around Ozona, Texas, Sol began to notice a few shrubby trees. "Finally, some scenery. I'm so tired of the desert."

Term kept his eyes on the landscape and seemed to enjoy it all.

He never did take a nap and didn't have much to say. Sol thought back to little Timoteo and his antics. Then he wondered about Paulette. She hadn't called since before the Fabens' stop. Maybe she'd given up on him.

He wondered how his shop was doing.

One thing was for sure, since Paulette was there with Eddie, his shop was in really good hands.

Eddie. The kid was gonna like his new tires.

But then an idea began to worm its way through Sol's thoughts. Maybe Eddie ought to pay for those new tires.

At the first San Antonio exit sign, Term spoke up. "Nice thing you did for Eddie, getting those new tires. I guess you learned, huh?"

"Learned? Yeah, about retreads." Actually, he'd done what he did, bought those good tires, for Timoteo's mom, for the boy's family. But as for Eddie—Sol turned the situation over in his head. He could get the money back.

San Antonio was coming up. Sol was starving. He pulled over at Leon Springs. "Let's find a steakhouse. Whaddya say, Term?"

"Fine with me."

"Then you can take the wheel."

But Sol didn't like the way his thoughts were turning. He should simply say the tires were for Eddie and forget the repayment. Eddie didn't have that kind of money, anyway.

"I think Paulette would be proud of you," Term said.

Sol frowned at the giant. His thoughts weren't private at all.

As for Paulette—she would have bought Eddie a whole new car.

As Matt escorted Coral back to Aunt Allie's, he stopped beneath the mulberry branches and gathered Coral close. He cradled her head against his chest and rocked her back and forth. "I'm sorry, Coral. I wasn't trying to pressure you. It's just that I…"

He smoothed her hair back and tipped up her face. "I wouldn't do anything to hurt you."

She nodded. "I know that, Matt."

"Back there on the boat, I hurt right along with you. I felt your pain. The betrayal. But I'd never be able to feel it to the depth that you do. I…"

Wordless, she rested her palms against his chest.

"I care, Coral. I care for you so much, and I never want to lose you. I've meant every kiss. Every word." Once again, he stroked her hair, bent, and brushed his lips across hers. "I only want your happiness." He straightened. "This decision, though—it's yours. And I'll honor that. If you want to go home, then home is where I'll take you."

He took her hand as they entered through the gate and stood before the steps. "I'll come back after Zeke and I take care of the boat. Do you want to go inside?"

She shook her head, her eyes downcast and lashes wet. "No, I just want to sit out here and think."

"I understand. And I know you'll come to the right conclusions. And keep this truth in your heart, m'lady," he said, dressing his words now with a light English accent. He lifted her hand to his lips. "Your wish is my command."

Matt prayed all the way back across the bridge. Prayed he didn't lose Coral. Prayed she didn't make a mistake and cut her dad out of her life before she had a chance to see the whole picture.

Three gulls sailed close overhead, laughing like a middle school gang in the hallway.

Just yesterday, Coral had been ready to tell her dad who she was. And now this.

He reached the other end of the bridge and loped across the back of the restaurant around to the boat where he found Zeke sudsing down the decks with a hose and mop.

"You polish the vinyl," Zeke hollered out as Matt leaped on board. Zeke was a fanatic about his boat, and nobody had a more spotless one. Before they finished, every chrome, vinyl, or waxed surface of the *Gulf Princess* would be wiped down and sparkling clean.

They still had a way to go—the galley, the heads, and even the fish cleaning station next to the end of the dock. Details mattered.

Matt's stomach growled. In all the excitement, he'd skipped lunch. Too bad they didn't have a shark today to trade for a free meal at the restaurant. Still, the Captain's Table gave Zeke and his employees a significant discount, and Matt wasn't about to burden Coral's ladies with feeding him every day. He enjoyed standing on his own two feet.

As Matt searched the cupboards for the vinyl cleaner and a rag, Zeke grabbed a towel and stepped his way. He dried his hands on a rag and threw it over his shoulder. "So... Coral's upset?"

"She heard up to the point where Ralph said he gave her mother money for an abortion. And she took off—with me chasing after her."

"Oh, geesh."

"Now she believes he's a murderer. There's got to be more to the story, Zeke."

"You betcha there is." And Zeke explained the man's regrets and immediate change of thought.

Matt continued wiping down the vinyl seats. He needed to wrap the job up and get back to Coral. "So Ralph never expected her to go through w…?"

Zeke interrupted, "He took off upstairs and wanted to make it right the next day. Only too late. She'd already left."

"I doubt if most guys would take charge and own up to their indiscretions."

"Maybe I'd just call it change of heart."

"Yeah."

"He's a man who's punished himself every day for twenty or so years, who mourns over the idea he's killed a baby—and maybe even the mother." Zeke grabbed the towel off his shoulder and wiped his face. "What brought it home to him was something that happened at the restaurant. A woman lost her baby and her life. Apparently, it set him off."

"So, he takes off, half-cocked, in that no-good boat. Sounds self-destructive, like a recipe for disaster."

Zeke scrunched up his face, confirming the thought. "Yeah, he can definitely react."

Matt knelt beside another vinyl seat and gave it a spray of polish.

But Zeke wasn't done. "I never mentioned a word about Coral to him. But I sure wanted to."

Matt looked up. "Yeah, and now I can't tell Coral about him. She won't hear a word. Stalemate."

"I asked him what if the mother just went away and found a life for herself and the baby. You should have seen his face." Zeke snapped his fingers. "Changed like that. Instant sunshine. I guess that possibility never even occurred to him."

Matt raised his eyebrows and returned to his work. "Man, to live all those years thinking you've killed a child."

"To hear him talk, if he just knew the child was alive, it would change his life."

"I hope that happens. But we've got a storm brewing with Coral."

Zeke nodded.

"She gets upset if I even mention it. Calls it pressure. I'm pretty sure she wants to leave town now."

Zeke pressed his lips together in an expression of deep thought.

"Listen, man, I know you're probably thinking I'll walk off the job. Try not to worry," Matt said. "I won't leave you in the lurch— unless I'm forced to. But I don't want to lose my girl. She needs to hear about this change in her dad. I'd hate to see her lose her only living relative."

Zeke gave him the side-eye, "*If* he is her father…"

"Cleared by an attorney."

"Well, maybe he's not the *only* relative."

"What do you mean?"

Zeke shrugged and raised one hand.

Matt stood. "You're saying he's *not* her only living relative?"

Zeke shook his head. "Not exactly. But think about it. For the girl to have been on foot, and the father to have scoured the town, the family had to live somewhere close by. And only Ralph would know."

Matt clutched the spray bottle even tighter.

Sol stood outside the passenger door and picked his teeth after the satisfying steak dinner. He tossed the toothpick to the side and fished out the keys to toss them over the roof to Term. "Your turn now."

They buckled up and took off.

"Sure does handle nice," Term said as he merged back onto I-10. "Take a nap if you like. I'll get us through the city tangle."

Sol suppressed a burp, a thing Paulette would have frowned upon. "A steak dinner under the belt. Trees to left and right, and another driver at the wheel. What more could a man ask for?" He lowered the back of his seat and closed his eyes.

"Too bad, you'll miss all the good scenery."

"*Pfft*," Sol said, his eyes still shut.

Three and half hours later, Term jabbed Sol's shoulder. "Wake up, Sol."

He cracked his lids open. While he'd slept, dusk had settled over the landscape, and their car was now parked at an all-night truck stop. He raised his seat. "Where is this?"

"East of Houston, it's called Cove, Texas."

The two climbed out and stretched. A truck stop meant a hot shower. Hot water for once. Man, was Sol ready for that. He reached into the trunk and found a new set of clothes. This time he picked the shirt Paulette had given him, a blue and white Hawaiian button-up. "In honor of you, honey," he mumbled.

Maybe she'd call him again.

Term still had on that same old yellow palm tree and surfboard shirt. Though he didn't smell stale, Sol was beginning to feel bad about his friend's limited wardrobe. "You know, you could get your-self some kind of souvenir tee shirt in there. They've got all kinds. Might find one that says something smart like *Remember the Alamo*."

"This bothering you?" Term said, pulling the fabric away from his chest. "Then I'll check out the shop.'

"Fine," Sol said. "You're 'bout to wear that one out."

Term turned left into the gift shop, and Sol headed right into the showers.

On the way out, he met Term going in with a coffee in one hand and a shopping bag in the other.

Eventually Term re-appeared. "Well, what do you think?"

He wore a crisp red, white, and blue button-up with a big Texas star on one side of his chest. The man seemed even larger than before.

"Nice shirt."

Term tossed Sol a spiral-bound book of state maps. "Stick that in your suitcase, you might need it one day."

Sol caught it in midair. "An atlas? Thanks." He tucked it under his arm.

"Let's go stretch our legs a little," Term said and pushed open the door.

What might have been a good stroll turned into a rapid walk around the outer edge of the complex. Mosquitoes buzzed around Sol's ears and landed on his arms, and Sol swatted them away. Term didn't seem bothered, but Sol couldn't tolerate it. Before long he tossed his cup and headed back to the vehicle. He swung in fast on the passenger side.

Term followed and once again took the driver's side.

"This is the longest dadgum drive I ever want to take," Sol said, settling back into the seat and checking the window to see that it was up with no cracks. "This is going to be one hot night. I wish I could just snap my fingers and be there."

"Well," Term said, "you could fly next time. It's much quicker."

Sol scratched at a bite and shook his head. "Never. Scares me to death."

Term placed his hands on the wheel. "Want me to keep driving?"

Sol couldn't believe his ears. This made Term even more worthwhile having around. "Absolutely. As long as you're not tired. Just make sure you don't go running off the road."

Term waved that thought away.

As they headed back onto the highway, Sol blurted out, "You know, I don't really have friends. But I might just miss you when you're gone."

After supper, while Grandma Rosella and Aunt Allie finished off their blueberry pie, I ran some dishwater and collected the dishes.

"You're tired, Coral," Grandma Rosella said. "Why not rest?"

I gazed into the bubbles. It wasn't that I was so tired. But I must have looked that way after today's disappointment on the boat and me acting like a crybaby. I felt like burnt toast.

But I hadn't let on about it to the ladies. No need to drag them into the situation. My brain hadn't even sorted things out.

"It's just a few dishes, and I don't want them staring at me later." I plunged my hands into the water and turned back to Aunt Allie. "I bet you're chomping at the bit to put those new glasses to the test." They'd planned an after-dinner game of rummy.

While I was out on the water this morning, Jessica had taken her and Grandma up to Crawfordville to pick up Allie's new eyeglasses. They had lunch out, ice cream, and topped it off with fabric shopping. A big day.

This coast was full of good-hearted people, and I counted it a blessing that Jessica's job was so flexible.

At the stove, I scooped a big helping of shepherd's pie onto Jessica's plate to save for when she came in later.

I glanced down at the two women. "Grandma, you and Aunt Allie act like two kids these days."

Aunt Allie pushed her empty plate aside and took her former husband's aged deck of cards from the middle of the table. She and Grandma grinned at each other like two schoolgirls.

"You deal, Rosella," Aunt Allie said. She slapped the deck of cards down in front of Grandma and leaned forward on her elbows, shifting like a cat about to pounce.

Who would have thought?

A single low-hanging bulb illuminated the two of them.

Grandma shoved her own dish aside and snatched up the deck, riffle-shuffling like a gambling pro. *Psing, psing, psing,* she tossed out cards like a casino mama. Wow. Her old Las Vegas life had carved out some edges I'd never been privy to until tonight. I tried to imagine her dressed in one of her old feather boas in a cloud of smoke, but her pink flannel gown and that braid around her head painted a different picture.

"You two…" I said as I covered Jessica's supper. "I'm heading outside to the porch.

"Have a good time," Aunt Allie said without looking up.

I held back a laugh.

There was no getting over Grandma's newfound energy—or Aunt Allie's either, with those new lenses. All thanks to Jessica. And God, of course. But Jessica and Aunt Allie were literal answers to prayer.

For now, though, I needed some solitude, and with them busy, I could head back outside for some quiet time. I wanted to rock, listen to the birds, and watch the last bits of color disappear from town—at least the narrow section I could see from the rocking chair—and think.

That's when Matt strode around the corner of the building. So handsome, even in his work clothes. I smiled, and then Zeke showed up a few yards behind. Oh, dear, a team. Zeke did not live on this side of the bridge. And he never came over after work.

When Matt had walked me home a little while ago, he'd been so—apologetic about pressuring me.

But Zeke, I wasn't sure what he'd come down here for.

Fresh from cleaning the boat, their wet tee shirts clung tight. They had to be cold and tired, but judging from their movements, they seemed a bit more animated than before. Clearly, they had something on their mind, I could tell by the way they pulled the rockers around on either side of me and sat down.

"Hi, Coral, how are you?" They said it together like two up-to-no-good boys.

"Oh, come on, guys. What?" I turned from Zeke and stared at Matt.

He shrugged and did that zipper-lip thing with throwing away the key and looked over at Zeke.

"Listen," Zeke spoke up. "I've got to get home to the family but wanted to stop over a minute to do a public service."

I couldn't imagine a more maddening or laughable scene.

"Do tell," I said. "I'm wallowing in the mully grubbs, and I don't feel like being pushed or pestered right now. So don't start."

Matt shrugged and stared at the ceiling.

Zeke opened his mouth. "We know things. I mean, I know things. Things that would change your mind."

Yeah. Nothing would change my mind about Ralph.

I turned to Matt. His lips clamped together so hard his dimples showed, and he nodded.

"We know things that would make you very happy," Zeke said.

Matt raised his eyebrows and nodded even more vigorously. Good for him. He'd kept his promise. However, this could still be classified as pressure.

"Well," I said, gripping the arms of the rocker. "I appreciate your kind and sympathetic public service announcement, guys. But you can stop."

It was time for me to call it quits here and go back home to Fort Myers. To forget I ever knew Ralph and get my life back to normal.

"I'm really sorry to disappoint you," I told them. "But this little—whatever you're doing—is not going to work."

Sol leaned back against the seat as Term pressed the gas pedal and sped them east toward Florida and their ultimate destination of Fort Myers.

Sol's destination, at least. He had no idea where in the heck Term planned to get off the ride.

When Sol had mentioned he might miss old Term when he was gone, Term had only returned a smile.

He wondered what that meant and figured Term probably wouldn't miss him. This problem car—all their burdens and delays—he couldn't blame the guy.

Since Sol's friend comment, despite the tires having devoured the miles, his words about missing Term still hung in the air. Sol's thoughts began to wander, and he pondered his next step—getting that executorship changed over to him before his mom died.

Then there was Paulette. He crossed his arms over the blue and white shirt she had once gifted him—a thing he kept in the closet, and had only worn about twice in the five years since she'd left.

Now that she'd called—he'd never even considered her coming back—he was glad he had it with him. Back at the truck stop he'd chosen it on purpose.

Paulette.

He did miss her. He did. But he didn't know how to fix it.

What change was she looking for?

He closed his eyes as the rumble of the highway worked its lullaby.

As he drifted off, he wondered if maybe it was already too late to fix things and whether Paulette was right, if maybe he was selfish.

Sol eased his eyes open and squinted at the bright morning sun that now blared through the windshield. Hours had passed. He caught sight of the new landscape flying by and sat up. Trees. Yeah. Real ones. Finally.

"Welcome back to the world," Term said.

"Did I snore much?"

Term laughed.

By the look in the giant's eyes, the bright look to his face, the man wasn't even tired. The giant still didn't need a shave. Sol felt his own stubble. Time to tend to it.

"You snored like a chain saw. All night long."

"Hah. Where are we?"

"Tallahassee exit's coming right up," Term said. "Ready for some fast-food breakfast? Then you can take a turn driving."

Tallahassee, yes! Sol's bladder was about to burst. "Find us a Burger King. They've got that two-for-five thing going."

Term nodded.

Sol waved an arm at the scenery. "Look at those trees," he said. "I never thought I'd be so glad to see trees."

"Need me to stop at one?"

"Very funny."

Term grinned. "Back in Texas you said you don't really have friends," he said.

"Not many. People don't really warm up to me."

"You mean like little Timoteo?"

"Ah, c'mon. That was just the bald spot. He thought I was his grandpa or something."

Another mile passed as Term located the exit, negotiated a few turns, and pulled into a BK parking lot. He turned off the motor and opened his door. But he didn't get out.

Sol cracked open his own door.

"Not sure why you think that's true," Term said. "Because back there and at Aunt Susie's you made the beginnings of several friendships.

"Oh, sure, I gave out some money. Bought a few friends."

"Nah," Term shook his head. "You know friendships don't work that way."

Sol stared at the giant. How could he say that? Money greased the wheels.

Term stepped out of the car but leaned his head back in. "The fact is, you cared. Both times."

"But…"

Term slammed the door and gazed over the roof as Sol stepped out. "And how did that feel?"

That crazy question again. Sol shrugged. It had felt good. But he wasn't going to just come out and say it.

"So, on your way back home, stop by those two places and check on how the families are doing. Check on that broken leg of Timoteo's. It's not the money. Yes, you could take a small gift. Something they might enjoy. Make it your business to care. That's the secret."

Sol wrinkled his brow.

Caring.

"Oh, and one more thing," Term said. "Don't even try to fake it. Make it real."

Care. Sol pondered the meaning of the word as they crossed the parking lot and pulled open the glass door.

How did one care?

After Matt and Zeke left me, I rocked on the porch a while more. Then I picked up my phone and searched for Peter in my contacts and dialed him up.

"Hello?" Peter's voice sounded unusually drowsy.

"I didn't wake you, did I?" It wasn't so late, but it wasn't early, either.

"Hard week, Coral. I was resting."

Peter, the man who always came through for me. "I'm so sorry. Is your family okay?"

"All fine."

"Why don't I call another time?"

"Go ahead. Spill it. You wouldn't have called if it wasn't important. I can get back to sleep."

"Oh, Peter. I am sorry. You said to call." Such bad timing.

"Everything okay?"

I paused on my end.

"Out with it. Something's wrong with Ralph? You don't like him? What did you find out?"

"Bad time to explain it all, but I was hoping to beg a ride home. Matt's tied up for a while."

Another pause. For a minute I thought Peter had fallen asleep.

"I could book a flight for you."

"No, no. Not that. I knew this was a bad time."

"I'd be more than happy to leave right now, but we've got a parade of witnesses this week. And I can't leave."

Peter, who like some kind of human angel had always been there for me, could not come. It was time to recognize he wasn't so supernatural.

I knew how things worked in the courtroom, and the last time Peter came up here, it had been a special favor at the beginning of the trial. I couldn't expect him to pull that twice, no matter what he'd promised.

I wished his feet weren't clay, but they were, just like everyone else's.

"I'll be all right. You get back to sleep."

He mumbled something about no trouble at all.

"And don't you worry," I told him. "It's not an emergency."

I clicked the red button and dropped the phone in my lap.

Not an emergency. No, but here I was stuck in the same town with a father who wanted nothing to do with his own child. An attempted murderer.

Ans Sol and Term finished up their Burger King breakfast in Tallahassee, Sol reached out his hand for the keys. "Thanks for driving all night, Term. But now it's time for me to take a turn and let you get some rest."

Term grinned. "Nice of you to offer," he said and climbed in on the passenger side. "I think I'll take you up on that."

Sol turned the key and put the car in reverse, glad the car Eddie had loaned him was an automatic. He looked over at Term. "Now, when I was a teenager, I drove a stick. Everybody did. I bet not one percent of today's teens could do that. Not if their life depended on it."

"My red Jeep was a stick shift."

Sol swung the car back and to the right. He wanted to get this show on the road.

Term extended a hand. "Be careful backing out, I saw some…"

"Yeah, whatever happened to that…"

Cruuuuuunch! Sol stomped the brake as soon as he heard it and craned his neck toward the right rear to see what they'd hit. But all he could see were lush green limbs of the adjoining woods.

He put the vehicle in park and hopped out, leaving the door hanging open. He circled around behind the trunk.

Term squeezed out too, but had little room.

Sol paused at the right rear tire, where a fat post—part of a low row of railroad ties—had his right rear fender pinned against one of his brand-new tires. His car wouldn't be going anywhere like this. He gave the post a good swift kick and let out a curse word.

"Dadgummit, Term. Why didn't you warn me?"

Term shook his head.

"Don't just stand there. Help me straighten this thing out."

"Better drive forward," Term said.

Once the car was clear of the post, he and Term pulled the fender away from the tire.

"See," Sol said. "No problem. Eddie will never know the difference." Besides, it wasn't Sol's car. It was Eddie's.

Term studied the sadly warped panel and the triangular gouge left by the impact. "Sol, I don't think Eddie could miss this. You think he's going to feel good about it?"

"I don't ca…." Sol took a few deep breaths, strode across to the landscaped area by the door, picked up a large smooth river rock and came back over. He'd already spent enough money on that new set of tires. "Gimme a minute. I can beat it back into shape."

When he finished the panel looked worse than before. Sol chucked the rock into the woods. "Forget it. Let's just go." Back in the driver's seat, he turned the key and got them back to the ramp for I-10.

The next time he looked over at Term, he caught him biting his cheeks to keep from laughing.

"Oh, stop that grinning. I'm tired of it now."

Term remained silent and turned away to watch the city of Tallahassee pass by on the way to I-75.

Sol insisted on having the last word. "Look at the bright side. It still runs. Right? We didn't hit a car. We didn't hit a person. Eddie ought to be happy about that, shouldn't he?"

Sol focused on merging into traffic while getting a look at the city of Tallahassee they were passing through. He glanced across at Term who hadn't said a thing since the last exit. "You think my car insurance would cover this little boo-boo?"

"Eddie's should."

Sol pulled his chin in. "I can't tell Eddie I messed up his car."

Term shrugged his shoulder. "You could get some body work, get the panel painted. But of course, by painting just one panel, it probably would never look the same."

Sol started to remind Term it wasn't his car, but at this point, that was beginning to sound pretty stupid. Hadn't he just about said he didn't care?

"What would you expect of someone who borrowed your own son's car and banged it up?" Term said. "Do unto others as you'd have them do unto you."

They passed another exit.

Only three exits in Tallahassee, and the next was Sol's last chance.

Sol thought back to Term's question about whether Eddie would feel good about this. Of course, dadgummit, he wouldn't feel good about it. Not the way Eddie kept his car cleaned and polished like a new penny.

And then, like Paulette said, Sol *had* bullied the kid. Eddie'd given in to the pressure and let Sol drive away in his car.

Against his will.

Eddie cared as much about his old car as Sol cared about his Mercedes.

And there Sol was, blurting out, "I don't care." Now that Sol thought about it, he could reflect back and hear his mother saying, "Don't be ugly, Sol."

Sol did care. He didn't want to see Eddie hurt.

He'd treated the kid as a chump, but now he was starting to see him as a champ. He'd always been able to trust Eddie. And now here he was trying to hold down the fort, even before Paulette showed up. And all for Sol.

He pulled off at the third exit.

Sol and Term parked in a gas station parking lot and used Sol's phone to research auto-painting shops in Tallahassee. Sol turned the screen toward Term and pointed out a listing. "Here's the cheapest one in town, and fast," Sol said.

Term crossed his arms, took a look, but didn't comment.

Sol pulled the phone back. "But I've seen their jobs. They don't last. Put the car out in that Las Vegas sun, and Eddie'll be painting it again in a coupla years," Sol said.

Sol pointed to another listing. "Five stars here. Let's find out what a paint job should cost and get a clear picture." They spent an hour studying the various reviews and cost expectations and then called around to find an opening.

They settled on one nearby who offered a medium grade paint job. "At least it'll last," Sol said.

"But what will you do for three days?"

"One day's drive and we could be in Fort Myers. I'm not sitting around in Tallahassee for three," Sol said.

Term agreed.

"Let's set it up and go find ourselves a Greyhound Bus."

The next morning, I sat out on Aunt Allie's porch once again. My favorite spot. Breakfast dishes were all done. Matt was out on the boat, and Aunt Allie and Grandma were out back in the chicken yard planning a flower garden. Grandma had made it down the steps holding the rail this time, but she agreed to use her walker out in the yard.

They'd been out there a little while when Millie stopped by before work. She stepped up and plopped down in a rocker. "Mornin', Sandy. Good to see you." Up to now she'd been somewhat aloof around me, but today she acted like an old friend.

"Mornin'. You're awful chipper today. What's up?" I said.

"Just stoppin' by," she said. "Did you see what all they brought home from Crawfordville—all that cloth?"

"They told me they bought some, but I never saw it," I said. "Guess we got busy."

"Oh, my, honey. Have they got plans!"

"Yeah?"

"Well, now that Aunt Allie can thread a needle… Let's see. They've got voile and eyelet for her new bedroom curtains…"

I started to say something, but she kept right on going.

"There's bright yellow gingham for the kitchen cupboards, something pretty for Aunt Allie's bedspread. That was your grandma's idea, Jessica's too…"

I opened my mouth again, and she added more. "Oh, yeah. Them two's a team. Then Aunt Allie thought they should all make look-alike flannel nightgowns."

"Goodness gracious," I said. "And they're out back right now planning a garden."

Millie practically squealed. "Oooeee!" She tapped her fingers on my knee. "I can't wait to see what them two come up with. They're like two peas in a pod, and that Jessica ain't far behind."

"Where'll they find time and energy to do all that?" I wondered aloud.

"You know that Jessica's a natural with that antique sewing machine. Ain't even electric."

I nodded.

She stood as if mission accomplished. "Well, let me get goin'. It's time to wait tables. Ralph's back you know. Just needed an IV. But that sunburn, now—I ain't lettin''im work too hard. He's red as a beet. He'll live, though. You take care, honey, and tell 'em all I said hey when they get back up—and bye all at the same time."

What a chatterbox. I'd never seen Millie so happy.

To tell the truth, I wondered how it would affect Grandma—and Aunt Allie—if I turned around and left right now.

That evening, Matt came down to Aunt Allie's after eating with Zeke at the Captain's Table. Another shark caught today. The boatful of guests wore him out today, and he ended up with a big batch of fish to clean. Late or not, I was glad to see him walk through the gate.

"C'mon around here," he said and reached out his hand. I took it, and he led me down the steps and around back near the chicken pen. The chickens clucked and fussed, but he ignored them. When we were out of sight of the windows, he turned me around and leaned me against the chicken pen for the biggest, warmest kiss yet. He came up for air. "I've been waiting for that," he said and then gave me another. He pulled me close and wrapped his arms around me, squeezing me and rocking me back and forth. "I've missed you so bad."

I smiled against his hard sweaty chest. "I've missed you too, Matt," I whispered. "All day long."

"Come spend another day on the boat with me."

I nodded, and he took me by the hand and walked me over to the light pole in the middle of the yard.

"Have a seat," he said, finding a seat for us on some nice soft grass. "I hate having to be so quiet up on the porch."

I sat beside him and leaned against the pole.

"First, tell me how Grandma is doing. I know she's improving."

"I've never seen her so happy," I said. "It's like a light switch has turned on. She's…she's…"

"Planting a garden, Millie says."

I swatted him on the knee. "You already know everything. I forgot about Millie. She stopped by here this morning talking ninety to nothing, and I didn't even get a word in. Told me all about the big fabric-store shopping spree. Did she tell you that, too?"

He nodded. "Grandma's not overdoing it, is she?"

"They sewed today, but tomorrow I'm taking them on a little picnic at the beach. Jessica's going to meet us."

"Jessica's a good kid."

"I won't let Grandma get too tired out. She does pace herself, you know."

He nodded, plucked a white wildflower and tucked it behind my ear, a serious look on his face. I could tell he had something on his mind.

"So." He allowed a long pause to follow.

I waited.

"Peter called me today," he said. "On break. That's quite a trial he's in the middle of."

I nodded, wondering what they had said.

"I told him, Coral. Told him all about what happened."

I picked a long blade of Bahia grass and twisted it around my finger.

"He told me you called. Wanted to go."

Tears formed in my eyes.

Matt took my chin and turned me toward him. "Don't go, Coral. Don't leave."

His gentle brown eyes searched mine. Were those the beginning of tears in his eyes, too? I took a shaky breath and hung my head to stare at my knees.

"I'll try," I said. "But no promises."

I stood at the kitchen table and finished laying out the turkey and cheese on our bread and closing them up. "Grandma, Aunt Allie, y'all are going to be all worn out before we get to our picnic," I said.

They were in the next room laying out fabric on the table, cutting, and pressing seams. Grandma stuck in another pin. "Oh, we're not sewing. We were just killing time while you finish up the picnic."

I laughed and packed the sandwiches in the cooler.

This time, Grandma descended the steps by herself. With me at the ready, of course, And somehow Aunt Allie squeezed into the backseat. Jessica planned to meet us there.

We headed west over the bridge, and I made a determined effort not to look over at the restaurant.

I never wanted to see that man again.

Down at the beach, tossed and buffeted by the breeze, we located a good table—there were plenty—a whole string of tables with turquoise-painted supports and roofing.

I'd barely gotten the ladies situated on opposite sides of the picnic table when Jessica pulled up in her little car and raced over to help me with the cooler.

"We've got to get a picture of this," I practically yelled over the wind. Jessica laughed and nodded.

There was no laying out supplies on the table, the wind wouldn't allow it, so, grinning and still just as happy, we ate straight from the cooler.

Jessica and I took turns taking shots of the small group, and selfies as well.

I pulled out my phone and studied the pictures, Grandma in her aqua-flowered hat—and same colored dress this time—and Aunt Allie in her blue—with the matching ocean behind. A picture worth framing.

But what struck me was their faces, so full of life, so full of joy.

Grandma had come so far, and so fast—and yet knew nothing of my bad news.

To tell her about my father would deflate her.

For now, I'd just have to keep it to myself.

When Sol got off the bus with Term in Fort Myers, it was the middle of the night. His Burger King breakfast had long since worn off, and Sol was starving. Term, though, had not complained.

They waited outside while the driver opened the outside hatches and pulled out the suitcases.

Sol showed the fellow his ticket and retrieved his lightweight bag. He stepped away with it. Part of his stuff had stayed in the red vehicle, but not the map. He'd brought it along. "Well, Term, what do you want to do? We could sit here all night at the bus station or go walking."

With the giant at his side, Sol had no qualms about being out at this ridiculous hour.

"You said you were hungry," Term said. "Let's find something good to eat."

At this hour they'd probably have to settle for a bar. "Lead the way," Sol said.

Term turned left, and Sol followed.

"What we really need to do," Sol said, "is cross back over that bridge and get back to North Fort Myers. That's where the lawyer's office is. Mom won't be at home, you know."

Term led the way across an intersection. "Do you know what hospital she's in?"

Sol stared at him. All this hullabaloo, and he'd not even thought about visiting his mom. Or calling. Hadn't done squat to check on her. What a jerk he was. All he'd thought about was that executorship thing.

Term pointed to the phone in Sol's pocket. Sol had given it a full charge on the bus. "Call around, maybe we can drop in on her."

Instead of a noisy bar, they discovered a Waffle House. They found a secluded spot in the back where Sol could make his calls.

He took out his phone and researched hospitals in Fort Myers, jotting down the numbers on a napkin. Then he set to work, one call after another. He hardly noticed when his food came, just kept calling and checking for the patient Rosella Flores.

But not one facility had her listed.

"She wouldn't be in some other town, I'm sure of that," he said. "She'd stay close. All her friends are here."

Friends. His mom had a gazillion of them.

Sol turned off the phone and set it down beside his plate of cold, stiff waffles.

"I don't know who else to call," he said.

"Don't beat yourself up. We'll find out more in the morning."

Sol ate but hardly tasted his food. His shoulders drooped. "What if I'm too late?"

"I know it's bothering you. But let's just wait until tomorrow." Once Sol finished, Term gathered up their clutter and tidied up. "We'd better get going if we're walking across the bridge tonight." He twisted around for a good look at the nearly empty restaurant. The cook was scrubbing up for the night. "The note on the menu said they close at midnight."

According to directions on Sol's phone it was only about three miles to get across the bridge. They could find a park bench to sleep on or some other place to hang out. It felt weird not having a car to climb into.

At least the bridge was well-lit. Term led the way along its narrow sidewalk, and they walked in single file.

Sol, unable to see around the giant, kept his eyes trained on the man's heels. The walk gave him plenty of time to think back to his last conversation with his mother, and the one before that, and the one before that, all riddled with his abusive language and bad attitude.

Mom was always sweet and never dished back to him what he deserved.

A knot formed in his chest.
He had no doubt she'd forgive him.
But at this point it might be too late to set things straight.

I sat up on the porch with Grandma and Aunt Allie. Millie stopped by on her way to work the next morning. "Come on up," I said. "Sit a spell. Aunt Allie and Grandma are sitting here drawing out their plans."

Millie stepped up and dragged over a chair, the squeaky one from the corner. "Show me what you have."

Aunt Allie handed over the notebook.

Millie nodded and studied the drawings. "Your vegetable garden?"

"Yes, but the weather's too hot right now. We'll have to wait till the fall," Aunt Allie said.

I sucked in a breath. Fall?

Aunt Allie turned to Grandma. "Rosella, I just realized. We won't be able to put our garden up against the house. That's the north side. No sun. We're going to have to put it past the chickens and find them a new area. Don't you think?"

Our garden? Oh, dear.

The more these two talked, the more ideas they came up with.

All I could think about was how our stay was growing longer by the day. *Wait till fall?* We'd be here forever. Trapped in a town with my father.

Millie smiled. "Those new lenses have done wonders for you, haven't they?"

"I've talked Allie into putting in raised beds with a watering system," Grandma said. She turned and patted my knee, "And we know just who can put that in, don't we?"

I offered a smile I certainly didn't feel. Now they were dragging Matt into it.

"Well," Millie said, handing back the notebook, "Miss Rosella, it looks like Aunt Allie is rubbing off on you."

"Oh, I love this lady like my long-lost sister. But no, she's not so much rubbing off on me, as I'm getting my old self back."

I nodded. Grandma was right. That old sparkle had returned. This was the woman I'd spent the last eight years with.

"Well, I just love all these ideas," Millie said. "But I'd better get along to work."

As she climbed down the steps, the very ones Grandma Rosella had ascended by herself yesterday after our picnic, she turned back to Aunt Allie. "I'd like to help out in your garden if you don't mind. I love that kind of thing."

"Anytime, Millie. Anytime," Aunt Allie said. "Bye, honey, and tell your Ralph to come down here too. Have a good day at work, now."

As Millie disappeared around the corner by the mulberry tree, Grandma Rosella turned to Aunt Allie, "We should all go down to Ralph's restaurant and have a meal together."

My insides wanted to scream, *No! Not that!*

But Aunt Allie had a quick answer. "No, I'm not going to do that, Rosella. But thank you anyway."

"No?" Grandma looked confused, and I wondered as well.

"I want Ralph to come to me."

Nobody spoke.

"See, I loved that boy like my own son. But something happened to Ralph. I don't know what. Whether it was the Army itself or his dad dying before he got out, or what. Ralph just stopped coming around. Never showed up again. Ralph stopped being himself. And I want him to know I still love him. But I'm not going to chase him down."

Grandma nodded.

But Aunt Allie wasn't done. "And if he thinks bringing those vegetables every week clears things up, he has another think coming."

Aunt Allie was no dummy.

But if I told her what I knew, it would break her heart.

It sure broke mine.

B efore lunch I found sewing equipment and fabric strewn all over the dining room. Grandma's and Aunt Allie's happy voices drifted into the kitchen where I opened cupboards and set about to make a peach cobbler from scratch.

It wasn't that I didn't enjoy sewing, but I didn't want to barge in and spoil their projects.

Grandma's happiness reminded me of how she used to be before Grandpa Eduardo passed away. Somewhere along the way, routines had taken over and that old personality had faded away. I'd almost forgotten the way she used to be.

She and Aunt Allie dove into their creative activities exactly like she said, like two long-lost sisters. Even last night she'd said to me, "You and Matt have been taking such good care of me. It's time you two spent some time together—like that day on the boat. Go walk on the beach. See the museum. Enjoy your stay. And don't worry about Aunt Allie and me. We are just fine."

She was giving me wings but shooing me away in part. "We plan on it, Grandma. But I didn't want to just desert you."

"You're not leaving anybody behind."

Well, I guess so then. After today I wouldn't worry again.

Just this morning I'd read that verse in the Bible about the joy of the Lord being our strength. And from what I could see, it was true. She was getting them both her joy and her strength back.

Truth was, I could spend all the time in the world out on that boat with Matt—and away from Mr. You-know-who. I'd get as tan as a coconut and catch the biggest and most fish of all.

There were plenty of ways to stay away from Ralph.

Within a few days, Zeke had an appointment out of town, and Matt had a day off. We visited the town's three museums and then by late afternoon headed back to Aunt Allie's to pack sandwiches for the beach.

While I made them, Matt spent time catching up with Grandma and Aunt Allie. They kept right on sewing as they chattered away. Jessica would be coming home soon to fix supper. Then there was the new Bible study, and Millie with all she was doing. They told of their gardening plans, the watering system they wanted him to put in, and the sewing projects. Between them they hardly took a breath.

When he returned to the kitchen, he chuckled at how changed Grandma was.

I put the lid on the cooler and he lifted it to his shoulder as we headed to the car.

"You're right about her," he said. "It's like a miracle. I can't believe all this stuff they're doing. Instead of being tired, they're all energized."

"I know. I know. I've been telling you."

Before long we were headed toward the beach as per Grandma's instructions.

The sun was turning gold when we dropped our shoes along the dunes, and Matt took my hand in his. We laid a trail of bare footprints in the warm wet sand as sudsy waves followed behind and washed them smooth again.

Very few shells littered the hard-packed shore. I suppose it would be different after a storm, but other shells, alive with leggy creatures, bobbed and scuttled beneath the amber waters. Still, I wanted to find a few to take home. We did collect a fistful, and I carried them along, though the breeze kept blowing my sun hat, and I had to hold it down at the same time.

Sandpipers, as if to keep us company, raced along ahead of us pecking here and there between the gentle waves and then fleeing as we closed in.

My sundress clung to my legs.

"There's always a breeze at the beach, but this one makes me think rain is coming," Matt said.

"But what about the clouds," I said. "There aren't any."

We paused there, and he studied the western sky, his tan face amber in the sun's waning rays. "We'll see by tonight. It just feels like rain, don't you think?"

I nodded, and he took me by the shoulders, "Coral. I know you don't want to be here right now. And I know you haven't asked me to help you get home because of Zeke. But would you like me to take you home? To Ft. Myers?"

I started to open my mouth.

"I could take a day or so off, run you down there. And come right back."

"Oh, no," I shifted the shells to my other hand. Wiped the sand on my skirt. "I can't have you do that."

Matt let out a long breath and then gave me a look that said, *Oh, come on, now.* He studied my eyes. "What about your call to Peter?"

It was my turn to let out a hard breath. "That—that was just a stupid impulse. And I'm glad it didn't pan out."

He brightened. "You've changed your mind?"

I tipped my head sideways and shook my head. "I didn't say that. Look, you've got obligations. To Zeke. To Millie. To Aunt Allie— those porch chairs—and now Grandma *and* Aunt Allie want that watering system. This is going to take a while."

"I'm sorry, Coral. I've made a mess of things, haven't I?"

"You—you've got to keep your word is all."

"But is that all?"

"Well, I was thinking—Ft. Myers would be pretty dreadful

without you and Grandma. And she's not about to leave here right now. She's having too much fun."

He took both my hands. "Is that it?"

The breeze caught the brim of my hat and flopped it across my face. Matt folded it back and looked deep into my eyes.

I still had no answer.

"Well?" he said, still searching.

I closed my eyes. Time to let it out. "I don't want to spend that time away from you."

I opened my eyes to meet that beautiful smile of his. He swept me up in his big strong arms and twirled me around. "That's what I was hoping you'd say. And I don't want to spend the time away from you. Ever."

My shells trickled to the ground as he gathered me into a kiss that matched a thousand setting suns.

S ol and Term spent their night on benches, the ones in front of an ice cream shop, and fairly close to the same law office Sol planned to visit. When the sun came up, they found a large tourist-centered gas station where they could clean up and change clothes.

But when Term came out in his red, white, and blue shirt, Sol shook his head. "You gotta get another shirt, Term. This is Florida, not Texas. That star's way out of place." Sol's own shirt was now a blazing orange with stripes of pink hibiscus. More like Hawaii, but very suitable for Florida.

Term laughed and headed back into the gift shop. "I'll see what I can find."

When he came back out, Sol nodded. Term wore a white tee with a palm, a sunset, and the words Ft. Myers printed across the bottom. And the way it accentuated his massive chest and biceps, he struck Sol as even more like the Terminator.

"Much better. Glad they had your size."

Eight o'clock arrived quickly. "This is when they open," Sol said, "the law office. And that lawyer, Peter Cordero, he should be there." Sol had good reason not to call ahead.

A short walk took them past the park and to the front of the antique law office with its tall rock staircase and colossal glass doors.

Sol stashed his suitcase under the hedges and then climbed a few steps. But Term stayed put. Sol turned. "You comin' or not?"

Term rested a hand on the brass banister. "Here's where I'm going to have to say good-bye, Sol. You won't be seeing me now. At least for a long time."

Sol took a step down to the bottom of the stairs. He couldn't believe his ears. "You—you're leavin'?"

Term nodded, gave him a sad smile. "You're going to be fine."

Tears burned in Sol's eyes, but he didn't let them out. A thickness filled his throat. "I—I hate to hear it. This is so—sudden. Why didn't you say something before?"

"I've enjoyed the trip, Sol. Thank you very much. For all of it. But you're going to be fine. Just fine." He handed Sol a wad of money. "A little something for gas."

"Fine? I'm—" Sol stuffed the wad in his pocket. He could hardly get the words out, his throat was so choked. "I'll sure miss you, buddy. You've been good company."

Term patted him on the shoulder. "And I'll miss you, too. Just think back to our conversations. Remember the new friends you've met along the way. And remember to care."

Sol started to hug the giant but shook his hand instead. He watched, mesmerized as Term strode east along the sidewalk then south. He turned and waved good-bye before disappearing past the building's tall shrubbery.

Sol gripped the banister and then dragged himself up into the foyer where he plopped into a chair, pulled out the wad of money, and flung it into the corner. He leaned over with his hands clasped between his knees, and stayed that way for a long time.

Matt brought the picnic over to the dunes where he and Coral had tossed their sandals and spread out a beach towel. There was hardly anyone on the beach right now, just a gent far down the shore frolicking with his over-sized poodle-mix, and the ever-present ocean birds, suddenly more interested in Matt and Coral's company than before.

They clustered when Matt threw them a handful of corn chips.

"Oh, now they'll bring their cousins," Coral said and laughed as she laid out their sandwiches and poured the tea.

The birds came close, and he shooed them away. "Yeah, maybe I should have thought that through."

He gazed at the sunset's salmon hue as it played across Coral's smooth skin and yellow sundress. "You are so beautiful," he whispered.

She glanced up from the tea pitcher and smiled, blushing. "Thank you."

"I heard once in a particular culture that if a person thanks you for a compliment, it means they know it isn't sincere."

She stared at him. "Then how can a person be polite?"

He shrugged. "You're welcome. But it's true—a sincere compliment."

She gave him a sideways smile and sipped her tea, the wind whipping strands of her hair. Everything about her pleased him.

"But it's who you are," Matt said. "You're so—so down to earth. So—oh, I just can't put my finger on it. You're a lot like Grandma."

"All right, now…"

"Her attributes, Coral, her ways."

"She's a beautiful person, and I thank you for that."

They ate in silence for a while, she thinking her own thoughts, and smiling when she glanced up and caught him staring at her—which he couldn't help. She was like an angel. He wanted to memorize the vision in front of him.

Matt finished off his sandwich and swatted his arm. "Good thing for this breeze or these little buggers would carry us off."

The sunset dimmed, and Coral swatted her leg. "It does feel like rain. Look, there at the clouds."

Matt turned. Purple clouds almost hid the sunset. It would be gone in short order. "Ready to go?"

She stood and began packing up.

He pulled up the beach towel and gave it a brisk shaking before rolling it up. "Coral, I just want to run something by you. Do you mind?"

She tipped her chin, interested.

He handed her the rolled-up towel. "Could you at least allow me tell you what Zeke said?"

Coral shook her head, immediately dismissing his efforts. "I'm okay with staying in town a little longer. But I'm done with Ralph. It's a closed book."

She turned and headed back to the car. He grabbed the cooler and both pairs of shoes and rushed to catch up. "But there's more you don't know. Important things. Things that could change your mind."

She swatted the air and climbed in the car. "How could there be? No, I don't want to hear it. At least not today."

Matt kept his mouth shut as he started the engine. He didn't want to ruin a lovely evening. If he hadn't already.

Well, he'd learned one more thing about Coral today.

She was also just as stubborn as Grandma.

At the lawyer's office, Sol stood. He glanced at the money he'd flung down, and thought better of it. He gathered it up and stuffed it back in his pocket. That lawyer wasn't getting it, for sure.

When Sol finally rounded the foyer partition and introduced himself to the receptionist, she leaped up in search of Peter Cordero.

Peter came out right away. "Good morning, Mr. Flores." We've been expecting you. Come in."

This wasn't the reception Sol was expecting, and it knocked him off balance.

Peter nodded at the receptionist and turned to Sol. "Come on back. Would you like a cup of coffee?"

"Uh, yes, thank you. Black is fine."

Peter led him back into his plush leather and polished wood office. Sol was still reeling from Term's sudden departure, his own raw regrets about his mother, and the realization that he might be too late to make things right. There was a lot to digest, and he was still struggling to sort things out.

"Please, have a seat," Peter said, and settled in behind his carved mahogany desk with his fingers steepled.

Sol perched on the seat of his winged chair and leaned forward. "Is she...?"

"No." Peter said with a direct stare into his face and an edge to his voice.

No wonder this man was so successful in the courtroom. He could off-balance a stone wall.

Sol stared right back and waited for more.

Peter crossed his arms. "She is quite alive."

Sol closed his eyes and leaned back, his hand on the armrests. He let out a sigh. "Thank goodness."

"I understand why you're here, Mr. Flores, to contest the assigned co-executors, but—"

"Where have they got her?"

"Where have…?" It was Peter Cordero's time to be off-balanced. "Let's talk about your inheritance first. First off, you should know you have nothing to worry about. You'll be well provided for and will get all her money. The cash will be yours. Nothing will be lost to you."

"But where have they got her?"

"She's fine. She's recuperating," Peter said.

Sol nodded.

"Concerning your mother, in light of your past conversations, she wanted a hedge against certain contingencies. So, she chose her grandson and a very close friend as executors to assure that her wishes are honored."

Sol nodded again.

He gripped the armrests. "Fine, fine. I've been a low-down jerk, and I need to make things right. Just tell me where the heck my mother is."

"I can assure you that won't change the circumstances of the executorship."

"Do you not understand, Mr. Cordero? I. Do. Not. Care. Where is my mother?"

Sol sipped the coffee brought in by the receptionist while Peter Cordero left the room to make his phone call. Absent for several minutes, the lawyer had refused to reveal Rosella Flores's whereabouts until he obtained her permission. When he returned to his office, the lawyer leaned against the front corner of his monstrous desk.

Sol drained his cup as the lawyer hovered over him.

"I'll tell you where she is," Peter said, "but she's very weak." He raised a finger. "Now if this is a ruse to connect up and harass her—I hope for your sake and hers that—"

Sol stood now and plopped his empty paper cup onto the shiny desk. He hoped it left a ring.

He leaned his face into the lawyer's. "Let me reassure you, Mr. Cordero," he said. "You can hope all you want, but I am not a dangerous man. I am not who you think I am. She has nothing to worry about."

Peter rose now, a whole foot taller than Sol. He lifted a palm in Sol's direction. "All right. Not sure what you're talking about. But as you say." He reached inside his coat and pulled out a business card. On the back was a scribbled address. He handed it to Sol.

Sol glanced down at the writing. An address in Carrabelle, Florida, wherever the heck that was. He'd figure it out later. "Thank you," he said and stuffed it in his shirt pocket. "I appreciate it. And I hope you have a nice day."

With that Sol made his exit, headed out into the sun and down the rock stairs where he recovered his bag from behind the hedges. He dug out the book of maps and tucked it under his arm.

As he strode back over the bridge toward the bus station, Sol finally had the space to think about his mother and feel the relief of not being too late. At the top of the bridge, he paused along the concrete barrier in the narrow shade of a light pole and set his suitcase down. He pulled the atlas from under his arm.

A semi plowed by and nearly blew the book out of his hands, but he found the page with the Florida map and squinted as he studied the fine print for the town of Carrabelle.

It wasn't too far from Tallahassee at all. But what in the heck was she doing all the way up there?

He shut the book. Somebody'd scribbled all over the cover. Probably some kid. He shoved it back under his arm and picked up his suitcase. He needed to get moving.

As he descended the other side of the bridge, he took time to consider Term, the things the man had said, and his abrupt departure, which saddened him all over again.

He replayed the phone conversation with Paulette, her fiery words and the fact she had come back to see about him and would be there at the shop for a while.

Then his thoughts turned to Eddie and his car, and the paint shop back in Tallahassee.

And then an idea struck. If the difference wasn't too ridiculous, maybe Eddie would enjoy some metallic sparkles in his paint. He could make it a surprise.

But Eddie might not like sparkles. Sol ought to check somehow.

Yeah. He'd call Paulette. She would know. And maybe he could figure out what kind of change she was looking for.

Another semi passed, and fluffed up his shirt. The atlas was beginning to slide from under his arm. He paused to straighten it and glimpsed once again the scribbles on its cover. It wasn't scribbles at all, it was writing.

He took a better look.

Remember to care. Term.

That choked him up. "I'll try, old buddy. I'll try."

Matt lay wide awake on his cot. Thunder rumbled in the distance. The smell of approaching rain filled the room. A good storm would probably cancel tomorrow's fishing trip. A loss for Zeke, but Matt would get the day off.

For several minutes he watched the curtains billow. Millie's cabin did have good cross ventilation, but if the breeze blew any harder, he'd have to pull the windows down. Probably should anyway, so things didn't get wet later.

But it could wait.

First, he needed to figure a way to get through to Coral. It would be a tragedy for her to miss out, to never learn that her dad would love her to pieces if she'd just go meet him or listen to the rest of the story.

If she'd just listen it would change everything.

This evening at the beach had ended poorly. Coral hadn't said as much. She'd thanked Matt and told him what a lovely time she'd had. But he could feel her shutting things down.

Matt was treading on thin ice and had better shut up. Even an apology at this point might make things worse. All he could do was pray.

Two encouraging things came to mind, though. First, she'd said, "At least not today." That seemed to leave the door open for the future. Maybe this just wasn't the right time.

And second, they had friends in Carrabelle now. There was good reason to return.

He took a deep breath. That gave him a little peace.

He flipped over on his elbows to pray.

Maybe this delay was for the best.

I rubbed a thumb across the smooth clicker and smiled at the memory of Matt at the beach—so poetic—with that tanned face, those earnest brown eyes searching mine, and our kiss bathed in the orange glow of sunset. No wonder Grandma had been so in love with Grandpa Eduardo—my Matt was the spitting image of him.

I crossed my arms and huddled against the cool dampness that always settles before a storm, but the goosebumps remained.

This coastal town was like a dream—in all but one way.

There was Jessica, who'd turned into such a sister-like friend. Maybe we'd spend more time together soon.

And Aunt Allie—I loved her so much. One wouldn't think of fooling with her or getting her riled, or she'd have them straightened out and apologizing before they could turn around. Feisty might be the right word.

I loved the way Grandma spent a lot of time with her, how it cheered them both up and pumped new life into them. But I wanted a chance to get to know Aunt Allie better too—to hear all her old stories.

And Millie, what a neat lady. I felt she'd gone through a short time of holding me at a distance, but whatever that was, things were better now between us.

And then there was my dad. If only I could keep my mind off him. The man who'd almost had me killed when he should have protected me and Mama. He didn't even know me, and he wanted me dead. My own father…

I had to forgive him, though—had to. The Lord's prayer is clear and says it all—forgive us our trespasses as we forgive those who trespass against us.

I sure didn't feel like it.

"You'll have to help me with that, Lord," I whispered. "I don't know how."

Forgiveness didn't mean I had to accept him, though, or get to know him.

I sighed. Thinking of my dad grated my nerves. Time to forget about it.

The clicker sat warm and smooth in my hand, and like a child's favorite toy, I didn't want to put it down. I rubbed my finger across it and imagined the teenage boys at Normandy, how they might have rubbed a thumb over their clickers in the same kind of way—but in pure terror. They'd probably made double-sure they had it on the string and absolutely sure they had that string around their necks. They checked and rechecked so as not to get shot.

My hand relaxed and I drowsed, woke, drowsed, and considered going inside.

But the air outside was so nice…and the mosquitoes were… the wind must be keeping them down…

I'd go inside.

In a minute…

A racket startled me awake, and my fingers squeezed the clicker. *Kapop*! I jumped, and the rocker squeaked. No longer drowsy, my eyes were alert, my nerves on fire.

Only then did my synapses call back the noise that woke me. Some kind of loud scrape.

I scanned the dark. But nothing seemed amiss.

"Don't shoot," the voice pleaded.

The voice, my dad's, came from the other side of the porch-post, and now I could see his raised hands. This was a stickup straight from a cowboy show with me the gunslinger.

"I'm only delivering vegetables," he said.

Dumbstruck, I spotted the basket of produce now and glanced from it to his back and his hands up in the air.

"Aunt Allie?" he said.

Pfft! Far from it. If only I were.

He'd earned every bit of my wrath. And I deserved the truth. I gritted my teeth. "Don't you turn around."

This was a standoff. Me with a little old clicker and him with his hands in the air.

"I'm just delivering produce. Okay?"

He eased through the gate. "Just leaving. Don't shoot." He'd nearly reached the stop sign.

Now wait a minute. I couldn't let him away from here without telling me the truth—all that stuff Zeke and Matt had been hinting at.

He should tell me himself. *Coward!*

I leaped off the porch, stomped through the gate, and marched up behind him—heck, I felt like David confronting Goliath with this clicker. Only I had enough sense to know he was no big danger.

But right now, I could have whipped a lion and a bear too.

But what should I say?

I let him reach the roadway where he turned toward the bridge. Took two steps.

"Just hold it right there," I said.

He complied.

"And don't you turn around."

He stood there frozen with his arms in the air.

"Now you talk." How ridiculous this was. He probably had no clue what he was supposed to talk about.

So he said nothing.

I spoke through clenched teeth, that clicker out in front of me like an outlaw's gun. Well, he was going to come clean and beg my forgiveness. *The heathen!*

He just stood there.

"You tell me," I said, "what else is there? Zeke says there's more to the story. What happened after you told my mama to kill me?" I was practically yelling now. "What more could there be after that! Tell me. I can't imagine."

He began a slow nod, a nod of realization. His arms began to lower.

"You keep those hands up."

He did.

"And speak where I can hear you."

"Your mama? Your mama?" Once again, his arms moved. But this time they shot straight up as in *glory be!*

I tucked my chin back. *What in the world?*

"This could only mean one thing, honey." Those arms straightened high in the air as if praising God. Then, at the top of his voice he leaned his head back and yelled, "Woooo hoooo!" The sound curdled my blood like that legendary Rebel yell that sent chills through those Yankees so long ago.

His hands punctured the air again. "Zeke," he hollered, loud enough to wake up the town, "Zeke! Where ever you are, you got it right, buddy! You got it right!"

I'm sure Zeke and all his family could hear him on the other side of that bridge.

He kept this up, right there by the highway, as if it were broad daylight, "Oh, thank you, God! She's alive! My baby is alive. She's alive!"

I stared. What had just happened?

He bent double, oblivious to my stupid little noisemaker. "That's all I need. Oh, thank You, God. She's alive. I didn't kill her."

I wrapped my fingers around the clicker as my hand dropped to my side.

Then he stood with his arms in the air, turning circles into the middle of the road and saying, "Oh, thank You, God, I'm not a killer. Oh, thank You, God!"

Now I didn't know what to think.

As the curtains billowed in again, Matt listened harder. He leaned
his ear against the screen and peered out in the direction of Aunt
Allie's. A man's voice. It seemed to be coming from there. Nearby,
for sure.

The words were muffled. But it sure sounded like Ralph.

Yelling.

Coral!

He yanked on his running shorts and slipped into his tennis
shoes with no socks, and slung open the door. His feet hit the gravel
and spun out toward the yelling—but it wasn't angry yelling, just
crazy. Crazy yelling.

Over the limestone he flew and then rounded the corner.

He pulled up short.

And stared.

There stood Ralph turning round and round with his arms up
in the middle of the road, and yelling thank You to God.

His Coral, looking a bit confused, stood to the side.

Thank God she was all right.

Nobody better touch his Coral.

Ralph, nearly dizzy, ended up in the middle of the road. He opened his eyes.

But the angry voice behind him continued her tongue lashing.

"What do you mean?" she hollered. "What do you mean, you're not a killer? Tell me!" she demanded.

He turned. And recognition hit. "It's you. It *is* you." He glanced toward the heavens. "Oh, God, thank You. I see it now."

He beheld her again—arms limp at her sides.

There was no gun. But just to set his eyes on her was… "Oh, honey, you look just like her—your mother."

She thumped her hands on her hips. Breathed hard.

"Listen," he opened his hands toward her. "It's okay. You're alive. You don't even need to forgive me."

She stared back, her jaw firm.

He lowered his voice, recalling that morning. "I took her the breakfast. Had it all planned out. I'd marry her, and we'd go someplace…someplace safe where her father wouldn't find us. I'd protect her forever."

The girl's arms slid back down.

He shook his head. "But she was gone. Just—gone."

I didn't know what to think. But something deep inside me seemed to break as a palm frond crackled loose across the road and tumbled across the asphalt.

His words faded as I considered how completely wrong I'd been about the situation.

A misting rain now fell, and I felt Matt's presence by the store before I glanced up to find him there. Poor thing, there he was, soaking wet and bare-chested in his sport-shorts and tennis shoes, arms poised as if to protect if needed. He smiled.

I wanted him here, but he held back, watching. This was my battle to fight. But it warmed me through and through to see him here.

Lights blinked on in several nearby windows and porch fronts. Oh, help me, Lord. We were on display for the world to see.

My dad stepped to the middle of the lane.

"I repented," he said. "Oh, believe me, I repented. Every single live-long day."

I blinked back tears and tried to figure out how things had so quickly bent sideways like a ruined nail. Had it been that way for him?

Then his voice cracked. "But I couldn't undo it. I couldn't."

The wind whipped up, and a strong gust backed me off the edge of the road onto the limestone. But my dad stood firm. I gazed at the road beneath his feet, wet in the bouncing mist and awash in streetlights.

"A reaction. A stupid inexcusable reaction," he said. "I failed the test."

With both hands, I wiped the rain from my face.

"Still and right away," he said, "I changed my mind. I didn't want her gone. I really didn't want it."

He wiped a shoulder across his eye. "But she was gone." He gazed up. "But God, what could I do?"

My voice splintered. "You—didn't want me dead?"

He looked down at me. Shook his head. "No, baby, not on your life."

"You didn't?" It came out as a broken whisper.

How could I not forgive this man who only wanted me to be alive?

Matt, stationed next to the store's front post, glimpsed the flicker of distant headlights coming this way through the trees and growing larger and larger. The sound of an engine accompanied them now, a big one.

"Truck coming," he yelled, "Get outta the road."

Ralph, his feet on the double lines and his mind on his business, ignored the warning, his sole focus intent upon the daughter he'd just discovered alive.

"You don't have to want me, Sandy. "Just knowing you're alive—I'll be fine for the rest of my life." He wiped the rain from his face again. "But what happened to Nadine, your mother?"

Matt strode across the rocks and waved his arms, "Get outta the road!" he repeated and gestured toward the approaching vehicle.

Now Coral looked up. "Come on! Get off the road."

Matt grabbed Ralph's slippery arm, missed, and then grabbed the back of his shirt to pull him over just as the driver laid on his horn, dodged left and skimmed off the left edge of the road.

A shower of warm road-water sprayed his legs.

Ralph seemed oblivious.

Still focused on his daughter, he waited for his answer.

Coral widened her eyes for a brief instant and caught Matt's gaze, aware of the near miss, and returned her eyes to her father. Back on track she shook her head.

"We lied. It's not Sandy."

Matt, his heart still pounding out of his chest, stared at Ralph. The man had no idea how close to death he'd come.

Ralph was barely aware as Matt grabbed the back of his shirt and yanked him toward the side of the road. He jumped and turned as the horn blared behind him. But he stepped on over to the limestone. Kept his distance from the girl. He didn't want to seem menacing. He'd done enough harm in his life and didn't want to cause more. He was just grateful he hadn't killed her as a baby. *Thank You, God. Thank You.*

So the girl had lied. He'd ask about that later.

But for now, he had to find out what happened to Nadine. "What about your mama? What happened to her? Please?"

The girl shook her head.

"She's…?"

A negative shake of her head. "Gone. Long miserable story."

Ralph's shoulders drooped.

"I'm so sorry, honey."

Matt gave them space again as Coral thrust her hands against her hips. The scene in front of him could go either way.

Coral could shove this man aside, a thing Matt couldn't blame her for. Or she could forgive him. But mainly he hoped she could find her way through, one way or the other. He never would have expected this whole thing to come to a head out in the middle of the road in the middle of the rain at what—midnight? This was messed up.

Whatever Coral decided, he'd be right here to support her.

Coral spoke now, her voice firm. "I grew up without you. On peanut butter and bread. Where were you when I wore those shabby torn-up clothes with lechers grabbing at my behind…and no lock on my own front door to keep them out? Where were you?"

Her eyes flickered downward before meeting Matt's gaze.

He sensed her shame. She'd never confessed these things.

Matt wanted to yell it was okay. Coral had to know this didn't matter, and Matt loved her regardless. He pressed his rain-soaked lips together and gave her a nod, as if to say, *You go right ahead, honey. I'm right here with you.*

She seemed to gain strength as she rallied with several ragged breaths. "I lived in dread of whatever else they might do if they caught me alone! And where were you all those times when I woke up in some different roach infested dump every other month or so? And had to start over at a new school? Imagine my life. Because you weren't there. But I was there, and I remember every ugly detail."

The jutting of her chin seemed to drill it in.

Ralph's head sank. "And I did this to my own child." He shook his head. "Oh, God, if only I'd gone upstairs sooner. Not given her that money. If only… Sandy. I'm sorry. I am sorry."

The rain slacked as he looked in her face and opened his palms toward her. "I can't undo it. I'm…" Once again he shook his head. "You don't need to forgive me. I don't deserve it." He raised his arm to wipe the rain off his neck. A peace settled over his features as he lowered the arm. "But you're alive. Alive."

Coral crossed her arms. "It's not Sandy."

Ralph nodded. "If it's not Sandy Shore, what is it? Your real name? Your mama would have named you that, for sure. She would have." He nodded. "She loved the beach."

Coral remained fixed.

"If—if it's not Sandy, then tell me what it is. Please. Just tell me that much."

She lowered her arms. "It's Coral."

He closed his eyes and threw up his hands. "Her favorite thing. Coral."

Coral frowned and stared at him.

Millie padded around the corner now, in her bare feet and nightgown, her eyes wide, taking in the scene in front of her. She stepped over to the covered wooden steps just as the rain picked up again. The wind blew it sideways, wetting her completely. She caught Matt's gaze and mouthed the words, "What's going on?"

Matt gave her a nod and turned back to the scene.

Ralph spoke again. "Your mom, she left three pieces. Of coral, I mean. Up in the window. And some shells." He bit his lip and turned as if to go. "I'll get them for you."

As Ralph stepped away, he raised his hands again, a smile on his face. "I'm just—this changes everything. Now the sun can shine! The waves can roll!"

Matt looked up as the store's double front doors creaked open and, visible by way of the streetlights, there stood Aunt Allie, Grandma Rosella, and Jessica in their long nightgowns. They helped each other down the steps and huddled under the overhang trying to figure out, Matt was certain, what in the heck was going on.

A few more lights blinked on up the street.

Ralph turned back to Aunt Allie's overhang and spread his arms. "Millie? Millie, honey? Do you hear that? Go decorate the restaurant. Decorate it inside and out. From corner to corner. Do whatever you like!"

Curtains parted and faces appeared between them.

Ralph blasted out a loud whoop and grabbed up a limestone rock. Then like a pro pitcher, he aimed it straight at the Captain's Table sign at the base of the bridge. *Kerblam!* It exploded in a damp drizzle of white, and he headed toward the bridge, a new and happy man.

Matt stood behind me as my brain spun like a whirligig. Since the very beginning my dad had actually wanted me alive. He had not planned to get rid of me. Not really. And I'd almost cut him off.

And here he was expecting nothing at all in return from me but that I had made it out alive.

Well, I wasn't about to lose him again.

"Wait up!" I yelled after him.

The rain thundered now, and he didn't hear me.

I raised my voice and splashed behind him.

"Wait up, Daddy!"

Ralph froze in mid stride. Turned, his mouth agape. "What did you say?"

Coral raced to catch up to him.

"I do. I do forgive you," she said, and ran into his arms. Dumbfounded, he embraced her. Caressed her hair.

Was he dreaming?

He held her at arm's length. "Daddy? You mean it? You sure?"

She nodded, rain washing tears from her face, and buried her head in his chest.

He closed his eyes and hugged her tight.

When Ralph looked up again, there stood Matt next to Coral, always the protector. A fleeting wisp of fatherly approval passed through Ralph's chest, her other protector.

He gazed up at the four women huddled under Aunt Allie's front awning.

"Well, lookie over there, Coral. I guess maybe this would be the right time to introduce you to everyone."

He wrapped an arm around Coral, walked her over to the edge of the asphalt as if it were his stage, and the women his audience. Matt stood between them and the steps.

He raised his voice to overcome the raucous downpour. "Ahem. Folks. This is my baby girl, Coral. Known to some as Sandy Shore. But this is my daughter, Coral. Say hi, everyone."

Clapping and cheering ensued. Millie's mouth hung open, "Your daughter? *Ah…* your *daughter*. All right, then!" She clapped and cheered as well.

As the ruckus died down, and the rain eased up again, Aunt Allie said, "Well, I'm shivering to pieces. This overhang hasn't kept the rain off anyone. Why don't we all come inside and build a fire and get dried out?"

"In the middle of summer?" Millie said.

"Yes, ma'am," Aunt Allie told her. "As good a time as any. God made fire for a reason."

Ralph stepped under the roof and raised his volume again. "One more thing. And this is important. Before we go in…Coral, would you like to meet your great-grandma?"

Coral glanced from him to Matt. "Wh-what are you talking about?"

Ralph took Coral by the hand and led her over to a thunderstruck Aunt Allie. He cleared his throat. "Coral. Honey. This makes Aunt Allie your great-grandmother."

Jessica threw up her hands and shrieked, "Your dream, Aunt Allie, your dream!"

All eyes settled on Aunt Allie with her hands clasped to her face. She hobbled over to Coral and with utmost tenderness transferred them to hers. "Oh… oh," was all she could utter. She leaned her forehead against Coral's and then raised her lips to kiss it.

"Oh, thank You, Lord. Nobody knows about that dream like I do," she said. She closed her eyes. "Dear Lord, give me some good long years with this, my beautiful great-grandbaby."

She leaned back to study Coral's face in the streetlight and then shook her head. "Oh, you're my little Nadine's child all right. And she was nothing but a child when I last saw her. I see it now."

She took Coral by the elbow and made her way up the steps but then turned her chin toward Ralph. "But you, Mister, you've got some mighty big 'splainin' to do."

He spoke now from behind the group. "I know. I know, Aunt Allie. And I'm glad the good Lord forgives. I just hope you can."

"Truthful answers, Ralph. That's all I ask. The truth. I will always love you, child."

Tears flooded Ralph's eyes. He couldn't hold them back.

Grandma Rosella took Jessica's elbow and climbed up the steps behind them. "Allie," she said, "I knew there was something I liked about you."

Matt, Millie, and Ralph followed them inside.

The women retreated to the back room for dry clothes while the men set to work building a fire.

Jessica fetched afghans, and before too long the cozy fire stopped their shivering, and Aunt Allie told them to go into the back and break out the soda pop.

"I don't care if this stove's burnin' in the middle of summer," Millie said, "this is awesome."

Ralph, soaking wet on an old orange crate beside her, rubbed his hands together and nodded his agreement.

"And I'm declaring to all here that it's time," Ralph said…

Curious eyes turned his way.

"…to make us a new restaurant sign."

Millie chucked. "What's that got to do with anything?"

"Gonna make us a new sign. Oh, yeah. And she's gonna say, Daddy's Place."

"In honor of your dad?" Millie asked.

"No," Ralph laughed. He kissed Millie smack on the mouth. "In honor of my *child*."

I couldn't help but see how pleased my dad was with this whole situation, and with Millie, and probably soon with Aunt Al—I mean, Great-Grandma.

Matt gripped my hand. His hair was still drenched, but together we wore one of the afghans around our shoulders. He glanced around the crowd and then at Ralph. "If it's okay, we'd like to help you create that sign."

Ralph smiled a big one, and everyone clapped. I felt the heat rise to my face as Matt leaned over and gave me a kiss like my dad had given Millie—only better.

As I came up for air, I thought of my little book of wise sayings. Maybe I should add one more after this: *be sure and listen to the whole story.*

Because I'm glad I finally did.

I have to say, this trip had turned out pretty good after all.

Acknowledgements

This book is dedicated to my Great-Aunt Allie Bentley, who actually did run a store like the one in this story. She was a feisty and outspoken woman of straight convictions. I was grateful to have known her, rocked with her on her porch, and listened to her stories for six years. She passed away in her eighties when I was twelve.

I will always miss you, Aunt Allie.

Many thanks to my beta readers, Chuck and Delores Kight, Danny Odom, Linda Cruey, and my editor Fay Lamb. Thank you for your input and candid remarks. I also want to thank my fellow writers of the Word Weavers Ocala, Florida chapter for all their varied input this time around. They are continually faithful. Thank you to Sarah Leppert, occupational therapist for her important advice on injuries, Sarah Bult, CNA, for her knowledge of miscarriages. Thank you Hope Laird, for your advice concerning recovery from Sepsis. Any mistakes in interpreting your advice are truly my own. Thank you, Mike Parker, the best publisher ever!

Special Notes

I love and thank the people of Carrabelle, all warm and friendly Floridians. I'm grateful, hoping you'll forgive me for rearranging and moving some of your wonderful buildings in my book *Along the Forgotten Coast*, and for inserting Aunt Allie's store in Carrabelle. Her store in real life was located in Martin, Florida.

Along the Forgotten Coast's characters are totally made up, (though I know you'll love them along with me), and so are some places like The Captain's Table, a restaurant at the base of the bridge, and Ralph's Marina in front of it. The Cozy Inn was inspired by a local bed and breakfast pushed around the corner and renamed. I am especially inspired by certain places in Carrabelle—among them CQuarters, the Fisherman's Wife, The Old Carrabelle Hotel, Camp Gordon Johnston WWII Museum, the Carrabelle History Museum, the Crooked River Lighthouse, Fathoms Steam Room and Raw Bar, and many other scenes, nooks, and crannies with no particular names.

Carrabelle is lovely and inspiring, right down to the docks and the sand on the beach.

About the Author

Jennifer Odom is a 5th generation Floridian. Her love of the land and its rich history reach back to the 1860s when her great great grandfather migrated to his new homestead in Central Florida near the railroad. Orange groves and farming busied the family while one child and her spouse established the general store and served as station-master for the thriving depot. Reflecting this love of Florida and its people, Jennifer has written human interest stories for the *Ocala Star Banner* and gardening articles for the *Ocala Gazette*. Her fiction is published in *Splickety* and *Clubhouse Jr.* magazines, as well as *Maine Review's Juxtaposition*. Her fifth novel, *Along the Forgotten Coast*, is the second volume in her heart-warming *Coral Series* and serves as the satisfying sequal to *Under the Mango Trees*. Her *Black Series* (suspense/mystery) includes *Summer by the Black Suwannee*, *Stranger with a Black Case*, and *Girl with a Black Soul*.

Jennifer is a multi-award winning veteran teacher and writer, selected as Teacher of the Year at her Florida Blue Ribbon School, and Writer of the Year at the Florida Christian Writers Conference. Connect with Jennifer online at:

jenniferodom.com